Ghosts of the World Fair

Parisian Ghosts

Janna Ruth

ISBN: 978-1-0670398-2-0 (eBook)

ISBN: 978-1-0670398-3-7 (Paperback)

PARISIAN GHOSTS 6

GHOSTS OF THE WORLD FAIR

JANNA RUTH

Grab your free copy

When an undead movie star asks you for a small favour, you know you're gonna be in deep trouble.

Seeing ghosts is just something I've learnt to live with. They're everywhere I go, especially since I chose to study history at the Sorbonne, one of the oldest universities in the world. While on a class trip to the Pantheon, where France's great men—and women!—reside, I get introduced to the fabulous Josephine Baker! One of her war medals has gone missing, and she wants me to find its whereabouts.

Who could say no to a flapper girl turned movie star turned war hero? Little do I know agreeing to do so will send me on a wild-goose chase across the country with a ghostly pet cheetah, hidden walkways, and a murder attempt.

·

Follow Alix on her first big ghost adventure two years prior to the events of Parisian Ghosts.

·

Sign up to my Story Seeker mailing list at <u>www.janna-ruth.com/ newsletter</u> and grab the prequel for free

A Note on Sensitive Topics

Dear Reader,

This is a book about ghosts, so naturally death plays a rather large part in it. If you don't like spoilers and are cool with everything, skip this note and start the book. If you want to be prepared, read on. I'm writing this because reading should be fun, not a nasty surprise.

There are a few things happening in this book. As part of the World Fair there's an exhibition of the Chevalier's experiments with necromancy, including reanimated animals, that might be unsettling. Alix and her friends will finally go after GoPol and uncover more of their dastardly schemes, all the while dealing with some PTSD stemming from what happened at the end of the last book. Meanwhile, Gaspar continues to grapple with his dark side, exhibiting both physically and emotionally abusive behaviour.

At the Ghost World Fair, a magical bomb threat is uncovered and thwarted before it can be carried out completely. In addition, there's also a kidnapping, a few heart-breaking sacrifices, and the typical dose of claustrophobia we encounter in the catacombs.

Finally, several people will nearly fall off the Eiffel Tower in a tense showdown at dizzy heights, and someone *will* die. It might even be a good thing.

This series has physical and mental confrontations between the living and the dead, but our heroine is scrappy and has a great group of friends.

Happy to tag along? Then join Alix on this new ghostly adventure as she visits the l'Exposition Universelle des Fantômes.

Love, Janna

Chapter 1

It's an honour to finally meet the one who'll raise the dead and bring chaos and destruction to the world.

Nostradamus' face, dominated by his ultra-long beard, begins to fray at the edges. The skin falls away, dissolving into wisps of cloud to reveal the skeleton beneath. Groaning, he stretches out his arms, reaching for me. Behind him—*is it still Nostradamus?*—other skeletons rise from their graves.

I scream and run the other way, only to be stopped dead in my tracks when I come across a glowing rectangle on the ground. Inside it is the shadow of a hanged man. Cédric.

When I finally manage to look up, all I see is my sister with her dead husband of less than three hours in her arms. Surrounded by a sea of white lilies, she glares at me. "You did this, Alix. You took him from me. I *hate* you!"

It doesn't matter that she's wrong, that it was GoPol who got to him long before I even came on the scene. In this moment, I feel her words seep into my bones with a truth that can't be denied. If it weren't for me, Sébastien would've never strayed. And if Sébastien hadn't strayed, he wouldn't have fallen prey to his parents' machinations. Then his father wouldn't have been distracted, and Cédric wouldn't have died alone with no chance of resurrection.

Bony fingers grip my shoulders and pull me backwards. I reach for Hélène, begging her to help me, but as usual, my sister is too preoccupied with her beloved Cédric. Or maybe she thinks I'm getting exactly what I deserve.

The white lilies blur as I'm yanked backwards and pushed in front of a mirror.

Discover the monster inside you!

But what I see in the mirror isn't me. Instead, there's someone else, too small for me to see clearly. I bend forward until my nose nearly touches the surface, whether of my own volition or from the dead pushing me. The figure grows quickly. I wish I could look away, but the skeletal hands are merciless and my eyes won't close.

"No, no, no, no, don't. Gaspar, don't."

But he does it anyway, and soon all I see is blood. The blood on his hands also sticks to mine. His murder is mine. Because he's my monster.

And so am I. The one who'll raise the dead and bring chaos and destruction to the—

"Alix!"

The grip of the skeletal hands is even stronger now. They're shaking my shoulder, dragging me away from Gaspar and the scene of his grisly murder. Light blooms through two slits and the voice returns. Odile's voice.

"Come on, wake up. You're scaring Malou."

Malou?

Letting go of the nightmare is like pulling my teeth out of hardening caramel. Only the promise of light, Odile's voice, and Malou's soft belly make it possible for me to let go. As soon as I open my eyes, Odile pushes the little hedgehog into my hands.

With her arms crossed, my little sister looks down at me. She's already dressed for school, her bag slung over her shoulder. "You had that nightmare again."

My fingers dig into Malou's fur, seeking the sweet comfort only an innocent pet can give. "I do every night."

Ever since we returned from our ill-fated trip to Provence, I've been struggling. So many terrible things happened that my brain is stuck in a loop. Cédric killed himself in the hope of becoming a ghost whisperer like me. Hélène lost her newlywed husband and, as usual, blames me for it. Sébastien sacrificed himself to his cruel and monstrous parents, and when I tried to free him... when I tried to...

Even though my fingers are buried in Malou's soft belly fur, they feel sticky with blood—blood I didn't shed, but might as well have.

My hands tremble and my breath accelerates when I see Gaspar in front of me again. My ears fill with the sound of him smashing Margot's head in. The blood…

Odile's fingers wrap around my wrist. "Stop thinking about it!"

She doesn't know all the details. Not because I didn't want to tell her, but because I couldn't without throwing up. All she knows is Sébastien's mother is dead, like Cédric, and I had to watch it happen. I couldn't even tell her it was Gaspar who killed her.

My monster.

"Don't take this the wrong way, but I think you need to talk to someone."

The last time someone suggested therapy, it was because of my ability to see ghosts. But it's not the ghosts who've messed me up. It's the living.

"Maybe."

"I'm serious. You're not coping." Odile says, running her hand over Malou's spikes. "No one is," she whispers softly.

That's right. I'm not the only one who suffered immense trauma in Provence. My sister lost her husband in the most senseless way imaginable and everyone's feeling the effects of it. Cédric meant little to me. So did Margot. It's Hélène who needs support, not me.

"I'm fine," I say, sitting up carefully, Malou in my hands.

Odile huffs. "You're absolutely not fine."

"Who am I supposed to see about this? Any shrink would send me straight to the psych ward if I told them about the ghosts." And it's impossible to get to the bottom of it without mentioning them.

"So, find a ghost shrink," Odile says with a shrug. "There must be dozens buried in your necropolises. You could talk to, I don't know... Jacques Lacan or someone. You could be open about the ghosts, and you wouldn't even have to pay them. Besides, they'd probably like to help someone after all these years of resting in peace."

I stare at her, stunned. "That's... actually, not a bad idea."

"See," Odile says with a grin. "I'm not half as dumb as you think I am."

"Odi..."

"Just kidding. I've got to catch the Métro and you need a shower! And get your ass to the Sorbonne. Happy first day!"

She's out of my room before I can fully process her instructions. Take a shower... My sheets are sticking to my skin, soaked with the sweat of my recurring nightmare. It's disgusting.

With a sigh, I take Malou and put her to bed in her cage, before grabbing my sheets and stuffing them in the washing machine as I've done every single day since my return from Provence. Fortunately, it's a Monday and my maman isn't around to comment.

I jump in the shower and let the hot water wash away the traces of my nightmare. The only thing it can't wash away is the blood on my hands. Gaspar did it for *me*. Only me. I created this monster.

Suddenly feeling woozy, I hold on to the wall and count my breaths. Maybe Odile is right and I do need to see someone. Add it to my ever-growing list of things to take care of.

Forty-five minutes later, I lock my bicycle at the Sorbonne and head up the stairs with the hundreds of other students. It's the first day of the summer semester and I've got a new set of classes to distract me from what happened in Provence. They better be as good as they sound.

"Alix!" Gaby calls, a tray of two coffees-to-go from *Chambelland* in her hand. "Bonjour!" She kisses me on the cheek before handing me one. "You look like you need this more than I do."

"Thanks," I reply sourly. Whatever offence I might have taken disappears as I take my first sip. "This one's good!"

"Marie made it extra strong," Gaby explains as she drinks from her own cup. "How are you holding up?"

I shrug. "Managing. Yourself?" Gaby was there, too, though we haven't really talked about it much since.

"Well enough." She waves it off, as if it doesn't matter. "So. Industrial Revolution with Renard. He did France's Revolutionary Way to a Republic in our second year, which I failed at the first attempt."

Now she's saying it, I remember the course. "Almost everyone failed that one."

Gaby gives me a long look. "*Almost* everyone…"

I happen to be one of four people who managed to pass the exam on the first try. I link my arm with hers and grin. "Don't worry. I've got you this time."

"You had me last time, too, so I'm putting my grade into your hands."

Before the make-up exam, I whipped Gaby into shape with my newly acquired knowledge of the 19th century, courtesy of the Panthéon ghosts. Turns out Victor Hugo made a better teacher in that regard than Monsieur Renard. "We've got this."

While both courses cover roughly the same time period, the focus is different. In the third semester, we had an in-depth look at the back and forth between revolutionary France and self-proclaimed emperors. A lot of people think we had one big revolution, and voilà, we freed ourselves from the shackles of monarchy, but it actually took more than a hundred years and several smaller revolutions until we came out the other end. Simultaneously, France had been swept up in the Industrial Revolution, which brought its own changes and challenges.

Gaby and I settle in a cautious third row of the seminar room. From memory, Monsier Renard hates nothing more than the entire class hiding in the back. Théo is even braver and takes the seats in front of us with his friends, which suits me just fine. He'll serve nicely as a buffer.

"Hey, how was—"

"Don't!" Gaby says immediately, and I shake my head grimly. We're here to be distracted from our troubles, not rehash them quickly before class.

Théo frowns and settles into his seat. "Are we still good?"

For two years, Théo and I had a bit of a row. I'd accidentally hurt him by choosing ghosts over him, and he'd retaliated by publicly shunning me for it. But now he's in the fold and totally cool with ghosts. He even helped me solve a ghost problem at the opera where his older brother works and has taken an oath on Malou to work with us. It dawns on me he's the only one of my friends who wasn't in Provence, and suddenly it feels like the gulf between us is back in full force.

Before I can think of a way to mend the rift, Monsieur Renard enters and puts down the slender case he always carries his lecture materials in. He's a rather young lecturer, forty at most, with thinning blond hair, a long nose, and grey eyes behind glasses. With a disapproving glance at the empty front row, he unpacks a pile of curious-looking envelopes and sets up his laptop.

"Alright, let's get started. For those who don't know me, I'm Monsieur Renard and this is The Industrial Revolution in France and Wider Europe."

The introduction is followed by the usual reminder of the expectations and requirements for passing the course. When he gets to the part about assessments, he pauses to count us quickly, squinting a little as he does so.

"There will be an exam at the end, which will be worth fifty per cent of your grade. The other fifty per cent will be divided between an oral presentation and an accompanying paper in groups of three."

A collective groan goes through the room. While it's cool the exam only counts for half of our grade, it's a bit daunting to know the other half depends on two other people. Gaby will obviously be one of them. As for the other...

"Do you want to team up?" Théo asks, looking over his shoulder at us.

"Quiet, please," Monsieur Renard asks. "You can discuss your groups in a moment. First, let me explain the task."

The room falls silent again, and the lecturer picks up the ominous envelopes and spreads them on the table behind him. "The written part of the assignment is due on the 31st of May, and we'll have oral presentations in the weeks after. The Industrial Revolution is well documented by the advent of l'Expositions Universelles, the World Fairs. We'll look at how they got started in a moment. Each group will pick an envelope and examine an integral element of the World Fairs and how that changed from year to year, focusing on three fairs that took place in France. In

June, we'll hold our own Exposition Universelle, and you'll be the guides for your respective pavilions."

For a moment, I was worried, but I can do tour guide. To be honest, this sounds a lot more fun than the usual essays and exams. It definitely has the potential to distract me from the dumpster fire that is my personal life.

"Alright, you may form groups now and grab an envelope from the front." Monsieur Renard already sounds like he's regretting it.

"So?" Théo asks, while his friends discuss groupings.

Gaby looks at me, as if it's all up to me. Since there's no one else we're particularly close to, and since Théo is an excellent student, I shrug. "Yeah, sure. Let's do it."

Théo grins. "I'll get our topic."

On his way to the front, he apologises to his friends, who quickly find other members among the rest of the class. It takes about five minutes for everyone to sort themselves out and sit back down with their assignments.

Curious, Gaby and I lean forward to look over Théo's shoulder as he opens the envelope. Inside is a pile of old illustrations and early photographs, copies of source texts, and the title page: 'Industries pavilion'.

He shrugs. "Beats the fine art exhibition."

I think it's perfect. It's *the* place to be for ever-changing technology, and will give us more than enough material to compare World Fairs between 1855 and 1937.

"Let's make an action plan after lunch."

The sooner we get started, the sooner I can worry about something else.

CHAPTER 2

After working out a research plan with Théo—I'm in charge of finding relevant ghosts—Gaby and I make our way to *Chambelland,* arriving just as Marie is about to close the café for the day.

She greets Gaby with a kiss, before asking, "How was your first day back?"

"Fairly relaxed," Gaby says. "We've got a cool new project to sink our teeth into. How about yours?"

Marie rolls her eyes. "I've got so much homework. Honestly, I'm not sure Law is right for me anymore."

"It isn't?" I ask, vaguely remembering how she once told me she liked the detail work and digging up obscure laws.

"Well, there seems to be a lot of stuff going on outside the law and nobody cares, so what's really the point, huh?"

I wince, strongly reminded this isn't just a friendly get-together.

As if on cue, the door opens and Sébastien slips in, followed by Dix. More kisses are exchanged, and we settle around a table in the back, which Marie has already set-up with coffee and leftover baked goods. I slip into a seat next to Sébastien while Dix hops onto the counter, his long legs hitting the wood without leaving a mark.

"How are you holding up?" Sébastien asks softly, his chair only marginally further away from mine than Gaby's is from Marie's.

"I wish people would stop asking me that."

"I take it not so good, then?"

Damn him. Here I was trying to brush it off, and he attacks with his caring side.

"Have you heard anything from him?" I ask instead.

Sébastien shakes his head. "As far as I know he's still in the catacombs, hiding."

"What if he's not?" I ask, my eyes burning. "What if he's out there, killing people at random?"

Gaby and Marie exchange a worried look, while Sébastien puts his hand on mine and squeezes it. I hadn't even noticed my hand was shaking until he stopped it. "It wasn't random," he says quietly. "He killed for a reason."

"For me."

The words are barely out before a whimper follows. I close my eyes and breathe through the wave of despair that threatens to engulf me. No one disputes me, but they all feel sorry for me, which just makes things worse, because it's true. Gaspar killed Margot to protect me, to keep me from making a deal with the devil, and now I'm sitting here dealing with the consequences.

"Is your father still keeping it under wraps?"

I wouldn't put it past Charles Roubert to pin the murder on me. But everyone in this café saw what happened, and while he could totally silence us all, he hasn't chosen to do so. Yet.

Sébastien takes a deep breath and nods. "Yeah, according to him, the matter is settled. He went back to work as if nothing happened. As if I hadn't found her in the first place and things hadn't escalated."

Now it's my turn to squeeze his hand. His father had planned to kill him many more times to make new whisper ghosts for GoPol's use, and would've happily murdered me if Margot hadn't intervened due to her bigger plans for me. Plans that will never come to fruition, thanks to Gaspar.

"So, what are we going to do?" Marie asks. "I know the law won't help us, but surely there must be something we can do. Or are we following GoPol's playbook? Ignore it? Pretend it never happened?"

I don't have a proper plan. Truth is, too much has happened to ignore it. I've had nightmares every night about the events in that lab and my supposed prophecy. But more importantly, Charles Roubert broke my family. He's persecuted me, eliminated part of my father under false pretences, and coerced my sister's fiancé into killing himself. If he isn't stopped, more tragedies will follow.

"We have to stop GoPol and find Gaspar before he... before he..." A huge frog in my throat makes it impossible to speak.

Gaby gives me a pitying look. "Those are two very different problems. Perhaps it would be best to concentrate on one of them. I'm almost afraid to ask, but which would be easier to solve?"

"Stop GoPol," I blurt out at the same time as Sébastien says, "Gaspar."

I glance at him. "You know how to fix him?"

Short of finding and *killing* Gaspar, I have no idea where to even start. Let alone face him after what he's done.

Sébastien shrugs. "No, but we know where to start, don't we?" When I continue to look at him, still clueless, he explains, "The Chevalier. We go to the guy who brought him back. First off, he needs to know what he did went wrong before he brings anyone else back, and secondly, we need to understand *how* he did it, so we can find out *where* it all went wrong. Finally, he's the most likely person to come up with a fix."

I sigh. All three points are excellent. I should've thought of them myself. Maybe there's a reason I resisted following the same line of thought—because I'm afraid the only solution *is* to kill Gaspar and start over. Unfortunately, there's no guarantee that just because he dies, he'll return to his former sweet self. The only good thing about it is he won't be able to hurt anyone else anymore. I can't believe I'm actually thinking about murdering my boyfriend, as if the act doesn't really matter, because ghosts and living people are interchangeable to me. Maybe I *am* the monster after all.

"Alix," Gaby calls softly, "get out of your own head and talk to us."

Good advice, but how do you talk to your friends about potentially having to kill your boyfriend? I don't want to take Gaspar's second life from him just because I'm more familiar with him as a ghost. Who am I to decide whether he has the right to live or not?

"We're going to get him back," Sébastien promises. "He's not beyond saving. Your Gaspar is still inside of him. We just have to get rid of the evil version."

"Just," I say with a huff, but the words help. I take a deep breath and sip of coffee, feeling a little calmer. "Okay. I'll go see the Chevalier—"

"Not alone," Sébastien insists.

"Yeah, we're not leaving you with that creep," Dix adds, in his usual upbeat tone.

I honestly don't think the Chevalier would want to harm me, but I'm glad not to have that difficult conversation alone. "Fine. We'll see him together, and hopefully, he'll know how to help Gaspar. Now, about GoPol."

"I'm gonna quit," Sébastien announces darkly. "I'll hand in my notice at the end of the week."

A few months ago, I would've wanted nothing more. It's good to know Sébastien has finally arrived at the point where he wants nothing more to do with the agency that ruined his life in more ways than one. But things are never that simple.

"Will your father let you go?"

"He'll make me sign an iron-clad NDA, of course. I know way too much to expect anything else, but I think he's as sick of me as I am of him at this point, so it'll probably work out."

"The last time you wanted to quit, it was on the condition he gets to kill you a dozen more times."

"See, that's the problem with History majors. They never forget anything," Dix quips.

I throw my head over my shoulder to glare at him. "It was last month."

As I turn back, I notice Sébastien swallowing hard. "I just want you to be safe."

"Will I ever be safe as long as he's around?"

The haunted look in his eyes makes me shudder. He's been through so much already, so much abuse, hidden in webs and webs of lies. He once managed to block it all out and concentrate on his job, using his purpose as a shield against cruel reality, but I took that from him. And while the truth might open the door to healing, I don't know how to fix him any more than I know how to fix Gaspar.

"Would you like some privacy?" Gaby asks.

It takes me a moment to read the look in her eyes as amusement. It turns sour before I have a chance to answer.

"I'm with Alix on this one," she says. "Obviously, I want you both as far away from GoPol as possible, but I don't know if resigning is the way to go."

"As for me," Marie chimes in, "I don't want to run away from GoPol. I want them to pay for what they've done. Your father shouldn't just get away with this."

Sébastien leans back and runs his hands over his face. "How?"

"We could find Gaspar and set him on Daddy Dearest next," Dix suggests. "That would take care of it."

This time, we both glare at him. "This isn't funny," Sébastien barks.

"I wasn't trying to be funny. Just pragmatic," Dix defends himself and jumps off the counter. "You have to admit, it would solve this particular problem."

"May I ask who you're talking to?" Gaby asks, slightly unnerved. She and Marie have no idea it's not just the four of us here.

"My infuriating younger self," Sébastien says. "We're *not* going to plot murder against our father!"

"Your younger self was happy to murder people?" Marie asks, nearly hopping onto Gaby's lap.

Sébastien sighs and shakes his head. "No, I wasn't, and I'm not now either. As for Dix..."

"He carries his own trauma," I say, ever so gently.

Dix glowers at me, but there's not much heat in it, just a hint I'm right on the money. Seventeen-year-old Sébastien hadn't thought about murdering anyone—though he'd certainly told himself it would be all right if someone murdered him. Eternally seventeen-year-old Dix, on the other hand, has just been murdered by his father and since then has watched life pass him by, never growing old, and worse, never again being respected as a human being. Is it really so far-fetched for him to want revenge?

Unfortunately, killing Charles is a hard no for me. I wish he'd just get into a car accident, but I don't want to bear that burden. And I don't want Sébastien or Dix to carry it, either, much less exploit Gaspar's darkness to do the job for us.

Dix walks over and sits on the table next to us. I don't know if it's because he can't move the chair or if it's because he's too cool to sit on something so mundane. "What are we going to do about him, then?" he asks. "I'm with Marie. He can't just get away."

"It's more important that you two get away," I tell him, putting my hand on Sébastien's arm. "That's our number one priority."

"You, too," Sébastien says softly, "because that's *my* number one priority."

Right. For a moment, I forgot how much Charles hates me. I may not work for GoPol, but that doesn't mean I'm safe. Far from it, actually. Charles has proven time and time again that if he can get away with it, he'll have me murdered and dumped at the bottom of the Seine.

Gaby clears her throat, and I let go of Sébastien as if I've been burnt. "Yes, so. Preferably, no one dies. But seriously, what can we do? Maybe, if we all go to the police—"

"My father's part of the police."

"Yes, but surely they'll want to know if one of them is corrupt—"

Sébastien shakes his head long before she's finished. "He's too far up the food chain. Let's say we do that. We get lucky and get an idealistic police officer with an unblemished sense of justice. As soon as the case gets to a higher commander, it'll get shut down. GoPol's mission is too important for this country's security. The higher-ups don't care what GoPol does so long as they do their job. My father would argue that Alix—and I—are a security risk and the government will agree. And believe me, they'll absolutely sacrifice one or two, or even four, innocents to keep GoPol going."

Marie crosses her arms and frowns. "That can't be right. Shouldn't the government, I don't know, protect *all* its citizens?"

"Not if they're a risk to national security." Sébastien sighs heavily. "Sacrifices must be made for the greater good." It sounds like something he's heard over and over again.

"Too bad the greater good doesn't include ghosts, right, History Girl?" Dix says sullenly, making Sébastien stiffen.

I get the whole argument. I'd have to be a fool and a very bad student not to understand it. You'd think we'd moved on from certain tactics, that we've somehow evolved and become better, but the truth is history repeats itself, and humans will be humans.

"So, to stop your father," I think out loud, "he has to become the greater security risk?"

Sébastien gives me a strange look. "I guess so, yes, but how do you want to explain that to his superiors?"

For a moment, I felt like I had a plan. Now it's slipping through my fingers again. "I have no idea."

The five of us stare at the table in sullen resignation. The truth is there's very little we can do. Charles has all the power and Sébastien is right. If the government wants to keep betting on GoPol, we'll be sacrificed. And nobody will be the wiser.

CHAPTER 3

I have to wait until my weekend shift before I get some quiet time with my ghosts. As I pick up the litter behind their graves and wash off dubious spills, I tell Victor the whole sorry story of what happened in Provence. The mundane task helps keep my voice fairly light, and I only choke up once or twice.

"And so, he killed her. It was pretty gruesome and—"

"How?" Victor asks. "You said Gaspar killed her?"

"Well, she was a ghost whisperer like me and..."

I bite my lip. So far, I've managed to avoid the truth about Gaspar's current status. My explanation is sound. Even as a ghost, he could've killed Margot. Just like, technically, any ghost could kill me. But do I really want to lie to Victor?

I sigh heavily. "Something happened to Gaspar, while... while he was gone."

Victor leans against the wall and looks down at me. "What do you mean?"

"He came back to life." There, I said it.

The change in Victor's demeanour is instantaneous. Concern turns to outright horror and indignation. His shoulders hunch, and he clenches his fists. "That's impossible!"

"It *was* impossible." I pack up my cleaning utensils and stand, rubbing my aching knees as I do so. "Le Chevalier d'Os has probably been working on bringing back the dead for years. He showed me his experiments." I shudder at the memory. "And offered to bring Gaspar back."

"And of course you took him up on it." Voltaire is suddenly there, his voice dripping with bile. "You have no idea what powers you're playing with, little girl. You just—"

"Shut up!"

Voltaire blinks at me. It's as if no one has ever shouted back at him before.

I really can't with his sanctimonious attitude today or any time soon. "I said no. We both decided not to mess with it. But then GoPol kidnapped Petite Alix and Gaspar thought he was going to lose me, so he went back to the Chevalier. Alone. I had nothing to do with it."

"Love knows no reason," Victor muses.

Voltaire snorts. "He should've waited."

"For what? Until I'm dead?"

Judging by Voltaire's silence that's exactly what he meant.

I turn my back on him. "Well, unlike some of the people around here, he actually cares about me."

Victor pulls a face, though he can't quite hide his amusement. "You know we'd be watching over you whether you could see us or not, kid."

"It doesn't matter. I didn't lose my powers. Gaspar just didn't know."

"Told you he should've waited," Voltaire mutters.

"And I said love knows no reason," Victor bites back before Voltaire can have another go. He looks at me kindly. "And you said it worked? He's really alive?"

I remember the day in Margot's lab when she'd tested Gaspar's ghost energy and came to a different conclusion. "He's something in between, I suppose. He can still walk through walls or appear out of nowhere, but everyone sees him. I was able to introduce him to my family and all." My voice begins to crack as I approach the last important piece of information. "There's something..." Let's try this again. "There's something very wrong with him." The words tremble all over the place.

"I bet," Voltaire grumbles.

Unnerved, I close my eyes and take a deep breath. Before I can open them again, I feel Victor's arms around me. He rarely touches me, so it comes as a bit of a surprise that he would initiate a full-on hug.

"Tell me everything."

And so, I do. It comes out in broken bits and pieces, and with a lot of tears and enough self-loathing to shut Voltaire up for good. When it's all out there, I feel emotionally drained. My head hurts and my eyes itch.

"I don't know how to fix this."

"Do you want to?" Voltaire asks. When he catches a look from Victor, he throws up his hands. "Yes, yes, love knows no reason. Have I ever told you how stupid love is? It ruins all progress of mankind. People *should* be guided by reason, not emotion. Our lives would be better for it."

"Our lives would be poorer for it, too," Victor says. "Just ask Zola."

Voltaire snorts and moves on—whether to actually ask Zola or sulk near his tomb and argue with Rousseau, I don't know.

Victor, meanwhile, wipes my tears and offers me his handkerchief. I don't think too much about the fact this handkerchief isn't real. It seems to work as long as I trust in it. Like Molay's wine back at the Boutique of Psychosis.

"I've never heard of such a case, but I'll inquire with certain mediums and other friends of the occult," Victor promises. "I have a few acquaintances in that field."

It's a good start. Apart from the Chevalier himself and perhaps Marie, I know no one involved. Just then, I remember. "Do you think Nostradamus could help? I met him in Provence."

"You met *the* Nostradamus?"

I nod. "Apparently he was working with Margot." Which should tell me asking him is a bad idea. "Most of the time, he spouts prophecies." My throat tightens as I remember another reason against him. "He had one for me. Two actually."

Victor pulls a face. "Real prophecies?"

Fresh tears run down my face. "One's already come true. He knew about Cédric's death."

"And the other?"

I need to take a deep breath. "He said I'd raise the dead one day and bring chaos and destruction to the world."

"And do you have such ambitions?" Victor asks with admirable calm.

"No."

His lips curve into a smile. "Then we shouldn't worry about it. Nostradamus may be right on occasion, but most of his prophecies are so vague they could literally mean anything. I believe he's little more than a fraud, and we should count ourselves lucky he rarely haunts Paris. Let us keep him in Provence and turn to more reliable sources."

I'm almost relieved to hear him say that. "And you have such sources?"

"A good handful, indeed." Victor's eyes widen slightly. "In fact, maybe one of those running the World Fair will have an idea. They're awfully clever."

Did I just hear that right? "The World Fair?"

"Oh yes, it opened a few weeks ago. L'Exposition Universelle des Fantômes."

"A Ghost World Fair?" If I didn't know Monsieur Renard gives his lecture every two years, I'd be worried about the coincidence. "Why haven't I heard of it?" Or *seen* it, for that matter.

Victor shrugs. "It's very much a ghost affair. I'm afraid Gustave would like to keep it that way."

"Gustave... Gustave *Eiffel*? The Eiffel Tower Gustave Eiffel?"

"And the Statue of Liberty, and a hundred railway bridges, viaducts, and railway stations. Oh, and the Panama Canal Gates or whatever he did there. Best not mention that one to his face, though."

Someone was a busy man. "And he's organising a Ghost World Fair?"

"Oh yes, see, he's only recently celebrated his ghost centenary, which has served to refresh his memory and re-infuse him with entrepreneurial energy. The 1889 World Fair was his crowning achievement, not that he organised it, mind you, but you can't blame the man for aspiring to lost greatness."

"He could be in the Panthéon one day."

"Possibly," Victor says, for once not arguing. "Which reminds me, have you had a chance to meet our newest members, Monsieur Manouchian and his lovely wife yet?"

"Yes, Victor. I had to learn all about them for the tour."

As their tombs have only recently been moved to the Panthéon, though, I haven't seen much of the resistance fighter and his wife yet.

Victor nods gently, and I see him drifting off. Before I lose his attention completely, I return to the subject. "Do you know where I can meet Monsieur Eiffel?" I could probably find out where he's buried—hopefully in Paris—but this seems quicker.

"Ask Marie. I think she's involved in the fair—showcasing some fascinating ghost radiation experiment, I'm sure."

I sigh. Normally, I try to keep my distance from *this* Marie. But Victor's right. Of all the inhabitants of the Panthéon, she's the most likely to have a connection with Gustave Eiffel. They're practically contemporaries and might've even crossed paths when they'd both been alive.

"One more question." I bite my lip again, unsure if I should really ask.

Victor's attention is firmly back on me again. "Yes, my dear?"

"Would you know a dead therapist or someone like that? Someone who's keen to continue... I mean who would consider giving therapy... to me. Just someone I could talk to about ghosts and Gaspar and... all that." As soon as the words are out, I wish I could swallow them again.

Victor's face softens and the pity in his eyes is devastating. "I'll find someone."

My confession has left me so exhausted I decide to take my bike into the Métro instead of braving Saturday traffic home. There's a lot to think about. Tomorrow, Sébastien and I will go down to the catacombs to talk to the Chevalier and hopefully come up with a plan. On the spur of the moment, I text Gaspar. Like all my other messages, it goes unread. Wherever he is, he hasn't switched it on or forgot to charge it.

Then there's the Ghost World Fair and Gustave Eiffel. Théo and Gaby agreed I should find them some ghosts to get a better idea of the World Fairs and what kind of inventions were exhibited in the Palais des Industries. If I can find out more about the ghost version, I can do them one better. Normally, I'd be thrilled and excited to learn more, but at the moment, it just feels like another thing on my list.

Yeah, I really need that therapy.

I try to gather some of the old amazement over ghostly lifestyles by trying to imagine what kind of inventions ghosts would come up with. Can they even work on a project long enough to make progress? Or do their ideas simply come into being, with no physics to limit them?

I arrive at my stop and get off the train. Carrying my bike upstairs, I wonder where they hold this Ghost World Fair. Probably in the catacombs. Or wherever Gustave Eiffel is buried. That reminds me to look it up, so I balance my bike as I pull out my phone. Levallois-Perret, which is a small cemetery just outside the western gates of Paris—not exactly close.

There's no point in cycling the short distance from the Métro station, so I use the time to gather a brief overview of the man who gave us so many iconic buildings. From the sounds of it, he was a real workaholic, although he somehow managed to father five children along the way. They probably never saw much of him as he jetted around the world for his various projects. It's a wonder he can stay focused enough in Paris to pull off an entire World Fair.

I lock my bike under the stairs in the hall and make my way upstairs, calling Gaspar one more time. Straight to mailbox. Since there are already fifty messages from me, I don't bother leaving another, and put the phone away again. And then I see them.

Hélène's boots.

With a heavy heart, I open the door and get rid of my shoes. From the living room, I hear muffled crying and my parents' hushed voices. I immediately feel bad. As if it's truly my fault her beloved Officer Cédric is dead. Hélène has been avoiding me ever since, but she made it clear I was *not* welcome at his funeral. I was fine with that as it saved me from having to listen to him whine about his bad choices, but it widened the gulf between the two of us even more.

He's been dead and buried for a few weeks now, which hopefully means my sister has had enough time to process her feelings and is ready to bear my presence again. Otherwise, what right does she have to force her hateful presence on me?

While I'm still considering whether to hide in my room or join the rest of my family in the living room, Hélène walks into the hallway on her way to the bathroom. She stops cold when she sees me, and I get to see what a giant mess she is. My sister is usually so well put together. Now she looks like she's been sleeping even worse than me, and hasn't washed her hair in a week, let alone combed it. There are deep shadows around her eyes and her skin is blotchy from crying. Most strikingly, she's wearing what I can only assume is one of Cédric's dress shirts over her pyjama bottoms. There are women who can pull off this look, but not with that lack of hair care.

Whatever tears she's cried dry on her cheeks as her expression turns to anger—not enough time, then. "You seem pretty smug."

"Do I?"

What have I got to be smug about? That my idiot brother-in-law turned out to be an even bigger idiot? That he backed the wrong homicidal horse? That she's as unhappy as I was when I'd thought I'd lost Gaspar?

"Isn't this what you wanted?" Even her voice sounds rough.

"Excuse me?"

Hélène sniffles. "He's gone. And it's all because of you and your ghosts."

And here we go again. "Fuck off, Hélène."

I refuse to be her punching bag. Cédric's death was of his own doing, and any guilt I might feel about it is all in my head. I don't even need therapy to tell me that.

I've turned my back on her and opened the door to my room, when she speaks again. "It should've been you. Then you could be with your beloved ghosts, and I'd have my Cédric back." Her voice breaks apart as fresh tears fall. "It should've been you."

Chapter 4

Hélène flees to the bathroom before I can even catch my breath.

Almost immediately, another door opens, and Odile pokes her head out. "What the hell?" she asks, looking absolutely bewildered. "Has she gone completely mad?"

At the same time, my parents emerge from the living room. "What was that about?" Maman asks.

One look at their faces and my breath catches in my throat. It's too much. It's all way too much. "Just focus on Léni." And with that, I flee to my room.

My whole body shakes as I lean against the door, Hélène's words running through my head. *It should've been me.* My sister wants me dead. She thinks I'd prefer it that way, anyway.

Less than half a minute later, a knock makes me jump. "It's me," Odile urges.

I don't know if I can face anyone right now, but Odile beats everyone else by a mile. At least, she won't blame me, too. Hopefully.

Still shaking, I open the door just wide enough for her to slip in. She takes one look at me and pulls me into a hug. I seem to need a lot of those lately.

"She's such a bitch."

"She's grieving."

Odile snorts. "That doesn't give her the right to be mean. Especially not this mean. You didn't put the noose around Cédric's neck. He did that all by himself. On his wedding day!"

"Don't…" I beg, trying to banish the horrible images of the day I found him.

"Pardon!" Odile lets go of me and takes a deep breath. "Malou cuddle time?"

Judging by the chewing sounds in the corner, my little hedgehog is already awake. "Malou cuddle time."

We don't really disturb her, just sit around the cage and watch her finish her breakfast. I envy her obliviousness. Malou has no idea of the family tragedies or the GoPol drama. She knows her ghosts, but that hardly stops her from living her best life. And when things get too much, she can just curl up in a ball and shut the world out. I *really* wish I could do that right now.

"I asked Victor to find me a therapist," I say after a while.

"Good." Odile looks as if she wants to say more, but it probably involves Hélène, so she shuts up instead.

I don't want to talk about it either, so I quickly change the subject. "Did you know the ghosts are organising a—"

Another knock interrupts me. *Please don't let it be Hélène.*

"Alix?" It's my father.

Maman probably sent him to calm the waves while she takes care of my sister. She always wants to keep the peace, but how we're supposed to come back from "I wish you were dead", I don't know.

I might as well get it over with. "Come in."

Papa opens the door and gives me an apologetic smile as he closes it behind him. "What are we doing?"

"Watching Malou."

Without further ado, he joins us on the floor. "Your maman sent me."

"I know."

"Listen, Hélène isn't doing well at the moment, but that was uncalled for."

"This isn't Alix's fault." Odile quickly launches into a passionate defence. "Just because she found Cédric doesn't mean she had anything to do with his death, and putting the blame on her, just because—Oh." She notices my raised eyebrow and Papa's unimpressed face. "You're not blaming her."

Papa grimaces. "Of course I don't blame her. Cédric killed himself. But he did it for a reason, didn't he?"

"But not because of Alix!"

He throws up his hands in defence and shakes his head. "I wasn't insinuating that." His gaze falls on me. "There's something I want to talk to you about. Cédric's death, but also other... ghost stuff. Maybe that's just something between the two of us?"

Odile warns me with an indignant look not to cut her off again. "Odi knows everything I know." Not really, but in spirit. "Besides, she'd be listening through the wall if you sent her out."

Papa snorts. "That's my daughter."

With a proud nod of her head, Odile crosses her arms, making it clear she's not going anywhere. "Alix and I are a team. And Malou."

"Very well. I want to help, Alix, but you have to be honest with me."

"Help with what?"

"Exposing GoPol."

My mouth drops open. I had a few ideas of what he might propose, but this wasn't one of them. "You want to expose GoPol?"

"In my opinion, they're the ones behind all this recent drama, and from what little I've gathered, there are more victims. Right now, it's just a theory, so first, I need to make sure I'm not totally wrong about this. Cédric's suicide is highly suspicious. People don't get married then kill themselves a few hours later without warning. Which tells me either something happened or he's been planning it for a while. You... you talked to his ghost, didn't you?"

The police never asked about anything other than how and when I found him. Apart from the tragic timing, there was nothing suspicious about his suicide. "He dreamed of becoming a ghost whisperer."

"Cédric?" Odile asks in disbelief. "He wanted to be like you?"

"More like Sébastien. He was obsessed with becoming a ghost whisperer and starting at GoPol. But he didn't know what it involved until I told him. Obviously, knowing didn't stop him."

"But why then? Why on his wedding day and why like this, when nobody could help him in time?" It helps that my father has been through the ghost whisperer process before and knows what it requires.

Part of me wants to keep the gruesome details to myself. I've already dragged enough family members into my little war with GoPol, but he just offered to help take them down, and Sébastien and I don't know how to. I'm not sure my father has a better plan, but it's worth a try. At least he's not trying to persuade me to forgive Hélène.

"Because he was tricked. Charles told him to do it on his wedding day, to prove his commitment. But when the time came, he dropped him to attend to... other matters."

My father raises an eyebrow. "Does that have anything to do with where you immediately ran off to?"

Sometimes, it sucks that Papa is an investigative journalist. He notices every detail. "Yes. Charles was… He was going to kill Sébastien."

"His own son?"

"He's done it before."

"He did…" Papa's eyes widen while Odile gasps. Apparently, I never told her about that part. After a moment, Papa stores the information away and begins his next line of questioning. "When?"

"His whisper ghost is called Dix, short for Dix-Sept."

"That's…"

"Murder?" I ask. "Child abuse? Utterly despicable?"

Papa breathes in sharply. "All of that, yes. But why would he kill him again? Or was it supposed to be all the way this time?"

"No, it… it's complicated. I suppose it was some kind of experiment. See how many whisper ghosts one could create?" I'm getting dangerously close to the subject I don't want to talk about, so I hastily dodge it. "So, yeah, it's Charles Hélène should be mad at. And Cédric, for being so gullible." That came out a bit harsh. "I suppose he's also a victim of a toxic childhood. According to Sébastien, Charles often pitted them against each other."

"I see." Papa runs a hand over his chin. "So GoPol actively murders its recruits? Raises them from childhood?"

"I'm pretty sure Sébastien was a special case. As far as I know, the other GoPol agents are people like me, who became ghost whisperers unintentionally but were deemed good candidates for their force. Most people with near-death experiences get relieved of their ghosts before they know any better."

He nods thoughtfully. "Like me."

"Like you."

"At the time, I was grateful and welcomed it, but you were right when you said I didn't know what I was bargaining away." He frowns, unhappy with himself. "It bothers me because I pride myself on being thorough and doing my research. But I did none of that. When Cédric offered to fix it, I just went along with it."

"You weren't coping well. At all."

"Yeah, but at least you didn't tell Alix it should've been her instead," Odile chimes in, still angry on my behalf.

I sigh heavily. The last surviving rational part of me wants to defend Hélène because it's clear she's not coping with the disaster her life has suddenly turned into, but the rest of me is sick and tired of being her punching bag. And talking about her. "So, you want to expose them for what they did to her?"

"To Hélène?" asks Papa. "What happened to her is just the tip of the iceberg. I know you tend to keep your cards close to your chest, but I'd bet my entire career that they've caused you a lot more grief. You've been involved with them for half a year, and in that time I've seen you reduced to tears every other week."

Only every other week? "Oh, they just tried to take away my whisper ghost, threatened me, and tried to kill me about half a dozen times."

My father looks absolutely horrified. "And you never thought to tell me?"

I shrug. "After what happened in the Boutique? I didn't want to upset you or get anyone else involved. Just ask Odi how resistant I was with her."

Odile rolls her eyes for dramatic effect. "Oh yeah, she cut me out *all* the time."

"You're not in this alone."

"I know, I've got Sébastien, and Gaby, and… Gaspar, I suppose." I suddenly have to blink hard.

Fortunately, my father has his own agenda. He puts his hand on mine and looks me in the eye. "And you have me."

"And me," Odile chimes in.

"Right." I manage to banish the thought of Gaspar. "You said you wanted to help expose GoPol—or Charles. How? He's practically invincible. According to Séb, the government will protect him, no matter what."

Papa's face darkens. "When the government fails you, you turn to the people."

"The people? Nobody knows about GoPol—or ghosts, for that matter."

"Yet."

My eyes widen and my mouth falls open. "Are you suggesting we *tell* people?"

Whenever the topic of ghosts came up in my life, I was met with ridicule or disbelief. Even Gaby needed real tangible proof before she believed me. And that's all before we get into the messy topic of people's beliefs around the afterlife.

"Not just tell them," Papa says. "Imagine an exposé in Le Monde or Libération. We inform everyone about ghosts and GoPol, and what crimes of theirs are kept from the French people in the name of national security. Naturally, we need irrefutable evidence, a whole lot of testimonies, and insider knowledge. A whistleblower. Do you think Sébastien would be up to the job?"

I still haven't recovered. What my father is proposing is *big*. He's practically putting his career on the line, risking immense ridicule, not to mention possible prosecution. "Do you think it would work?"

To pull this off, we'd be forcing people to readjust their entire belief systems. The ghostly afterlife is not exactly the reward and punishment system of most religions. Never mind the fact we're asking people to believe something they can't even see.

"The court of public opinion is extremely powerful. And if they find out the government has been keeping this from them, there might be riots."

Violence in the streets is about the last thing I need right now. "But would they believe it?"

In my experience, people don't tend to readily believe in ghosts. At least not the way they really are.

Papa shrugs. "That's why we need proof and insider knowledge. If Sébastien can get us files and mission details, maybe pictures of their setup, we stand a pretty good chance. Plus, testimonies. We need to find as many independent or former ghost whisperers as possible."

"I could put out an appeal on social media," Odile suggests cautiously. "And sift through the frauds to find the real ones."

"Good one! But be subtle. We don't want to alert GoPol to what we're doing until we've put it all together. We can't risk them putting an embargo on this and blocking our outlets."

I look back and forth between the two of them. Slowly, my father's plan is taking shape in my mind. It's scary—terribly so—but it might actually work, and for the first time in months, I feel something like hope. GoPol has been tormenting and toying with me for most of the year. It's high time I fought back.

"Very well. I'll talk to Sébastien. He'll probably be reluctant, but Dix will be all for it. Maybe together we can convince him that it's worth it. It's just a lot of... trauma."

"Understandable." Papa nods wisely. "We can probably do it without him, find someone else willing to talk, but he's Charles' son and knows GoPol better than most. Besides, you two are in this together, aren't you?"

How much does my father know already? Inexplicably, I think of the kiss—or rather, kisses—Sébastien and I shared. A relationship is out of the question, what with Gaspar and all, but I can't deny I've grown very fond of him. Maybe even too much.

"He wants this as much as I do. I just have to convince him this is the right way." It certainly beats an assassination attempt.

"Good." Papa claps his knee before standing. "Shall we go and deal with the minor matter of Hélène's misplaced anger now?"

"Do I have to apologise?"

Papa shakes his head. "Not in my book, though it probably wouldn't hurt to tread on eggshells for a bit."

I get up with a groan, while Odile just waves us off. "You deal with Léni. I'll keep Malou company."

"Coward," I hiss, as I follow Papa into the living room.

There, Maman and Hélène are sitting on the couch. Hélène has her head on Maman's shoulder but straightens when she hears us approaching.

"Did you have a good talk?" Maman asks, a kind smile on her lips.

Papa and I exchange a glance. We had a good talk, but probably not about what Maman had hoped.

I sigh, and decide to get this over with quickly, so Hélène can leave. "Léni, I'm sorry about what happened to Cédric. It must be so hard."

Her face falls so quickly it's almost frightening.

"I know you blame me for it, but I had nothing to do with his death."

She snorts. "Yeah, right."

"Darling, please," Maman says in a soft tone. "We talked about this."

Hélène takes a deep breath and sits even straighter. "I'm sorry for what I said. I didn't mean it."

I almost respond with, "Yeah, right," as well, but manage to bite my tongue and wince instead. "You're in a lot of pain. I understand that."

"That's right," Maman says, smiling gratefully. "Léni and I talked about it, and we've come to the conclusion she should move back here. Just for a little while, so she doesn't have to be alone in her apartment, where everything reminds her of Cé—"

"If she moves in, I'm out."

The smile melts from my mother's face. "Alix…"

"I mean it. If you don't want Hélène to be alone, why don't you just move in with her? I'm not going to share my room after the way she's treated me." So much for apologising. As all three stare, I throw up my hands. "I'd better start packing, then."

Chapter 5

I'm lucky to have the best friend in the world. Gaby didn't even bat an eye when I called and asked her if I could stay for a while. She's so nice, she even made room for me in her drawer, then listened to me rant about Hélène all night long.

But now morning has come, I can't see it lasting long. Even though I've brought the bare minimum with me—toiletries, two changes of clothes, study materials, and Malou—her shoebox apartment looks cluttered. My clothes are in the drawer and my school stuff stayed in my bag by the door, but my toiletries are scattered everywhere, along with my catacombs gear, and Malou's cage takes up considerable space on the kitchen counter, blocking off the life-sustaining coffee machine. Add to that the empty bags of snacks and dirty dishes, and I feel terrible for imposing on her.

"If you're up, could you grab me a new shampoo bar from under the sink?" Gaby calls from the shower, which is barely an arm's length away.

I get out of bed and promptly trip over a pair of shoes. Managing to avoid any sharp corners, I step over my bag and grab the item and hand it to Gaby.

"Thanks, ma puce! I'll be done shortly, then you can jump in the before your date."

"It's not a date," I say, rolling my eyes, but it reminds me I should text Sébastien my new address. Now, if only I could find my phone.

A few stumbles later, I unplug it from the charger, only to realise it was unplugged at some point in exchange for Gaby's. My phone's at a measly twenty-two per cent. I send a text to Sébastien before checking Gaby's phone, which is now fully charged, and give mine a few more minutes. Then I climb back, put Malou on the bed, and empty out the coffee machine, before freshly filling it. Meanwhile, Gaby finishes her shower, and we shuffle past each other as I take her place.

Gaby laughs at the awkwardness of it all. "This is fun."

I grimace slightly. It's not the first time I've stayed at Gaby's—far from it, but now I've been invited to live here, it seems much smaller than before.

"It won't be for long, I promise."

Hopefully, Hélène will get over Cédric soon enough to move back. If she can afford to keep the apartment. I sigh. If not, she'll probably move home for much longer.

"You know you can stay here as long as you want," Gaby says, as she rummages through a drawer she's pulled from under her bed to hand me a towel. "Or you could move in for real. You're old enough to leave the nest." Her eyes light up. "We could have a slumber party every night. Just you, me, and Malou."

"And what about Marie?" I ask. "Am I supposed to stand in the shower when she sleeps over?" There's no room for privacy in this tiny flat.

"Marie will understand. And I can visit her when I want some alone time."

"Doesn't she live in a church?"

Gaby pulls a face. "Yeah, there's that. Never mind. We'll think of something. Now go!"

I take a quick shower, put on my cataphile gear, and have barely enough time to finish my coffee when the doorbell rings. A quick glance out the window shows me Sébastien's familiar bike.

"It's him."

"Of course, it's him. He's always on time!" Gaby giggles. She's lying on the bed with her coffee in her hand. "You two have fun crawling through the catacombs, while Malou and I have a girls' day."

"She's sleeping."

"Yeah? Maybe I'll take a nap, too." She yawns for good measure. "I definitely didn't get enough sleep last night."

"Sorry."

Gaby throws a sock at me. "I had *fun!* Now, you go and have some, too."

With where we're going—or rather, why—fun is a very unlikely outcome.

I fill Sébastien and Dix in on my father's plan as we walk down the dark corridors and squeeze through tight tunnels. As expected, Sébastien starts grimacing and biting his lip, clearly holding back choice words, while Dix grins widely.

"Imagine if everyone knew about ghosts!" the whisper ghost exclaims as he pulls me through one of the windows.

Clearly uncomfortable, Sébastien pulls a face before he climbs in after me. "I don't see what's so good about it. Most people won't believe it, even with scientific proof. Not if it goes against their beliefs. And then you've got the people who *will*. They have their own ridiculous ideas about ghosts. You'll get countless people claiming to be ghost whisperers and scamming others. Never mind the *real* ghost whisperers, who'll be up to all sorts of shenanigans."

I wipe dust off my forehead. "You still want to regulate who can be a ghost whisperer and who can't?" Are we really taking a step backwards here?

He winces. "Partially. Like, obviously, I don't want to continue the policy of taking away everyone's whisper ghosts, but there should be some regulations, don't you think?"

"Why? What's the big deal if some people can talk to ghosts? I do it."

"Not everyone's like you," he says, still sounding a little tortured. "You help ghosts, and you treat them like real people. All in all, it's no more dangerous than hanging out with the living. But there's huge potential to use these abilities for nefarious purposes."

I'm not too impressed. "You mean like spying on people?" With an eye roll, I continue down the path.

"Maybe I'm biased," he admits. The tight tunnel forces us to walk in single file, so I can't see his face. "The things I've seen on the job... Espionage is pretty serious. It's not just about over-hearing an important conversation or catching a glimpse of a state secret. Those are bad enough, but being a ghost whisperer makes other crimes so much easier. Assassination, for example. Some-one's whisper ghost can quickly find out everything about your daily routine and plans to prepare a strike. Or grand robberies. No combination would be safe. Kidnappings, data theft, acts of terrorism..."

There's a whole side of GoPol I haven't come into contact with yet. With all the drama surrounding my whisper ghost, it's easy to forget they actually play a vital role in our nation's defence force. Sébastien's right. My experience with ghosts is wildly different compared to what he usually has to deal with. Perhaps I'm being too optimistic when I imagine the rest of the world would act and react the way I do. If I've learnt anything over the past few months, it's that the world definitely *doesn't* work the way I'd thought. Still…

"I get it. It would be a massive change." Even my father mentioned riots. "Maybe we don't tell the world…" I pull myself through another window into a wider corridor.

There, my gaze lands on Dix, who looks at me with a strange mixture of hope and fear. It would be so easy to agree with Sébastien and keep the peace by maintaining the status quo. But that's how we got into this situation. Just because the world doesn't know about ghosts, they won't cease to exist. They'll still be here, longing and suffering—or in some cases, like Dix, even being exploited. Things *have* to change.

"It's not up to us to decide who knows what. Nobody has the right to keep the rest of the world in the dark. And yes, it's a process, probably a messy one, but so was every change in history. Things never magically improve from one period to the next. There's always strife and chaos. I mean, just look at how long it took us to carve out this nation."

"Listen to History Girl. She knows her stuff," Dix says.

But I shake my head while I help Sébastien through. "No, listen to Dix. And all the other ghosts. We ignore their needs because it's easy to do so, but just because something is easy doesn't mean it's right. In fact, doing the right thing can be a lonely path."

He straightens and rolls his shoulders. "It can also be one of the most dangerous."

"As Voltaire would say, it's always dangerous to be right about things important people are wrong about. However, he also said it only takes two or three courageous people to change the spirit of a nation. So," I hold out my hand, "are you in?"

Sébastien takes it before he's even made up his mind. Or maybe his decision was already made when he threw his lot in with me. "I asked you to follow my lead, and it ended disastrously for both of us. I trust you. And your father."

I can't help smiling. The doubt is still visible on his face, but his words ring true. I'd be lying if I said the prospect of the chaos my father's article will unleash doesn't frighten me, but even as my heart beats like a drum, I see a glimmer of hope for the future. A glimpse of a better world for the living *and* the dead.

"I can't promise it'll be safe," I tell him. "In fact, if you agree to be the whistleblower, you'll have to keep working for GoPol. You'll have to get close to your father again, get him to trust you. At least partially. It could all blow up in our faces, anyway."

He squeezes my hand tighter. "This is what we trained for." With a horrible grimace, he adds, "All my life."

I want to pull him close and hug him, maybe even kiss him, but Dix seizes the moment to chime in. "Now C-Trente is gone, it should be so much easier. We'll get him, Séb. He won't get away this time."

Sébastien lets go of my hand and the moment passes. "Let's not get ahead of ourselves. As Alix said, processes like this take time. We won't earn Papa's trust back in a day, and we'll have to be selective about the kind of evidence we use. I don't want to put people at risk."

"You're such a bore," Dix complains. "Just blow it all up."

"And become the security risk Papa claims we are?" Sébastien argues.

"I think if we go through with this, we'll become exactly what he's so afraid of," I admit. "But he'll be a lot easier to sacrifice."

"Maybe," Sébastien muses. "He's having a bit of trouble."

I raise my eyebrows. "Trouble?"

"Word of what happened in Provence reached the higher-ups. He's got some explaining to do and is swamped. That's why I thought he'd be more open to letting me go."

Now that's something I like to hear. "Could you talk to the higher-ups? Get our version of events out, maybe?"

Sébastien winces predictably. "I..." He sighs heavily. "I guess, if I'm staying on, I might as well build some relationships of my own."

I know how hard this is for him as a lifelong loner. His father isolated him from all his peers and at work. If it weren't so important, I wouldn't ask.

"Thanks."

We fall silent as we arrive in the ruins of Lutetia. All around us, the crumbling, 2000-year-old walls alone bear witness to ghosts long forgotten. My historian curiosity still itches at the thought of all that knowledge down here, but there's something else buried in the heart of the catacombs.

It only occurs to me now that Sébastien has never been to the Chevalier's laboratory and has no idea what horrors await him. The Chevalier might not be too happy to see him, either. After all, Sébastien was involved in the raid on the Monastery of Bears. I probably should've warned both.

But it's too late now. We've already reached the hidden trapdoor in the ruins, and every word about what we might find behind it is stuck in my throat. I hated this place with its creepy reanimated animals since my first visit, but I seem to keep coming back. Mostly, because, according to the catacombs' ghosts, it's where the Chevalier spends his time.

With a heavy heart, I knock on the door and call, "Romain? Are you in there?"

For a few moments, I hope he isn't, but then the trapdoor opens, and the Chevalier sticks his head out. "Alix?" He squints at Sébastien. "And the young Roubert. What's this? An arrest?"

"Is there anything you should be arrested for?" Sébastien asks, just as curtly.

"Nobody's being arrested today. We just had a few questions."

The Chevalier frowns. "I'm rather busy."

"It's about Gaspar. Please!"

My pleading tone seems to soften his heart, but instead of inviting us in, the Chevalier comes up and closes the door behind him. Planting his feet on it, he asks, "What is it?"

I share a wary look with Sébastien before taking a deep breath. "Something went wrong with his resurrection."

"Care to be more specific?"

My stomach turns just thinking about it, but I force myself to explain. "He's not himself. I mean, sometimes he is and then he's all sweet and lovely, but sometimes... he's mean. Really mean. Like, he wants to hurt you."

The Chevalier frowns and takes a deep breath. "Did you really come to me to complain about your boyfriend's mood swings?"

"He killed someone," Sébastien says, before I can protest.

That gives the Chevalier some pause. "He did?"

I nod, my eyes stinging once again. "He did it to protect me, but still... I know Gaspar and that wasn't him. The Gaspar I knew wouldn't hurt a fly." I hug myself as the memories begin to form vivid images. "And these aren't normal mood swings, but full-on Dr Jekyll and Mr Hyde switches." I didn't come here for some mundane relationship trouble. "Something went seriously wrong when you brought him back, and I was wondering…"

"If I could turn him back into a ghost again?" the Chevalier asks, not sounding too impressed.

My cheeks heat up at the notion. It's too close to the last resort, which I don't even want to think about. "No, no, that's not what I'm asking. Just… fix him?"

For a moment, it looks like the Chevalier is going to laugh, but then he frowns instead. "Thanks for bringing this to my attention. I can't make any promises about Gaspar, but it's valuable information for any future experiments."

"Future experiments?" Sébastien asks, his voice a low rumble. "Who else are you trying to bring back?"

"Who knows?" The Chevalier shrugs, clearly unbothered by the question. As if he doesn't really care.

In a way, he reminds me of Margot—she even said they worked together for a while—but as much as he loves his science, I know there's a bigger plan behind it. Something that has to do with the places of power he's trying to claim.

He dismisses Sébastien and turns his attention back to me. "I'll look into it, but I'm a bit busy right now, and like I said, I can't promise a solution that isn't… rather permanent."

A shiver runs down my spine. It seems death truly is our only option. But it can't be. No matter how I feel or how much it hurts, I can't do that to Gaspar. He may have only agreed to the resurrection for me, but this is his *life*. His second life, but his life, nonetheless. I have no right to take that away from him, just because I miss the way he was as a ghost.

"Is that all?"

I swallow hard. The Chevalier has never dismissed me so quickly. Usually, he's eager to share his aspirations and plans—at least, to some extent. Is it because I brought Sébastien? Or is there something else going on I'd rather not know about?

"If you see him… would you tell him I miss him?"

He sighs but shrugs. "Sure. I'll be in touch if anything changes. Otherwise, I'll probably see you at the fair."

"At the fair?" My eyes widen. "You know about the Ghost World Fair?"

"Of course. Any ghost friend worth their dime knows about it. So long." And with that, he disappears back into his laboratory, closing the trapdoor on us.

"What's this about a Ghost World Fair?" Sébastien asks. He's got his arms crossed, clearly not impressed with the interaction.

Meanwhile, Dix crouches near the trap door. "You know, I could check inside?"

Before I can protest, Sébastien gives a little nod, and Dix falls through the door.

"That's rude," I call after him

"He's clearly hiding something." Sébastien loosens his stance and starts heading back the way we came. "So, about this Ghost World Fair—"

The trapdoor screeches behind us, just as Dix flies out again. "You won't believe this—"

But before he can tell us anything, Gaspar appears. His hair is dishevelled and his face is smeared with something dark, as if he's dug himself from a grave. He's still wearing the clothes he was wearing when he killed Margot—they're still stained with dried blood. But worst of all is the burning look in his eyes, as if he hates my very guts and the world's, as well.

"I hear you want to get rid of me?"

Chapter 6

"Gaspar!" Despite his frightful appearance, my body moves on its own, and I run to him. I throw myself into his arms, burying my fingers in his dried-out hair and hiding my face in the crook of his neck. "I missed you so much."

Instead of putting his arms around me, Gaspar snorts. "Doesn't look like it."

When I tip my head back, I notice him glaring at Sébastien. Meanwhile, Sébastien's face has darkened, and he has a hand at his side—near his weapon.

Shocked, I stumble back. Is this how far Gaspar has fallen? Is he now a danger to everyone?

"Must hurt that she's still all over me despite everything," Gaspar says in a deep drawl unlike anything I've ever heard from him.

"Stop that!" I say, nudging his shoulder.

Gaspar reacts with lightning speed, grabbing my wrist before I can pull it away. His fingers tighten and I yelp as he squeezes it hard enough to hurt.

Almost as quickly, Sébastien is at my side, breaking Gaspar's grip with an enviable ease. He shoves me behind him as he and Dix form a wall between us. "Don't you lay a hand on her!"

"She started it," Gaspar says, the mockery audible in his voice. A step back and he raises his hands. "Whatever. You can have her. I don't want her anymore. Just leave me alone."

Every word is a punch in my gut. Even though I know this isn't my sweet hedgehog boy, they're gut-wrenching. It sounds like the Gaspar I knew is well and truly gone. The resurrection killed him more than death ever could.

I half expect Sébastien to take a swing, but all he does is maintain his protective posture, refusing to take the bait. "You done?"

"Long ago."

"She came here to help you."

"*Fix* me," Gaspar hisses back. My own words are reflected back and I feel my stomach turn. "She's just sad her toy won't work the way she wants it to anymore."

I can't take this any longer. Squeezing my hands between them, I push through Sébastien and Dix. They let me pass, but I earn concerned looks from both. Maybe I should heed their silent warning, but I just can't give up on Gaspar. All the things he's saying to hurt me come from a place of pain deep inside. This dark side isn't just a caricature, it's all his anger, fear, and pain rolled into one.

I start with an apology. "I'm sorry I misspoke. 'Fix' was the wrong word. You've been through something so traumatic, I'm struggling to grasp the extent of it."

He looks at me irritably but doesn't interrupt.

"We've both been through so much. You more than me," I add quickly. "Listen, Victor is going to find me a ghost therapist to work through all the Provence stuff,"—and probably much more—"maybe you could tag along? Talk to them, too?"

Gaspar makes a face and spits out, "Oh, great, now you want to fix me with therapy?"

"You're hurting, Gaspar."

He leans forward. "Not as much as you'll hurt when I'm done with—"

Sébastien puts his arm between us and pulls me back again. "That's enough! Let's go, Alix."

"Yeah, go with him," Gaspar says, with a sneer. "If anyone's broken, it's the two of you."

Tears sting in my eyes as Sébastien gently pulls me away. Meanwhile, Dix looks at him in confusion. "Why do you want to hurt her so badly? You love her."

"Never have, never will."

Blinded by tears, I stomp stoically through the catacombs. Soon, the passage is narrow enough to pull myself forward, though I stumble over my feet. My fingers scratch along the rough surface, catching on shards or bones, but I don't care. Keeping going is all I can do while Gaspar's words run through my head like an out-of-control bulldozer.

He hates me. He really truly hates me. Is it because he became a murderer for me? Or because he's stuck in this existence, neither dead nor alive? Either way, I'm the cause of all his problems.

Mercifully, Sébastien remains silent behind me, as if he knows even the slightest word now would shatter me. We crawl back through the catacombs in complete silence until I reach a small window. As I climb through it, my backpack catches on a corner, and I hang in suspense for a second or two before crashing down and knocking my knees on the rough-hewn stone.

"You okay?" Sébastien asks.

I burst into tears. It doesn't even hurt that much, but I'm unable to hold back any longer. I crawl out of the way, ravaged by sob after sob. Look at who needs fixing now.

Sébastien climbs through and crouches next to me. Once again, he's silent, but he puts an arm around me and holds me tight. I lean against him, hiding my face in his chest and crying through his shirt. Almost shyly, he runs his thumb up and down my back before finally putting his other hand on the back of my head. He doesn't say a word as I let it all out, all the pain and despair.

From time to time I hear Dix shuffle his feet, but he stays quiet, too.

Eventually, I manage to calm down enough to let go and wipe my eyes. Sébastien's shirt is a complete write-off at this point, but he doesn't complain.

"Sorry."

"Don't be."

I nod, unable to form any other coherent words. The tears have stopped for now, but they're not sealed away. Just thinking about Gaspar and what he said makes my throat tighten and eyes burn again. I tell myself the Chevalier will find a way to make things right, but Gaspar's words invade my thoughts. He's not mine to fix. He's not mine at all.

Sébastien raises his hand and wipes away a single tear with his thumb. "We'll find a way."

I shake my head. "Say something else."

He pulls himself up before helping me. "Do you want to talk about that Ghost World Fair?"

That, I can do. "Apparently, the ghosts are rallying behind Gustave Eiffel to organise a World Fair reminiscent of the 19th century ones. You know, where they showed off the Industrial Revolution's innovations?" This is working. My voice stabilises with each word.

"Sounds boring," Dix says, folding his arms behind his head and yawning for good measure.

Sébastien rolls his eyes, and I manage a half chuckle. "Is it just nostalgia or are the ghosts presenting new innovations?"

"I don't know," I admit. "All I know is it's happening, Gustave Eiffel is organising it, and Marie Curie is apparently planning on attending. Oh, and apparently, the Chevalier will be there, too."

"He can't see ghosts," Sébastien says, his face instantly darkening.

That's true, which means... I look in Sébastien's eyes and realise he seems to have had the same idea. "There'll probably be ghost whisperers in attendance."

"But who?" He frowns, then winces. "Don't shoot me for saying this, but it sounds like something GoPol should investigate." When I raise my eyebrows, he quickly amends, "What I mean is this is the perfect piece of information that could buy me a sliver of my father's trust. Take it to him, set up a mission. Plus, if we meet those ghost whisperers, they might agree to help with that article of yours."

It takes me a moment to realise what he's suggesting. "You're right. This is a golden opportunity. Just promise to take me with you. Mission or not, I'm dying to see it. It would also benefit my homework."

We talk a bit about the fair as we walk down one of the underground boulevards. Most of it is speculation about what innovations ghosts would come up with, which on Sébastien's side are purposely ridiculous to make me laugh.

When my heart feels like it's been glued back together enough to last another day, I tell him about Hélène's struggle and how that led to me moving in with Gaby.

"You know I have space."

I stare at him, and he looks surprised he's said it out loud. "In Gaspar's room?" As soon as I say it, I regret mentioning his name.

"It's empty at the moment. But you can also sleep in my room... While I sleep on the couch, of course!" he adds, so quickly I can't help grinning.

"Would you now?"

In the light of my headlamp, his cheeks are deliciously flushed. "I'd sleep on the floor if necessary. I miss your visits," he adds softly.

Before we all went to Provence, I had dinner there almost every day. But that was when Gaspar lived there. Now it would be just the two of us. Living together.

I swallow, suddenly reminded of the kisses we've shared. With all the drama lately, it was easy to push my feelings for him aside. It'll be harder if we're living together.

Once again, Gaspar's cruelty sours my thoughts. The way he passed me on to Sébastien, as if *I* were a toy he was tired of playing with... You could say our relationship is well and truly dead, and yet I can't help holding onto the belief he's not the same. Simply moving on without him is out of the question. The guilt alone would kill me.

"As friends..." I begin.

He nods immediately. "Yes, absolutely. You need a place to stay. I've got one. This is just until Hélène moves out or you get your own place."

I nod more slowly. That's right. It's only temporary, and as much as I love Gaby, her apartment is too small for the two of us. We both know that.

"Okay. Thanks, I mean."

"No problem."

I find myself smiling, a real, warm smile that heals a part of the heart Gaspar shattered earlier. Together, we make our way across the Banga and walk through a few corridors until we reach the wider one that will eventually lead to the overgrown gully. I can already see the rectangle of light at the end when I hear the patter of someone running behind us.

"Alix!"

My heart immediately falls to pieces, the glue not yet strong enough to hold it together. It's Gaspar's voice, but unlike before, it's soft again, painfully reminiscent of my hedgehog boy.

"Alix, wait. Please." He enters our circle of light, panting from running.

As Gaspar leans forward to catch his breath, I share a look with Sébastien. He's cautious, but this time, his hand stays away from the concealed weapon at his hip.

"I'm sorry," Gaspar manages to say. He looks up at me with his brown puppy eyes and whatever shield I might have scrambled together falls apart. This is him. His true self.

He takes another breath and straightens up. "I'm so, so sorry about before." His gaze flickers to Sébastien. "I have to apologise."

Sébastien tenses for a moment, but then he nods. "I'll give you two some privacy." As he turns, he touches my shoulder. "If he switches, just shout out. Dix will be there in a moment, and I'll follow shortly after."

Gaspar looks absolutely miserable as he watches Sébastien leave. "He's mad at me, isn't he?"

"You said some pretty hurtful things," I say, crossing my arms to keep them from flying around Gaspar's neck.

He looks down again. "I'm so sorry, Alix. I... It's happening more and more. It's like a... switch," he says, using Sébastien's word. "I can't control him anymore. Not for long."

"Him?"

"The other me." Gaspar snorts. "Gosh, that sounds like such a lame excuse. I'm there, you know? I can see you and hear you, but every word I say gets twisted in my mouth, and my body moves on its own. It feels like... I don't know, can ghosts be possessed?"

I shrug noncommittally. "You're not a ghost anymore."

"Right. There's that." He takes a deep breath. "Listen, I don't know how much time I've got left, so I wanted to apologise. To both of you. Please tell Sébastien I'm sorry. I like him. I like him very much. With you."

I let my arms fall. "What are you talking about?"

"He's a great guy, Alix. And he loves you so much, and he can give you everything I never could."

"But I want you." Annoyingly, my voice is on the verge of choking again.

"You want him, too," Gaspar says with a terribly kind smile. "You don't have to deny it. I see you together. You've grown fond of him."

The damned tears are back. "Gaspar…"

He shakes his head. "No, no, don't cry. This is good. I'm glad you have each other. Really glad." His smile widens. "Do me this favour, love. Move on with him. Don't look back. Don't try to…" At last, the smile becomes painful. "I can't be fixed. But I can stay away from you both. Please." He takes a step closer and gently runs his thumb over my cheek to wipe the tears. "Let go of me."

Before I can even catch my breath, he turns around and jogs away, quickly disappearing into the impenetrable darkness below.

My throat is too tight to call after him until it's far too late. My feet feel like lead as I turn away from the catacombs and follow Sébastien into the light.

It's a cloudy afternoon, which makes the light a little easier on my tear-strained eyes. Dix is playing with the bike at the top of the gully, while Sébastien is waiting for me right at the exit, looking as if he's been holding his breath all this time.

"You good?"

I nod shakily. In truth, I'm so far from good I no longer know what good even feels like. "It was his good side. He says he's sorry. And... and... and that I should let him go."

Sébastien regards me carefully. "Will you? Let him go?"

It's not even on the table. "Of course not." The sour taste of stubbornness fills my mouth, erasing the tears. "I'll find a way to bring him back."

Sébastien looks almost relieved to hear me say it. He holds out his hand and smiles grimly. "Together."

I take his hand, grateful for his strength. "Together."

CHAPTER 7

The next day, my father helps me move my things to Sébastien's apartment. I'm not taking everything with me. My furniture is staying where it is for now, as are most of my books and keepsakes. Instead, I'm bringing the majority of my clothes, everything I need for school, and Malou's things. The latter has caused a bit of drama with Odile, who's already seeing her Instagram account failing, but I've promised her regular content creation visits that double as sisterly hangouts. Right now, she's documenting Malou's big move, complete with a miniature suitcase she's pulled from the depths of her accessory drawer.

Meanwhile, Sébastien, Papa, and I are unloading the car and carrying the boxes up the stairs. Or rather, they're carrying most of the boxes, as Sébastien refuses to let me lift anything heavier than a potted plant.

"I don't know about this, Chouchou. Moving in with a man?" Papa asks on one of the rare occasions we're alone in the stairwell.

"What's so different about it from moving in with a woman?"

Papa snorts. "Touché. Although, I'm more comparing Gaby to him here. We've known Gaby for years. She's like our fourth daughter."

"Gaby's apartment is too small, and before you say we could look for something bigger together, have you ever tried to find an apartment in Paris?"

"I know. It's why we never moved into a bigger place." He shrugs awkwardly, a box in his arms. "And soon there won't be any need for a bigger place. What with all my birds getting ready to fly."

I shift the bag of Malou's treats I'm carrying to my other arm and give him a quick one-sided hug. "You've got Hélène back."

"And lost you in the process," Papa says, the pain evident in his voice.

We make some space as Sébastien comes jogging down the stairs. "Anything left?"

"Two more boxes," Papa tells him. "I'll help you with the last one."

"No need. I've got them both." And with that, he's already past our flight.

Papa giggles softly. "I'll admit, he comes with benefits." A long look at me follows. "Maybe even more benefits?"

I groan at the blatant insinuation. "Sébastien and I are just friends. No benefits whatsoever."

That only makes him laugh harder. "If you say so."

"I mean it!" We reach the top floor, and I push open the half-closed door a little more forcefully than intended. "Seriously, Séb and I... oh, hey Dix."

Dix is leaning against the wall, looking a bit bored, since he can't help with the move. Now he grins, though. "What's that with you and Séb?"

"Nothing!" I groan again, making both my father and Dix laugh.

I drop Malou's treats in the spare room—Gaspar's former abode—and join my sister and hedgehog in the living room. The move had roused Malou from her sleep, but now she's curled up around one of Sébastien's potted plants, prompting Odile to take a million photos. I have to admit, she does look quite cute. But then again, when doesn't she?

"Men are so annoying."

Odile laughs. "And yet you're moving in with two of them."

"Dix's not a man."

"Hey, I heard that!" the ghost complains. Since his footsteps make no sound, he's perfect at sneaking up on people. He appears beside us and looks down at Malou. "Can I hold her?"

He sounds rather disinterested, but I know he's been waiting for this ever since he heard about the little hedgehog.

"If you promise not to wake her up." I tell Odile what's happening as I gently pick Malou up. With a stern "Sit!" to Dix, I hand him the hedgehog.

Despite being a ghost, Dix can hold her easily. And just like Gaspar, the transformation is almost instantaneous. A moment ago, he was a sullen teenager. Now he's a puddle of joy, cradling the little creature in his hands and exploring all the tactile pleasures of her spikes and soft belly fur. Within seconds, he looks the youngest he ever has, and I catch a rare glimpse of the child he and Sébastien once were.

"You know it's creepy when you smile at the thin air like that," Odile whispers, ruining the moment.

I roll my eyes and pull her up. "Let's give them some space."

Enough time has passed for Sébastien to arrive with the remaining two boxes, and I find him and Papa in my room, discussing what looks like a serious matter.

"So, none of the bad ghosts can enter the apartment?" Papa asks.

"Not without my knowledge, no." Sébastien shows him a pouch of salt on the bedside table. "And if they get in here and cause a problem, this will slow them down."

In terms of ghosts, it's the equivalent of sleeping with a gun under your pillow.

"She's safe here," Sébastien says. "The only place safer than this would be in the Panthéon itself."

"And you'll protect her?"

I clear my throat to make my presence known, but that doesn't stop Sébastien from replying, "With my life."

Papa looks at me over his shoulder. "Sounds like you picked a good one."

I lean against the door frame and cross my arms. "Happy now?"

He comes to me and smiles. "I'm still sad knowing you won't be around home, but such is the nature of your kids growing up, isn't it?"

Odile throws her arms around him. "You still have me." After a short pause, she adds with a grin, "Until the summer."

The heavy sigh that follows makes us all laugh. Or at least everyone except Sébastien. I catch him looking at us with a painful longing that twists my heart. He never had a family like ours, with its share of squabbles, but also love and laughter. Someone needs the Malou treatment just as badly as his whisper ghost. Not that he'd ever let himself relax as much.

"Shall we go into the living room and have some coffee?" Sébastien suggests. "We can talk about what you need for that article."

Papa and Odile part and we settle around the dining table as Sébastien gets the coffee sorted. Dix hasn't moved a muscle, still engrossed in his newfound happiness. If Sébastien notices, he doesn't comment.

"I have to apologise," my father says out of the blue, while we're still waiting for our coffee.

"What do you mean?"

He sighs. "All these years we didn't take you seriously and ignored your struggles." He reaches out to squeeze my hand and gives me a sad smile. "We failed you, Alix."

Uncomfortable, I don't know what to say or do except shrug. "You didn't know any better."

"But I never *tried* to know better," Papa says. He shakes his head and continues, "You were always the quiet, withdrawn one, so I guess it was easy to ignore you. Not completely, of course, but to ignore the things you might have struggled with. Between Hélène's high demands and Odi's eagerness to make her mark on the world"—my sister narrows her eyes at him, trying to work out whether that was a compliment or veiled criticism—"you just fell through the cracks. And I'm sorry for that."

I still don't really know what to say, my mind blank. "Sounds pretty standard middle child to me."

Papa snorts. "Yeah, but doesn't make it right, you know? You're allowed to be the problem child now and then, Chouchou."

"What's that supposed to mean?" Odile complains loudly. "I'm usually the one causing trouble?"

"It's not so much about making trouble, mon chaton. It's about the child who worries you the most. Lately, it's been Hélène, and what she's going through is beyond anything I ever imagined for her, but Alix has been through just as much, and she's done it all on her own." He looks at me, the guilt obvious. "For that, I'm sorry. Like I said: we let you down."

It's surprisingly nice to hear him acknowledge it. I honestly didn't think my parents had failed me before, but maybe that's because I've long since accepted I'm a bit different and there are things in my life I can't share.

Sébastien clears his throat, looking like he'd rather be anywhere but here as he serves us coffee and macarons. "Sorry. If you'd like some privacy, I can take Dix for a walk."

"I'm not a dog!" Dix complains, pulled from his Malou reverie. He gently puts her back on the potted plant and joins us at the table, sitting on a corner like an animal, because all the chairs are currently occupied. "Besides, we have important things to discuss, don't we?"

I pull away and sit up. "That's right, we need to talk about our plan of action." I look at Papa. "What exactly do you need?"

He switches back to business mode without missing a beat. "Well, there are several elements to the article. I did a bit of thinking over the weekend, trying to imagine what the result would look like. I figured we have to be a little more conservative about mentioning the ghosts. It'll require a delicate approach and irrefutable evidence.

"Ideally, we get proof of how GoPol monitors and tracks ghost whisperers and takes their ghosts away. So, if we can find more people who've been affected, that'd be a start. Unfortunately, that alone won't be much of a scandal. At worst, people will think it's all made up or fail to see the problem. What we need are stories like yours"—he nods at Sébastien—"and what happened to Cédric."

"Or the Chevalier," I think aloud. When Papa cocks his head, I explain, "He's a former ghost whisperer, Charles' ex-partner. They had a falling-out when Charles threw him under the bus and had him arrested—after he'd almost killed him trying to create multiple whisper ghosts."

Papa narrows his eyes. "Do you have a name? I can check the court case, see if I can find any inconsistencies."

"Romain Coullier. I used to have his whole file, and I've memorised parts of it…"

"We need actual proof. So, unless you've taken pictures?"

"I did!" How could I forget? I took photos to show the Chevalier I had what he wanted. But as I scroll through my phone, my heart sinks. "They're gone." GoPol must've hacked into my phone and deleted them. "So much for that."

Papa sighs. "In that case, it won't be much use unless the man himself comes forward and has some kind of proof. You're in contact with him?"

I shrug noncommittally. "Sort of."

Fortunately, my father understands the privacy of informers. "Well, see if you can get him to join our cause. We might find a lot more if we talk to other active or former whisperers. One tragedy is a shame, but a bunch is systematic." He looks at Sébastien. "Is there anything, files or transcripts, you could provide us with? Maybe even recordings?"

I see Sébastien struggling with the idea. We're not just talking about simple theft here but full-blown treason. If he's caught before we manage to shift the narrative, he could spend years in prison. Never mind the emotional conflict of turning against not just his only family but everything he's ever worked for.

Still, he meant it when he said he was all in. "I can't promise a quick turnaround—"

"Not asking for that," Papa quickly assures him. "These things take time. We'll publish when we're ready."

Sébastien winces but continues, "I'll try to gather as much as I can. There won't be any reports about what he did to me—"

"Or me," Dix chimes in.

"And Dix. If there are any, I don't know where he'd keep them."

"I can look," Dix offers, a little more helpful this time. "Old C isn't around anymore, so the upstairs will be a lot safer."

"Be careful," I tell him. While it's true C-Trente is no longer there, I still remember how he messed up Gaspar, even though he was still a ghost then. "Knowing your father, he'll have come up with something to replace his lapdog. Other whisper ghosts, an alarm system..."

Sébastien nods. "Alix is right. The upper floor won't be un-guarded."

Dix rolls his eyes. "I'm not a bloody beginner. I'm just as much a special agent as you." He snarls at Sébastien for good measure. "Besides, aren't we on Daddy's good side now?"

"I don't know about that," Sébastien says before suddenly noticing my father and Odile look confused. We both seem to have forgotten they can't hear Dix. "Sorry, just a little discussion about Dix. He wants to spy on our father to find out where he might have hidden the more sensitive files. Like the file on Coullier. Or the one on Roubert," he adds quietly, a muscle in his cheek twitching.

"If he can do that, that'd be wonderful. He can't take them, though, can he? Or take a photo of them?"

Sébastien shakes his head. "No, but I might be able to figure out how to get my hands on them, if I know where they are."

"What did he mean you're 'on Daddy's good side again'?" I ask, impatiently. I've been worried about it ever since Dix mentioned it.

"Oh, just what we talked about in the catacombs. I told him about the Ghost World Fair, and he'd agreed to take me out of suspension to work on the case. Apparently, there's been sightings of foreign whisper ghosts." Sébastien licks his lips. "This is all sensitive information, of course."

Papa nods seriously. "Absolutely. I don't need any details of active cases unless they're evidence of the crap GoPol gets up to behind the scenes. Let's keep the article clean of everything else."

Sébastien lets out a huge sigh of relief and leans back in his chair. "Okay. So, proof of how GoPol, or rather my father, plays fast and loose with people's lives. That's it?"

"That's it."

"Cool," Odile exclaims, reminding us all of her presence. "So, what do I do?"

Papa grimaces. It's written all over his face that he'd rather not have two daughters involved, no matter how proud he is of her investigative nature. "You could help me sort through the evidence and write the article?" he offers half-heartedly.

"Or you could come with me and meet some ghosts, get them to join the cause and let us know about potential whisperers," I suggest. It can't hurt to have her around and it gives us a chance to hang out more now I'm no longer living at home.

With a smug smile, Odile nods. "Both."

Papa and I share a look and snort at the typical Odile answer.

"All right, I better get back to work then." Papa gets up and knocks on the table. "Thanks for the coffee, Sébastien. I hope you take good care of my girl."

"Like I said, I'll guard her with my life."

The words should've made me smile or swoon. Instead, they feel like lead in my stomach. I've already lost Gaspar. I don't want to lose Sébastien, too.

A few minutes later, Papa and Odile have left, and I'm alone with my new flatmates. An awkward silence spreads.

"Do you want to... I don't know watch a movie?" Sébastien asks.

I glance at the couch. An image of the two of us—sitting side by side, his arm lying on my shoulders as I snuggle up against him—flashes in front of my eyes, and I quickly avert my gaze. "Um, I actually need to unpack."

"Of course," Sébastien says, so fast, as if he's had the same ridiculous vision.

"And then I have homework to do."

"If you need anything, let me know."

I manage a smile. "Will do."

As I retreat to my new room, my heart beating a hundred miles an hour, I hear Dix say, unimpressed, "Well, that was awkward."

Chapter 8

Fortunately, my new living arrangements don't remain awkward for long, and we soon settle into a sort of easy routine. Sébastien usually leaves for work before me, but he always provides me with coffee and breakfast, which is really sweet. In return, I take care of dinner. Between my schoolwork, the Panthéon, and our investigation, there's little time for long, awkward silences and we don't see too much of each other during the week.

During one of the quieter afternoon shifts at the Panthéon, I gather the ghosts to tell them our plan—partly because they might know about other ghost whisperers, and partly because I want to make sure we're doing right by them if we expose their existence to the world.

"I don't know if I ever told you this, but my father is an investigative journalist—"

"A noble profession," interjects Émile Zola. "Just make sure the chimney sweep doesn't get paid off to skip yours."

It takes me a moment to make the connection. I wish I hadn't. "Assassination. Dreyfuss affair. Got you."

We may no longer have chimneys to worry about, but the threat of assassination is just as real today. I wish I could still trust in the law to dismiss the idea, but I know better than to believe my father is safe from retribution.

"He knows the risk. He once told me we're both adults and capable of making our own decisions." I take a deep breath. "Thing is, we're all in danger. Whether we stand up to Charles Roubert and his agency or not. And I'd rather go down fighting."

Without his manipulations, Cédric would still be alive, happily married to my sister, Gaspar would've never have risked his soul to stay by my side, and Sébastien would be whole. And I wouldn't be nearly as messed up as I am right now.

Victor nods, though I see conflicting emotions on his face. "When dictatorship is a fact, revolution becomes a right."

Voltaire snorts. "Is this a revolution, though?"

"Well, here's the plan," I say, ignoring Voltaire's latent hostility. "In order to expose Charles Roubert, we have to give the people some context. Which means, essentially, they'll have to learn about ghosts."

There's an immediate uproar. Some ghosts gasp, others nod with grim faces, and Voltaire and Rousseau launch straight into one of their arguments.

"You want the knowledge of ghosts to be available to the ignorant?" Voltaire bellows. "That superstitious lot who think every whisper of the wind is a ghost? Who talk of unfinished business and haunted houses? Look what that knowledge has given birth to at this so-called ghost police. Instead of respecting our autonomy and imprint we left on this earth, we're nothing but tools."

"It's ignorance that's the enemy here," Rousseau protests. "What you deplore is born of the darkness in which these minds are held. Wasn't it you who urged men to think for themselves?"

Voltaire snorts. "There is a difference between people thinking for themselves and people thinking about *my* existence. I've seen the minds of this age. They're quick to judge and eschew expert knowledge in order to conduct their own *research*." He shudders as if the very idea gives him the creeps. "I'd rather you didn't hand them the tools to bother us."

"But aren't they bothering you already?" I manage to squeeze in before Rousseau launches into another tirade. "Is it worth preserving what you have? With GoPol using and discarding ghosts as they please? With the Quarry Department dispersing spectral energy by inflicting mindless torture on ghosts resting in peace?"

"Isn't that the thing, though?" Voltaire asks. "We're not resting in peace. Are you prepared for the crisis of faith this will unleash?"

"I don't think so," Victor muses. "We know nothing about what happens after the living have forgotten us. There might still be a heaven awaiting lesser men." If so, it's a cruel fate that keeps some ghosts tied to the world forever.

Rousseau holds up a finger. "Who's to say our souls haven't gone on and all we're nothing but a remnant of our time on earth?"

Voltaire rolls his eyes. "Why don't you explain that to the living when they see their whole world shaken? Oh, that's right. The living are blessed by not having to listen to you."

Frustrated, I rub my face. "I hear your arguments, and as usual, you're much wiser than me. But by lying to everyone, aren't we just prolonging the inevitable? How are new ghosts dealing with awakening neither in Heaven nor Hell or Nirvana or wherever, but right where they left Earth?"

Victor sways his head thoughtfully. "Some wail. Some are relieved. It really depends on the ghost."

"They get over it," Voltaire barks.

"Exactly. So, why can't the living? Sure, some will refuse to believe it until they die and experience it for themselves, but..." I pause to take a deep breath. "You're all men and women who, in one way or another, have changed the ways of the world, the way people *think* and *act*. You've challenged the status quo and championed progress. Especially you two!" I glare at Voltaire and Rousseau for good measure.

"Well said, Alix," Victor says, nodding. "To the weak, the future seems impossible. To the fainthearted, it is unknown, but to the valiant, it is ideal. Perhaps now is the time where we marry the world of the living with that of the dead."

"You want the living to dictate our afterlife? Because they'll try." Voltaire shakes his head. "There's a natural balance in things as they are right now."

I roll my eyes. "Maybe for you. But for the other ghosts, the ones who are disrespected and forgotten, exploited and discarded by the ignorant and knowing alike, the afterlife isn't so rosy."

Rousseau mocks Voltaire with great glee: "You're becoming the very thing you once opposed."

Anger takes over his features and I half expect to see steam coming out of his ears. He hates being wrong. He lets out a big sigh and complains, "I've not had enough coffee for this discussion." He promptly summons a cup—his eighth since my shift started—and sips it.

"Alix is right," Victor says, with reassuring calm. "As the leaders of our fellow undead, we have a responsibility to see after their needs. And hasn't every one of us complained about the world being blind to us? How much it misses my latest book or your grand speech." He points to Voltaire, then looks at Rousseau. "Your thoughts on inequality. So much of what we create is lost in the dark. Without impact, can there be a purpose?"

"Funny you should say that." Rousseau puffs out his chest and holds up his index finger. "I happen to have some thoughts."

Voltaire groans and rolls his eyes. "Oh, please don't."

I can't help giggling. Meanwhile, Victor sighs. "I'm sure you do, Jean-Jacques, but let's leave that discussion for after Alix's visit." That seems to satisfy Rousseau for the moment, and he wanders off, already lost in philosophical mumbling as he prepares his argument.

"I hear you, Victor," Voltaire says, suddenly much more relaxed. "This could be a chance to once more be a part of the world again, instead of just a spectator."

"Exactly." Victor nods proudly at me. "Thank you for giving us ample warning, Alix. Change like this may seem scary, but it's inevitable for society to evolve, and a society that doesn't evolve is dead. Truly dead. We should see the opportunities in this, not just the dangers. As a ghost whisperer, you'll have an important role to play in this future. I have complete confidence you'll do right by us."

Let's not get ahead of ourselves. Right now, I'm just protecting myself and those I love from a behemoth-sized enemy. The only role I want to play is the one who ends Charles Roubert's atrocities and avenges all those he's wronged, starting with the little boy entrusted in his care, and ending with my own flesh and blood.

"If you know any other ghost whisperers," I say, more determined than ever, "or anyone with tangible proof of Roubert's wrongdoing, let me know."

Jean Moulin tips his head to me. "You'll have a full report by the end of the week."

Once that's sorted, I take a deep breath and walk past the writers' alcove to the tomb inhabited by Pierre and Marie Curie. I usually stay away from its ghostly glow, but both are so busy with their experiments I rarely have a chance to speak to them outside their tomb. Besides, Petite Alix loves spending time there, helping Marie in the spectral lab.

I knock on the wall next to the display of Marie's old lab book. Petite Alix sees me and almost drops the crystal she's carrying in her eagerness to run over. Marie takes it from her, and we reunite. While my whisper ghost is merely a toddler, something always snaps back into place when we connect. Thanks to GoPol's intervention, we haven't really had the chance to explore our connection. I still struggle to see her as a part of me. Rather, she's her own entity, an eternal three-year-old with an ingrained fear of water, thanks to twenty years of drowning.

She doesn't talk much, but she wraps her little arms around me and nestles into the crook of my neck, almost as if she needs our connection more than I do.

"Madame Curie?" I ask.

Marie Curie has already turned her back to me, assuming I've only come for Alix. "Oh, did you want something?" Even after almost two centuries in France, I can still hear the Polish accent.

"Victor says you're involved in the World Fair."

She continues to work, examining the crystal Petite Alix has brought her, but her eyes light up. "Oh, yes, I'm going to present the ectoplasmic radiometer and my ghost resonance crystal. You should come to my lecture on the Spectral Stabilisation Field. It's a most fascinating subject with great potential in ghost anchoring."

My head is swimming. "I'm sure it is. When's your talk?" Not that I'll understand even a tenth.

"Next Sunday in the Industries Pavilion on the big stage... Oh, wait a minute. You're not a ghost."

"Not yet," I quip.

Marie winces. "Sorry, darling, but you'd have to get a special ticket."

"A ticket?" How am I supposed to get a ticket to a fair that doesn't even exist in the world of the living?

"See, Gustave has done something truly astounding. Not only has he found a way to project the old glory of the fairs into our time, he's also managed to block out all living. Even whisperers like you—or maybe, especially whisperers—because no one else would be any wiser. Sorry, love, but if you don't manage to get a ticket, you'll probably miss my presentation."

Although I'm not particularly keen on the lecture itself, the prospect of missing the Ghost World Fair as a whole makes me sad. It sounds absolutely marvellous, full of things beyond even my wildest imagination. Besides, I was hoping to gather information for my group project.

"So, this fair is strictly ghosts only?"

"Oh no, they've invited whisperers, too. Not many, but a few."

My heart rate quickens at the mention of other whisperers. Could they be former GoPol agents? Or are they the foreign threat Sébastien is investigating? "Can't you invite me? I really want to go."

"Wanna go too!" Petite Alix babbles happily.

I smile and bop her nose. "You can. You're a ghost. But don't go alone."

Marie Curie grimaces at me. "Sorry, darling, but only one of the organisers has the authority to do that. I'm just a presenter, so I can't help you there."

"So, I have to ask Gustave Eiffel?"

"The very same."

"And I can find him...?"

Another grimace. "Oh, he'll be hard to track down, always busy with a new project and, of course, the fair itself. Try the Eiffel Tower, perhaps? Or maybe his wind channel lab." She puts on a pair of safety goggles and approaches the crystal with a test tube containing blue smoke. "You'd better stand back in case there's an exothermic reaction. Unbound spectral energy is a bit unstable."

I don't need to be told twice, even though I have a lot of questions about spectral energy and the nature of this crystal, which definitely doesn't exist for the rest of my fellow living.

Instead, I return to Victor and hand him Petite Alix. "I'd better get going."

I still have to go over today's lecture notes and prepare a literature review for tomorrow. Hopefully, Sébastien has taken the initiative and cooked dinner.

"Do you have time?" Victor asks.

I pause. "Is there anything else we need to discuss?"

"Come. I'll take you upstairs."

Intrigued, I follow Victor out of the crypt and up to the staff room. Before we enter, he says, "You're important to us, Alix, so we wanted nothing but the best."

"The best?" I'm confused.

"You asked me to find you a therapist."

My stomach tightens as I begin to understand.

"Normally, he'd only be available for sessions at the Cimetière Communal de Guitrancourt or in his former consulting room on the rue de Lille, but I've been able to architect an exception and offer him a temporary office in the Panthéon to ensure your safety and privacy."

Knowing how precious the Panthéon ghosts are about their place of power, this means a lot. They don't open their doors to just anyone. And while this therapist is clearly not invited into the crypt, Victor has arranged it within the walls of the Panthéon. For me.

He smiles and opens the door. "Alix, I want you to meet Jacques Lacan, one of the most prolific and influential psychoanalysts of France and a student of Freud."

Before I lay eyes on him, I'm struck by the change Victor's brought to the break room. Instead of a row of lockers and a lonely table, there's a couch and a reclining chair. The discrepancy between what my brain expected to see and what it actually sees is giving me vertigo.

I blink hard as I try to adjust, and only then do I notice the friendly looking older gentleman with the bow tie.

"Mademoiselle Dubois, it's a pleasure to meet you. Why don't you take a seat? Either is fine," he says as he offers me the two options.

Victor smiles and nudges me forward. "I'll make sure you're not disturbed." Quietly, he adds, "None of us will eavesdrop on what is said in this room."

Still stunned, I stagger towards the couch. Its seating area roughly overlaps with the bench in front of the lockers, which makes me trust it more. It also feels safer than leaning back in the armchair.

Despite Lacan's friendly smile, I have the feeling I've already failed some kind of test. If so, he doesn't say anything as he settles in the chair I've passed on.

"Alright, why don't we start with you telling me what made you seek out a ghost therapist?"

I can't help but laugh helplessly. "How much time do you have?" My voice sounds a little meek and terribly close to tears.

"Literally all the time in the world," Lacan says, with another smile.

I swallow hard. "In that case... You'd better get comfortable."

Chapter 9

The next day, Gaby, Théo, and I gather around a table in the library to begin our research on the World Fairs. To divide the work between us, we've each chosen a different one. Mine, of course, is 1889, because that's the one for which Gustave Eiffel built the Eiffel Tower, and which the ghost community is trying to recreate.

The Exposition Universelle of 1889 was unique in that it celebrated the centenary of the Great Revolution. It was a rather controversial theme, leading most of the European and other monarchies of the time to officially boycott the fair. This opened the way for many less prominent countries to step onto the big stage, and while they didn't officially take part, the boycotting countries still sent individuals as part of a private commission.

There was much to see that year. The Palais de l'Industrie, which we're going to focus on, was the first building to use electricity on a large scale. The illuminated fountain was a major attraction, and the Eiffel Tower drew crowds of tourists. Two captive balloons amazed people, as did Buffalo Bill's Wild West Show. There was an exhibition on the history of human habitation I would've loved to have seen and, of course, a reconstruction of the Bastille.

With pavilions full of innovations, art shows, and musical displays, it's easy to get caught up in the splendour. But the World Fair was also a child of its time. For the first time, France showcased its many colonies by inviting the natives to live in the most clichéd representation of their abodes for the duration of the fair, just so rich Europeans could marvel and pat themselves on the back for bringing civilisation to these poor people. Just the thought of the human zoo makes me want to barf. We're learning about the history of colonisation in a different course, and it really makes you lose hope in humanity.

Hopefully, the ghosts aren't so stuck in the past they've recreated that part, too.

"How's living with Sébastien?" Gaby asks, apparently bored by the 1855 World Fair she's researching.

Théo glances up from his 1937 research material, but he keeps his head down, knowing better than to come between us.

"It's quite nice. He's a surprisingly tidy fellow. None of the typical guy stuff. Plus, Dix spends a lot of time with Malou at night because he doesn't sleep. She's got full range of the apartment."

"Oh, she'll love that. I must come and visit. See how you're settling in."

"Sure. I have space now," I joke.

Gaby laughs and slaps my arm. "I like my cosy apartment."

Théo bites his lip, but he can't hold it in any longer. "Are you and Sébastien a proper couple now?"

"No!" I say, a little too fast. "We're just friends. My sister moved back home after..." I sigh, suddenly overcome by dread. "Her husband killed himself on their wedding day."

Théo's eyes bulge. "What? Oh my god, that's terrible. I'm so sorry."

"Well, yes, it's all very terrible. But she's blaming me for it, so living together is not an option. I get that she's grieving, but I'm not her punching bag."

"Hear, hear," Gaby says, proudly.

I shrug. "So, I moved in with Sébastien while she recovers at home. It's only temporary."

Théo nods, still full of sympathy for my sister. "Why is she blaming you for her husband's suicide?"

Gaby sighs and rolls her eyes. "Because that's what Hélène does. It's always someone else, usually Alix, never herself or her precious Officer Cédric."

"Do you know why he did it?" Théo looks uncomfortable and stutters slightly. "He's a ghost, isn't he? Like he could tell you?"

"I know why."

"Because he's an idiot," Gaby says. "Always has been."

Now it's my turn to sigh. Looks like we're not going to get much research done. "He was misled. He thought by killing himself he'd prove his loyalty and commitment to GoPol and Sébastien's father would be there to bring him back and make him a ghost whisperer. Problem is Charles is a monster and never cared about Cédric. So, Cédric truly died, and has regretted his decision ever since."

"Told you. He's an idiot." Gaby's not taking prisoners today. "Is he still bothering you?"

"No, I think he's mostly sticking to Hélène or, rather, hanging around their apartment."

While I'm sure the mere memory of him makes it hard for my sister to stay in her own home, I'd bet my abilities Cédric's making it even harder by haunting the place.

"He's still fairly new to ghost existence, so he'll be drawn to the places he frequented in life and his grave site. Or a person." Gaspar had latched on to me after his death. "Fortunately, I'm not that person. Nor did he ever study, visit the Panthéon, or spend any meaningful time in Sébastien's apartment."

Gaby nods thoughtfully. "That's good. After everything he's done to you, the least he could do is stay the hell away in death."

Knowing Cédric, he'll seek me out sooner or later. When I left him in Provence, he tearfully begged me to bring him back, as if I had the Chevalier's power. I wonder if Hélène would accept the whole resurrection business if it would bring Cédric back to her. Probably.

Théo shakes his head, as if his mind wandered places he didn't want to go. "That sounds intense."

"Welcome to my life."

Gaby puts her arm around me and hugs me. "You're going to need therapy after all this."

"I actually started therapy last night. Odile suggested it, and Victor went out and got me Jacques Lacan."

Théo whistles through his teeth, earning himself a few dirty looks from the surrounding students. "The master himself."

"How was it?" Gaby asks.

"It was an absolute shit fest. I did a garbage job of summarising the whole thing and, within minutes, turned into a blubbering mess on his couch. At some point, I told him about a girl who died in high school. Like seriously, what was I thinking?"

That first session had made me feel like I was failing at therapy, which would be quite the feat. But Lacan assured me I'd done nothing wrong and encouraged me to carry on. I don't see it working yet, but it felt good to get some of the weight off my chest. Me not having to explain anything—especially not about ghosts or my drowned toddler-self hanging out in a crypt all day—was a tremendous relief.

Gaby grins. "Sounds like it was a good session, then. Are you going to continue?"

"Well, I can't give up on it after one session, can I?"

In the end, we barely scratched the surface, and I didn't even get to what happened in Margot's lab.

"That's my girl!" Gaby says proudly. "Tell Odi she had a good idea."

If I tell Odile Gaby said that she might float for the rest of the week. "We'll see."

We fall silent again to look at our research material, and I begin to read about the various exhibitions in more detail. Théo was right to groan when he picked out the "Industries" envelope for us. With all the innovations of the industrialisation, there's a ton of material in one world exhibition, let alone three. It'll be a pain to filter out the most important innovations, but at least it'll be interesting to see the difference between three World Fairs so far apart from each other.

My mind drifts a little as I read about fantastic presentations such as a moving sidewalk and Edison's phonograph. In fact, Thomas Edison had an entire pavilion dedicated to him, housing his nearly five hundred inventions. Electricity was the queen of the fair, and the colour-changing fountain in front of the Palais du Trocadéro attracted thousands of spectators every night.

At the mention of Eiffel's prefabricated metal housing, I decide to skip ahead and look at the history of habitation. That's when one name catches my eye.

"No way!"

Both Gaby and Théo look up.

After nearly four years of studying history and even more of dealing with ghosts, it shouldn't surprise me so many famous people were contemporaries. I know this in theory, and yet it's always a revelation when two names appear in a document together, like puzzle pieces fitting together.

I point at the book in front of me. "The 1889 housing exhibition. It was organised entirely by Charles Garnier."

"Opera Charles Garnier?" Théo asks immediately. His brother's a tenor at the opera, and he's got a part-time job in the archives.

"The very same."

Théo shrugs. "Well, he was an architect, so it makes sense he'd be running an exhibition"—he looks down at my book—"on housing."

"Oh, but it's so much more than that." I grin at them. "He was one of the organisers, and he just so happens to owe me a massive favour."

Gaby's face lights up. She gets it. Then again, I've already told her about the Ghost World Fair. "You mean—"

I nod, still grinning. "I think I just figured out how to get us tickets to l'Exposition Universelle des Fantômes."

Chapter 10

Later that afternoon, I meet up with Sébastien at the Palais Garnier. On our way in, multiple ghosts thank us for dealing with the whisper ghost that had been haunting them.

"And the other one," says one of the divas. "God-awful music, I tell you."

My chest aches, and Sébastien slips his hand in mine to comfort me. The one with the "awful" music is my very own phantom, Gaspar. And like the real Phantom of the Opera, he's very charming, but most definitely a psychopath. At least on his bad days.

Théo lets us into the archive so we can have a quiet chat with Garnier. While he's completely oblivious of the number of ghosts around him, he's now aware of their existence and has no trouble arranging a meeting between me and the dead architect of the building.

"Do you want me to leave?" he asks.

"This won't take long. If you don't mind listening to horribly one-sided conversations, you're welcome to stay."

"I've had worse," he jokes and starts sorting his work for the day at a nearby desk.

Meanwhile, I concentrate on Garnier. Or rather, I try to. Turns out the other ghosts have already informed him, and he walks into the archive just as I'm about to call him.

"Mademoiselle Dubois," he exclaims, leaning in for kisses. "And Monsieur Roubert. What an honour to have you back at the opera. What can I do for you? Would you like tickets for another performance? A tour? Backstage passes?" He leans in and wriggles his eyebrows.

"Actually, we *do* need tickets. To the Ghost World Fair. History suggests you might be one of the organisers, unless..." If I remember correctly, Garnier was one of a handful of signatories who protested the Eiffel Tower's construction, calling it a travesty and eyesore. It doesn't help Garnier lost out to Gustave Eiffel in the competition to create the fair-defining monument.

"Unless I'm to let that old quarrel interfere?" Garnier waves his hand. "All water under the bridge. Not one of his, just a nice normal, Eiffel-free bridge."

Sébastien snorts softly. "So, are you one of the organisers?"

Garnier straightens his jacket and puffs out his chest. "Oh, absolutely. This is a group project. After all, Eiffel has never organised a fair before. I don't even know why he claims the 1889 as his, just because he built that little tower." After his rambling, he deflates. "The man's too busy to do it all by himself, so he asked me and a few others to help. Can you imagine? A famed architect with such a grand building to his name, relegated to administrative duties."

"Did you not have your own exhibition?" I ask, concerned.

"Just the old one. But nobody's interested in the history of housing anymore."

"I am!" It's not even a lie. Anything that has to do with history immediately fascinates me. Still, I'm not here to talk to Garnier about housing. "Too bad. I won't be able to see it without a ticket."

Garnier's eyes widen. "Mon dieu, non! That would be a travesty. You, Mademoiselle Dubois, should be the guest of honour. Let me rectify this oversight immediately. You, too, Monsieur Roubert. Arms out."

Sébastien and I share a look, both surprised at his strange request. I shrug and hold out my hand.

Garnier opens a pouch and pulls out two white strips, the kind you see around the pool or at a festival. "This is all part of Eiffel's resonator project," he explains, as he wraps the strips around our wrists. Unlike sticky paper strips, these click together like magnetic bands.

"Just need to tune it to your frequency." He presses a finger into the band.

I yelp as I see it sink into my skin, leaving behind a silver shimmer and a smooth, cool sensation. "What is this?"

"Resonating bands. Basically, they'll give you a spectral signature when you're near Eiffel's resonator, which will allow you to see the fair." Garnier pats my wrist, which still feels cold. "There, there, all done. Let me know when you plan to visit and I'll show you around my exhibition in person."

A little later, Sébastien and I get off his bike near the Eiffel Tower and stow our helmets. We're at the far end of the Champs de Mars, the whole park in front of us. The Eiffel Tower rises on the other side, near the river, surrounded as usual by tour buses.

Sébastien looks down at his wrist, trying to catch the silver gleam of the bracelet. "Do you think it'll work?"

"We'll see... or not."

I feel a bit miffed about the whole thing. After a lifetime of seeing ghosts, I'm offended there's something I *can't* see. On the other hand, I'm intrigued to find out how they did that. All of it!

When I first heard about the Ghost World Fair, I thought it might be held in the catacombs, somewhere away from the living, but Garnier has quickly dispelled those thoughts, claiming it had to be in the old place for it to work.

At the moment, I can't see anything unusual about the Eiffel Tower and its surroundings. It's a sunny day, so it's quite busy, but if there are any ghosts in the crowds, they're far outnumbered by tourists.

As we wait to cross the road, Sébastien updates me. "Dix had a little look around the fair. According to him, it's all boring stuff, but that's Dix for you, I guess."

"Teenagers," I complain, thinking of Odile, whose interest in the fair would go no further than the ghosts who visit. "Did he find ghost whisperers?"

"Yes, but none have a connection to GoPol, as far as he can tell."

"Overheard any criminals?"

Sébastien gives me a long look.

I throw up my hands. "Let me guess, classified information?"

"For now," he admits. "But I guess I can tell you that, so far, we haven't identified any notable security threats."

"Apart from the security threat we all know about."

"Apart from that," Sébastien concedes with a tip of the head.

At last, we have a chance to cross the road without being run over. We dodge cars and make it to the Champ de Mars. I suddenly feel a chill on my wrist as we step onto the green. Just as I'm looking at it, the grounds around me shift. It's like the wavering heat of summer on asphalt, giving me a glimpse of something I can't quite catch.

Sébastien inhales sharply and stops cold, staring ahead.

I take another step and suddenly it's as if a curtain has parted. The sound of cars is drowned out by a chattering, excited crowd in period dress. In front of us, several buildings rise from the ground: small stalls and colourful pavilions selling drinks, food, and goods from a bygone century.

Beyond the first row, a breathtakingly beautiful palais rises, almost blocking the view of the Eiffel Tower. It's a behemoth of glass and steel with sweeping arches, bigger than the central station, yet as delicate as a stained-glass window. Inside, a multitude of huge machines are on display, which gives me a clue that this is the Galerie des Machines. What little I see of the Eiffel Tower behind is no longer light brown but a deep saturated red, and in the sky I see at least one large balloon.

Thousands of people stroll through the gates behind us, laughing and gawping at the displays. Ladies in fancy hats, puffy sleeves, overskirts, and little parasols gossip as they're trailed by children trussed up in their Sunday best. Gentlemen in suits queue at an old-fashioned cotton candy machine, discussing the fair with serious expressions.

One foot onto the Champ de Mars and I feel like I've stepped back in time.

"This is incredible," breathes Sébastien. He's frowning, but his mouth hangs open in surprise.

Overcome by exuberance, I grab his hand. "Come on! Let's have a look around."

Laughing, I pull him with me and join the hustle and bustle of the Ghost World Fair.

CHAPTER 11

"This is amazing!" I can't even decide what to look at first. The beautiful gallery of machines, the red Eiffel Tower, or all the little stalls. My neck twists this way and that as I recognise fashion and objects I've only ever seen in history books. "It's like a dream come true."

Sébastien chuckles, still holding my hand. "It's pretty impressive, I agree."

I barely hear a word he says as I spot yet another little detail that makes my historian heart flow over. "That girl's taking her doll for a walk!"

It's one of those incredibly detailed, handmade dolls, sitting in a black miniature pram that the girl, dressed almost identically to her doll, is proudly pushing along.

A group of boys run after a small dog that's broken free of its leash and is following a ghostly butterfly. While many of the ghosts look as if they jumped straight out of my history books, there are also a lot of non-period ghosts enjoying the fair, and the crowd is thankfully more diverse than it used to be 150 years ago. Still, the atmosphere is very much Industrial Revolution, like a superimposed image everyone has agreed to play along with.

Together, Sébastien and I enter the Galerie des Machines. Normally, an exhibition of large agricultural and industrial machines wouldn't excite me, but there's something in the air, like a sense of excitement. What's old to me was new and sensational back then.

People bend over backwards to see a steam engine in action, enamoured by the black smoke, whereas all I can think of is the pollution it will eventually cause. Beside the machines on the ground floor, there's a slow-moving platform that carries a tightly packed group of visitors from one end of the gallery to the other. The waiting platforms on either side are filled to the brim with eager fairgoers waiting their turn.

We exit into a beautiful dome that feels like a breath of fresh air after the smokey gallery. In the centre is a fountain decorated with a larger-than-life sculpture. Plants and benches have been placed along the sides. While it's a place of thoroughfare, it's also a place to recuperate.

Not that I'm ready to sit just yet. Instead, I crane my neck looking at the copula above me as I drag poor Sébastien out of the dome and into the Ville de Paris, a park-like area with a little pond and lots of artfully arranged greenery. In between and beyond are more booths and pavilions, among them those of the various visiting countries.

Sébastien and I walk down the rows to marvel at all the innovations on display. Unlike the Galerie des Machines, most of the inventions here are definitely of a ghostly nature. Ghosts line up at the Phantom Portraiture Booth, which allows them to take pictures of themselves in various period costumes. It looks like a lot of fun, and if the queue wasn't so long, I'd drag Sébastien along.

Instead, I learn about ecto barometers that measure spectral energy, ghost lanterns that feed off spectral energy to serve as lights where the living have installed none, and listen to a piano that plays on its own with the listener's memory, like a ghost jukebox. One of the larger booths is advertising the Hauntshifter 3000, which allows ghosts to travel to places they never went in their lives—all within a small-ish radius. They're about to draw the winner of the prize draw and send a happy couple to the English Channel. Not my preferred beach holiday, but ghosts don't feel the cold the way I do.

"Oh, there's Marie!"

Sébastien doesn't even have a chance to get a word in as I pull him towards a pavilion dedicated to Marie Curie and the wonders of spectral radiation. The pavilion's emitting a blue glow, which makes me a little wary, but none of the other ghosts have let it stop them, and I decide to stop being a chicken and approach with the same interest and wonder.

Marie's pavilion is an interesting mix of turn-of-the-century ex-hibits and modern poster displays. Her husband, Pierre, is wandering around, giving tours and explaining the process of spectral radiation to the fairgoers. From what I gather, it's related but different to living radiology. Instead of unstable isotopes, I learn about spectral signatures and the ghostly energy every ghost emits as a by-product of their existence. One poster, entitled 'SSF — Spectral Stabilisation Field', claims to have found a way to stabilise and anchor a ghostly form, allowing them to remain in the afterlife longer than the memory would otherwise allow.

At the front, Marie is explaining her latest findings to a mottled crowd of interested ghosts. "—with the Ectoplasmic Radiometer, we can quantify a ghost's health and determine the time until they start fading. Now, we all fear being forgotten, and it will happen to all of us eventually. But with the Ghost Resonance Crystal"—she picks up the crystal she was working on in the Panthéon and lets it float in front of her—"we can store some of our essence to preserve it, and thus prolong our existence."

She looks through the crowd and points at someone. "You, sir, please come on up."

I look around and see the crowd parting, but it takes a moment to catch a glimpse of a ghost moving towards Marie. How she even knows it's a man is beyond me. Since his form is flickering so much, it's just like smoke in the wind.

"What's your name, sir?" Marie asks, when it looks like the ghost has made his way up the stairs.

If he says anything, it's too quiet for the rest of us to hear.

"Étienne! Nice to meet you, Étienne." Marie grabs another crystal from behind her. This one isn't shimmering blue but milky and empty. "Please hold on to this, Étienne, and think of everything you can remember about your life. The names of your parents, any loved ones, a day in the sun, even your death, if that's easier. Just remember yourself, Étienne."

I assume she repeats his name so many times to strengthen him. I hold my breath as I watch the flicker in the wind cling to the milky crystal. Wisps of blue are sucked into the crystal, drawing gasps from the crowd. And then it happens. Suddenly, a surprisingly young man in a blue coat appears, three bloody wounds on his chest. A student, perhaps one of the revolutionaries from 1830.

A smile of wonder and relief spreads across his youthful face and I join the thunderous applause that erupts in the pavilion.

When we step back out into the sunshine, I'm positively buzzing. "Can you imagine. They don't have to fade just because people stop remembering them. That's groundbreaking."

"Well, she did say, they have to fade eventually," Sébastien points out, always the downer. "I'm not sure what to make of that, playing with the natural balance of... I suppose, afterlife and fading."

I snort. "Oh, please, as if the living don't do that all the time. With that line of thinking, you'd have to give up all medical research. This is just ghost health."

Sébastien scratches his head. "I suppose. Sorry, I'm still getting used to this whole... afterlife thing."

I give him a pitying look. His whole life he was taught ghosts were nothing but tools for him to use in order to protect the country. Instead of learning to respect them, he learned how to manipulate them. The idea they're not just eagerly waiting for a GoPol agent to fill their afterlife with purpose but have rich, fulfilling existences, completely separate from the living is a lot for him to wrap his head around.

But I know he's trying his hardest to unlearn his father's lessons and open his mind to a world he's seen and yet been completely blind to, so I squeeze his hand and continue our stroll.

It occurs to me there are so many ghostly things to see that I've completely lost sight of the actual people gathered around the Eiffel Tower. It's as if I've truly been transported to another time—or perhaps another place. Now that I'm looking for it, I can make out the crowds of tourists, but it's surprisingly difficult, like a hologram where you see one image from one angle and another as you walk by. I wonder if it's the same for them and we're like ghosts ourselves. And then I'm distracted by the fair again.

There's a stall selling so-called wraith wear, spectral cloth that allows ghosts to wear whole outfits they never got to try on in real life. And ghost pets.

"Oh my gosh, that's so cute."

I crouch down next to a booth full of spectral puppies. Unlike real ghost pets, of which there are shockingly few since their memory is so short and dies with their owners, these are shimmering blue. I reach out to stroke one and it leaps right through my hand, leaving behind the fleeting memory of soft fur. Much stronger than the physical touch is their personality. A wave of overflowing joy and love washes over me as the puppies swarm me, eager for my attention. Within seconds, I'm in love.

"Can we have a ghost pup?" I look up at Sébastien with what I hope are my very own puppy eyes.

A helpless smile spreads across his lips, and he shrugs. "I don't know. *Can* we?"

It's a good question. I have no idea how they exist. Are they truly memory or imagination? Do they need a crystal like Marie's to stay in existence or are they gone once their spectral battery runs out?

Hard as it is, I give them a few more cuddles before I get up and hang onto Sébastien's arm instead, laying my head on his shoulder while I watch them play with other ghosts. "Malou probably wouldn't appreciate a dog, anyway."

"Maybe." His voice sounds strangely forlorn, as if he desperately wants one, too.

Finally, he manages a deep breath and turns us away. I slide my head off his shoulder but keep my arm linked with his as I throw one more glance at the ghost puppies before I find something new to feast my eyes on.

A girl with a basket approaches us and offers us so-called 'chill bloomers'. "They change colour near different auras," the ghost girl explains. "Would you like to buy some?"

"Do you take credit card?" Sébastien asks, eyeing the flowers.

The girl laughs. "Only coins, I'm afraid. Francs, livres, euros. Don't you have any real money?" Apparently, credit cards aren't quite tangible enough for ghosts.

"I do!" I pull out my wallet while Sébastien hesitates.

"Do you really think you should—"

I pay the girl with a fifty-cent coin. Thanks to inflation, I get a bunch of flowers.

As soon as the girl has left, Sébastien frowns. "You just gave real money to a ghost."

"It's only fifty cents."

"She won't be able to keep it for long," he argues.

I shrug. "So, some lucky kid finds a coin. Meanwhile, I've got a nice bunch of flowers." Unlike real flowers, they don't smell, but they *do* change colour as we move through the crowd.

Sébastien sighs. "I wanted to buy them for you," he admits softly.

I don't think he wants me to acknowledge it, so I hide my ridiculous little smile in the flowers and fight the heat that floods my stomach.

We're near the base of the Eiffel Tower when Dix finds us. "You're here. Good."

"Hey, Dix," I say coyly.

He looks from Sébastien to me, from the flowers to the linked arms, and suddenly, his cheeks flush. "I don't want to interrupt your date, but..." He leans forward and whispers into Sébastien's ear.

Sébastien sighs and pulls away. "I'm afraid I've got GoPol business to attend to."

"That's okay. I have a whole fair to distract me."

Indeed, my eyes are drawn to a pavilion just below the Eiffel Tower. The entrance is guarded by a red rope, but the door is open to allow visitors to peek inside. Signs pointing that way say 'Ectowave Resonator', prompting me to recall the tales of Eiffel's resonator.

"I've already found what I'm gonna look at next."

"You guys can see it now?" Dix asks.

Sébastien nods. "Alix managed to get us whisperer tickets." He holds up his hand to show off the shimmering band around his wrist. Then he turns to me. "Sorry, but I'll have to go with Dix. Will you be okay?"

"See you later." My feet are already dragging me away. I look over my shoulder and grin. "But I can't promise I won't come home with a ghost puppy."

Dix looks confused, but Sébastien bursts out laughing. A beautiful, warm laugh that makes my cheeks glow and puts a spring in my step as I head over to Eiffel's invention.

Chapter 12

The Ectowave Resonator is a complex machine with a distinctly steampunk vibe. It's hard to imagine it's purely ghost-made with its shimmering copper and brass elements. Between two antennas at the top, attached to an intricate structure of gears and coils, a storm is gathering, which seems to be the main reason for the required safety distance. Somewhere, a pump wheezes and blue smoke billows around the entire structure. A large dial occupies the lower part with a heavy-looking lever turned to near maximum.

"What does it do?" I ask no one in particular.

"Funny you should ask."

A man in a dark suit appears beside me. His eyes are pale-blue and he has a well-trimmed moustache and beard. His wavy, blonde, greying hair is swept upwards to keep it from falling into his face. The suit is similar to most of the men around him, a sign of fashion of the late 1800s.

"Monsieur Eiffel," I greet. "It's a pleasure to meet you in person. I've heard you're very busy."

He tilts his head. "I'm afraid I am. There's lots to do at a fair of this magnitude. Besides, so much input gets my own gears turning. Have you been up on the tower?" He nods towards the old-fashioned elevators that run up the tower's legs. They've been modernised in my time, but not by much. Eiffel's general principle has stood the test of time.

"Many times. I'm a local."

He takes another look at me. "You're a whisperer. Wait, don't tell me. You're the Panthéon whisperer. Hugo's protégé?"

"Alix Dubois, at your service." I do a fancy little curtsy, not even thinking how this might look to the many tourists around me. I doubt they even notice, taking their selfies.

Eiffel frowned. "I forgot to invite you, didn't I?"

"You're a busy man. Don't worry about it." I nod at the resonator. "So, this machine... What is it?"

Whatever social awkwardness was happening before, it vanishes when he starts talking about his invention. "This is the Ectowave Resonator, a spectral amplifier I've spent many years perfecting. It uses collective spectral energy and memory to recreate historical environments and project their presence into the living world."

My eyes widen. "Is that how you managed to recreate the World Fair?"

Eiffel nods proudly. "It is indeed."

He proceeds to tell me about electrical waves and stabilisation fields that had to be calculated, and from there dives into the capacity of human memory and spectral reflection.

I very much tune out after the first few words, but that doesn't stop me from watching the whirring object with unbridled awe. If I understand correctly, the projection is made possible not just by the intricate ghost mechanics behind it, but by the presence of other ghosts. That's why so many of them are people who actually visited the World Fair. They and the old machines are needed to stabilise the projection so everyone else can enjoy it, me included.

"And how do you block it off?"

"An unplanned but very welcome side effect, I'm afraid," Eiffel admits. "The projection only truly works on ghosts, and so long as the ghosts stay inside the field, they're obscured, too."

"What about me? Am I obscured?" Am I a ghost right now?

"An interesting question. Shall we test it?"

I stare. "How?"

Eiffel offers me his arm. "Come with me."

I take his arm, not knowing what to expect. Or how he'd even begin to test such a thing.

He leads me to the old-fashioned elevator on the southern leg of the tower, the one usually reserved for staff, and opens the door. "Step inside."

"I can't. That's trespassing."

"I'm inviting you."

"But..."

No one's watching me. If anyone's keeping an eye on the staff elevator, they're not interested in me. Does that mean I'm invisible? Is the cabin invisible? Will it even carry me or will it drop me from the sky?

Eiffel smiles at me. "Trust the resonator, Mademoiselle Dubois. It's so close, nothing will fray."

My heart is hammering against my chest, and my pulse is rushing, filling my ears with static. I half expect someone to shout as I step into the cabin, but no one does. No one even looks at me.

The doors close and there's a sudden jolt, which nearly makes my heart stop and create another whisper ghost. Instead, the cabin begins to move, pulled upwards by Eiffel's remarkable hydraulic system. We're about halfway up to the first platform before I manage to loosen my grip on the bars.

Eiffel chuckles softly. "I'd say, yes, you're obscured, too. At least partially."

I remember the way the tourists shimmered through the spectral reality and wonder if it's the same for me. Is there a kid looking up, catching a glimpse of me floating up the leg of the Eiffel Tower?

There's another jolt, signalling we've arrived. Despite the successful journey, my legs are shaking as I step onto the platform. Up here, it's harder to ignore the crowds of living people. Together with the dead, it's a little too crowded, but Eiffel leads me up the stairs until we reach the weather station he installed to prevent the tower from being demolished in the early 1900s. It's hard to imagine the Parisians once hated what's now a national symbol.

The wind ruffles my hair as I look around. As usual, the view is breathtaking on a sunny day, but now it's even more so. Even though I've already spent hours with Sébastien at the fair, there's so much more to see. On the other side of the Eiffel Tower are more gardens and national pavilions and, apparently, a stage. Across the river, there's the illuminated fountain I read about in front of the Palais du Trocadéro, which overlaps the modern-day Palais de Chaillot. The old palace is a beautiful piece of art with Moorish and Byzantine influences.

The exhibition continues along the river to Les Invalides, where the colonial village used to be. I can't see much from here to confirm whether it's been recreated or replaced by a modern or ghostly display. Not just one, but two balloons are hanging in the sky, and a little railway takes visitors from one end of the World Fair to the other.

When I've had my fill of the sights, I turn to Eiffel, only to find him tinkering with his weather station. A busy man indeed.

"It's very impressive," I tell him. "I've never seen anything like it."

"Nobody has," Eiffel says, distracted. He rubs his beard. "I suppose that makes it impressive."

I giggle a little. He may be one of the greatest engineers who ever lived—or died—but he hardly ever seems to pause long enough to look at his own achievements.

"So, what's next?" I ask, deciding to humour him.

"I want to develop the resonator further, create portable versions, so we can recreate other events or just places in general," he explains as he continues his work. "You see, every time our surroundings change—a new house is built, another is torn down, that kind of change—the ghosts become a little untethered. It's hard to exist in a world that bears little resemblance to the one you grew up in. The living experience it, too."

I think of the old who struggle so much with advances of technology. Some have the energy and willingness to learn new things, but so many never even try, until they slowly grow out of touch with the world and are left with nothing but nostalgia. It used to annoy me when I was younger. Now I see the wealth of information they've had to process and how much the world really does change in a lifetime. Especially these days.

"And by recreating the places, you anchor yourself?"

Eiffel strokes his beard. "A little. You've been to the catacombs, haven't you?" When I nod, he says, "We extended the World Fair below to accommodate Nexus' demands and the many ghosts living down there. The resonator doesn't work very well below, but it doesn't have to, since the catacombs haven't changed much."

"Is that why there are so many ghosts down there?"

I've always wondered what drew them there despite their remains—especially since so many have been removed.

"Indeed. It's a place of little change, away from rebuilds, modern machinery, and the masses of the living. Its own little world. Personally, I've always embraced change, but I understand there's a strong need for nostalgia in those unlike myself."

I nod, completely absorbed in his tale. "That tracks with what I've learned."

"You're a curious one," he says, at last leaving his instruments alone. He crosses his arms on top of the measuring station and studies me. "Most of the ghost whisperers who asked to be let in aren't interested in the fair at all. They're all here for the Chevalier or to use the fair as a distraction to meet and discuss whatever it is whisperers discuss. But you—you take it all in. You ask all these questions."

It's not the first time I've noticed how different I am from other ghost whisperers, so I shrug. "Maybe that's the historian in me. We're going through the Industrial Revolution right now." I probably should've taken some notes while I was walking around the World Fair, but I guess there's plenty of time for that on another day.

"And what is it about history that interests you so much?"

At first, I want to groan, because it reminds me of all the times I had to endure the question from my family, but then I realise he's not interested in talking me out of it but gently nudging me towards a realisation.

"It's the ghosts. I studied history because of all the ghosts I met."

Eiffel laughs softly. "As I thought."

I blush a little. When I'm with ghosts, it's the greatest thing, but among my peers I always feel singled out. I once thought meeting other ghost whisperers would help me feel a little less alone. Instead, all I found was trouble.

"Do you think it's wrong? Like, our very existence as whisperers? Would it be better if the dead and living didn't mix?"

He grimaces and shakes his head. "Nonsense. We'd be nothing without the living and you'd be nothing without the ghosts of the past. If anything, we need more people like you, Mademoiselle Dubois. People who can bridge the gap and bring out the best in all of us."

"Lots of people are afraid of big changes. You just said so yourself."

"Lots of people are stupid." And with that, he ducks his head and continues his tinkering.

I chuckle at his response and feel a little better about myself. While I didn't need his approval to go ahead with my plan, he's given me confidence that we're doing the right thing. Maybe the world will need some time to catch up, but it will eventually. It always has.

I'm about to return downstairs when he curses and shakes his hand, causing it to flicker.

"What happened?"

Eiffel sighs heavily, staring sullenly at the instrument in front of him. I walk around the weather station to take a look and find a miniature version of the resonator, though this miniature version is still the size of a portable freezer.

"It doesn't work." He looks absolutely disgusted with it. "Something about the field being coiled so tight and overlapping makes it suck up *my* spectral energy instead of the latent one in the atmosphere."

"Is that a big problem?"

He throws me a long glance. "It basically means it'll eat any ghost who gets too close."

"Yeah, okay, that sounds bad."

Frustrated, he takes a step back. "It's not the only problem. There's no one here, and if there were, they wouldn't see anything different. It's still the same tower." He puts a hand on the steel behind him and looks up at his creation. "But everywhere else, it superimposes an image of the past on top of the present."

"Didn't you say that's its purpose?"

"The shield doesn't work," he admits. "With the big one, it's fine unless you turn it up too much, but I haven't worked out how to recreate it on a smaller scale. And if the shield fails, the past will *literally* be superimposed on the present. It will *affect* the present.

Maybe even destroy it. Or kill someone. And then who knows?" He gives me a wry smile. "This is one of those things where the dead and the living *should* be kept apart."

I take a step back, as if the resonator will come to life on its own and suck me in. "You're going to figure this out, aren't you?"

"Eventually. Hopefully." He rubs his chin and leans in closer. "Let me just try this..."

And with that, he's back to his experiments. I take another look at my hometown before deciding to head back down, going with the stairs this time. As great as the resonator sounds, I don't quite trust it without Eiffel around.

I'm just about to leave the platform when I notice movement in the shadows. Startled, I crane my neck, but whatever it was, it's already gone. Weird. For a moment, I could've sworn I saw a person.

Shaking my head, I turn back around, only to let out a yelp as someone *actually* appears in front of me. I fall backwards, hitting the stairs. Panting and digging my fingers into the step, I look up at someone I know far better than I ever wanted to.

"Cédric!"

For a ghost, he looks rough. The rope marks on his neck are still bright red, as if he hung himself only yesterday. I would've expected him to be wearing his uniform, but instead, he's still in the light trousers and white shirt he wore at his wedding, only now they're dirt-stained and dusty. His hair is dishevelled, and he's grown a scruffy beard, which makes no sense, because he was always clean-shaven in life. I guess that means he *wants* to look like shit.

"Are you okay?" he asks with his annoying puppy eyes and holds out a hand.

I stare at him. "As if you care."

Everything he ever did served his own misplaced ambition. I was just the pawn with which he tried to buy his uncle's love.

Ignoring his hand, I pull myself up and dust off my pants. "What are you doing here? Did you love the Eiffel Tower or what?"

"It's where I proposed to Hélène."

I roll my eyes hard. "Of course."

Only Cédric would do something as clichéd and touristy as propose on top of the Eiffel Tower.

"How is she?"

"You know how she is."

The misery on his face makes me want to puke. "Alix, please. You've got to help me."

"No!" I shout. "I don't *have* to do anything for you."

"But you grant favours to ghosts. I heard the others talking."

I can't believe this. All he's ever done is exploit and betray me, and now he wants me to grant his wish, as if I were some fairy godmother.

"I help genuine ghosts. If I can. I don't have to do anything."

I really wish I could push past him, but Cédric fills out the stairs, blocking my path. He nods hastily. "You're right. You don't have to do anything, and I'm not asking for myself. Really."

"Is that so?"

"I won't... I deserve to be dead."

At least, he's got that right. Unimpressed, I listen for more.

"But Hélène doesn't deserve all this pain. She doesn't deserve to be a widow at twenty-seven and—"

"I'm not going to resurrect you because it would be the best for Hélène!" As if framing it around my sister makes it any less of a favour.

Cédric shouts back in despair, "I'm not asking you to resurrect me! I've heard the rumours about Gaspar. It's not something I want for your sister."

My heart nearly stops. Somehow, he's twisted it all around. Noble Cédric would never go to such depths as evil Gaspar. I hated this sanctimonious jerk when he was alive, and death hasn't done him any favours.

"Get out of my way," I growl, regretting the stairs. Falling from a ghost elevator would be preferable to dealing with this jackass.

While he lets me past, he cries after me, "Help her, Alix. Please. You're the only one who truly understands what she's going through. She needs you."

"No, thank you."

There might have been a time when I would've run to my sister's side, but Hélène has well and truly burnt that bridge, whether it's an Eiffel one or not. If she wants my help, she'll damn well have to ask herself.

Chapter 13

"They had ghost puppies," I gush to Odile as we make our way across Père Lachaise.

On our first weekly hangout, we're visiting the cemetery to say hi to our grandmother and take a few spooky photos with Malou. According to Odile, she wants to hop on the ghost trend before it blows up big time. I doubt anyone will pay much attention to a cute hedgehog in a spooky setting, but whatever floats her boat.

Malou is definitely enjoying her walk. I suppose the cemetery is full of tasty worms. If I didn't have her on a lead, I'd probably never see her again.

"Ghost puppies?" Odile says, with big eyes. "Can I have one? I'm lonely without Malou."

"You wouldn't even be able to see it."

"You know, you really make being a ghost whisperer sound so cool."

I bite my lip, not quite sure how to take it. "It comes with a lot of trouble."

Odile sighs heavily. "Yeah, I guess that's true. Can't your ghost create something so a mere mortal like me can see the fair?"

I can't help laughing. "I'm still very much mortal, you know?" More than I care to be.

She waves me off. "You know what I mean."

We walk a few steps in silence. On the way here, I told her all about the World Fair. It's all I can think about at the moment, having already given Gaby and Théo an info-dump after class. I'd have done the same with Sébastien, but if he even came home at all, it was long after my bedtime, and he left again before I woke up.

I push aside the pang of worry and try to return to the ghost puppies again. Instead, I remember Cédric.

"Um... how's home?"

Odile gives me a long look. "If you mean with Hélène, it's... it's actually quite sad. She hardly ever comes out of her room, and I hear her crying all the time. She tried to go back to work this week, but when I got home from school, she was already back in bed. Maman's constantly worrying about her because she's not eating much."

Although I should know better by now, I feel sorry for her. For some inexplicable reason, she truly loved Cédric. But that only makes me hate him more. If it weren't for him, we'd still be close, but no, he had to poison her against me and for what? His death is pathetic. I bet in a few months he'll be picked up by GoPol and find fulfilment spying for them, ignoring they're the reason for his death.

"Does she still blame me?" I ask sullenly.

Odile's sigh tells me all I need to know. "Papa mentioned doing this thing for you and she went on a rant about how we're all letting you drag us down or something, then she burst into tears and ran away. After that, Maman and Papa had a serious talk."

I try not to make a face, but my eyes are watering and my throat has suddenly started to hurt. In a nasty, devious way, Hélène is absolutely right. I *have* dragged the whole family into my ghost drama. At best, Cédric and I share the guilt.

"She's wrong," Odile says, surprisingly vehement. "Stop accepting her nonsense. You didn't drag anyone into this, least of all her. We're family, Alix. We'll always have your back."

As harsh as her tone is, her words are quite sweet. They ease the pain in my throat, and I even manage a smile. "Thanks."

We reach our grandmother's grave. Since the GoPol attack on the cemetery, she's slowly recovered from her salt wounds, but there are gaps in her memory. Things she's experienced with Beatrice, her budding relationship with Alexandre de Beauharnais, and everything I told her about. When I first came to see her, she didn't even recognise me.

"Alix," she says with a smile as I approach. She and Beatrice are having coffee while working on some ghostly shawls. "What a nice surprise. And who's this young lady?"

"That's Odile, Grandma." I describe the scene to Odile who smiles vaguely at the gravestones, missing the ghosts by a hand width.

Our grandmother's eyes widen. "No, never. Little Odi Bébé? My, what a pretty lady you've become."

I relay her words to Odile but leave out the baby part to save her the embarrassment.

"Well, I'm eighteen now, Grandma." She looks at me. "Should I tell her what I'm up to?"

Seeing our grandmother's eyes light up at the thought, I encourage her to do just that. In the meantime, I sit next to Beatrice and ask quietly, "How are things?"

"Oh, you know. She's still Estelle. We're having a lot of fun getting to know each other again. It's quite exciting to start over, you know?" Her face soon falls. "But poor Alexandre. She doesn't remember him at all. Instead, she's suddenly talking about her Antoine, as if that old crook still cared about her."

Our grandfather has moved on since her death and fallen in love with a nice lady he met at his gardening club. They don't officially live together, but she's always there when I come to visit. According to him, they love maintaining their own little spaces while going on adventures together—coach trips to the surrounding gardens and castles. It's going to be a little awkward when he dies eventually.

"He always speaks fondly of her," I say.

"Haven't seen him in ten years," Beatrice complains. "But that's okay. We don't need him. Even back then, Estelle mostly felt sorry for him, seeing him so sad. She was glad when he moved on. It meant she no longer had to worry and could enjoy her afterlife to the full. As she should. Now she's back in that whole mourning phase. And poor Alexandre is forgotten."

"How's he taking it?"

Beatrice sighs. "Like the gentleman he is. He drops by now and then, but keeps his distance, hiding his aching heart behind pleasantries and politeness. Oh well, if it's meant to be, it'll be. We have all the time in the world, haven't we?"

Not all the time, I think to myself. Even though he predates our grandmother by 150 years, Alexandre might out-after-live her in the end. Eternity is not a given. I look up the hill, to where Abelard and Héloïse have their mausoleum.

"Their relationship didn't survive."

I whip my head around. "What?"

"He lost all of it. All eight hundred years."

"But they loved each other before that."

Estelle nods. "And he loves her, but he's very much a man of his time now, and Héloïse has gone *with* the times. She can't stand his views and his attitude. He's no longer the man she loved. They're still bound to each other, of course, but they're done. She broke up with him."

Tears flood my eyes. Eight hundred years of love and it was all snuffed out in one cruel night by people who couldn't care less about ghosts.

"This is my fault."

"No." Beatrice reaches out and pulls me to her chest. "Oh, no, my love. You did a wonderful thing for them. For a few weeks, they knew true peace."

"But I knew the risks. I hid Petite Alix there!"

"And they knew the risks, too," Beatrice says. "Remember, Abelard fought to defend her with everything he had. He loved that little girl more than himself. And if he… if he remembered, he'd do the same thing again in a heartbeat. You didn't do that, Chouchou. Those evil men did. The ghost police." She hisses the words, a sound I've never heard her make before. "It's their fault and theirs alone."

Our grandmother reaches out and brushes the tears from my face. "Oh, ma petite, it's all going to be fine. We ghosts are a resilient bunch."

But they're not. One load of salt and everything about them is lost to the nether. The ghost community at Père Lachaise was wounded that night and it'll take years, if not decades, to recover.

Odile looks at me, worried, and I wipe away my tears. "We're going to bring them down," I announce bitterly. "Papa has a plan.

We're going to expose everything they've done. Not just what they've done to the living, but what they've done to the dead, too."

Papa might not agree, but this report wouldn't be complete without all the cruelty GoPol has dealt to the ghosts. People are precious about their loved ones. Even the dead ones.

"What do you need?" Beatrice asks, her voice just as hard.

My heart pounds in my chest as I lift my head. "Whispers. I need every whisper of GoPol. Who have they wronged? What have they done? Where can I find evidence?"

I look around and see the ghosts of Père Lachaise have drawn near. There's Héloïse with a grim face, Frederic Chopin and Jim Morrison side by side, Oscar Wilde... and a whole lot of ordinary ghosts whose afterlife is more limited, but just as rich.

In front stands Alexandre de Beauharnais in his revolutionary uniform, one hand on his sabre. "Say the word and we'll march on GoPol itself."

CHAPTER 14

We don't plan to storm the GoPol headquarters that night, although I might consider it to give Sébastien a chance to recover as much hard evidence as he can in the chaos. Instead, we set up a spy network that surpasses anything GoPol could ever dream of. In order not to overwhelm me, the ghosts will report to Jean Moulin, who will in turn follow up leads and filter out the important information.

While the ghosts get to work, I take Gaby and Théo to the World Fair so we can work on our project, but mostly so they can discover it with me.

"I don't see anything," Gaby says as we arrive at the Eiffel Tower. She purses her lips and looks a bit disappointed.

Meanwhile, Théo exclaims, "Woah, this is trippy."

"Can you see the fair?" I ask, confused.

He shakes his head. "No, but I also can't really see you. Like, I know you're there and I can hear you just fine, and when I look straight at you, you're there, but out of the corner of my eye, nothing."

"He's right," Gaby confirms. "Is that how ghosts look to you?"

It's interesting to hear their experiences. It matches what I saw of the living when I visited the fair with Sébastien. Gaby and Théo, however, are clearly visible. Maybe because I know they're there.

"Well, that's disappointing."

Before we came here, I asked Garnier to give them both similar entry bands and they both claimed to have felt a chill, but there was never any silver shimmer, and it's not working as I'd hoped.

Gaby gives me a quick side hug. "It was worth a try. And this will still be helpful. You'll just have to describe what you see."

"I'll take notes," Théo says, pulling out his phone and opening an app. "Look, I also found a map in the archives. The Palais des Industries should be here." He pulls a face. "Damn, that's across from Les Invalides. Where's that old fair railway when you need it?"

"Right there." I point to the station near the Eiffel Tower. It used to be such a novelty, and it's packed with ghosts. "But I suppose you can neither see nor ride it?"

Gaby pulls a face. "It's a walk for us."

"How does that even work?" Théo asks as we walk towards the banks of the Seine, the site of the fair's maritime exhibition. "Could you take the train even if it's not there?"

"It works here. Normally, there aren't many installations like this, and when there are, they're unstable, so I wouldn't be able to use it. Ghosts can often summon objects they were familiar with in life, but they're like reflexes, a part of them. So, if they gave it to me, it would flow through my fingers and disappear. Thanks to Eiffel's resonator, I can interact with all of it."

"That's so cool." Théo shakes his head in awe. "I'm so sorry I gave you such a hard time with the whole ghost thing. If the dead can still come up with new things, evolve, and pull off things like this, they deserve more respect. Way more respect. When are we going to fix the catacombs issue?"

I laugh and shrug. "Maybe after my father's article hits the stands. Once everyone has had a chance to come to terms with it and maybe even appreciate a petition."

"A petition. Yeah, that sounds about right."

Gaby looks a little more pained. "Do you really think people will suddenly believe in ghosts just because of one article?"

"Probably not, but it doesn't have to stop at one."

"But you'll be mentioned in it?"

We haven't actually discussed the details yet. My father may very well try to keep my name out of the papers to avoid the obvious connection between the two of us, but I have a feeling it's inevitable. "Maybe."

"I'm worried," she admits. "People will start harassing you."

"More than now?"

She winces. "Touché. Guess it beats GoPol's assassination attempts."

"It'll be okay," I say, hooking my arm into hers. "I have a strong support system."

"Oh yeah, they mess with you; we mess with them," Théo claims, sending Gaby and me into fits of laughter.

Over the next two hours, we spend time in the Palais des Industries, which is a bit tricky since the building has since been replaced by the Grand Palais and the two don't exactly match. Somehow, we get through without hitting a wall or a display. I try to focus on elements that have been nicked from the original World Fair, but I get distracted by all the ghost inventions sprinkled throughout.

There's an ectoplasmic pen used to write secret messages that can only be read by ghosts or whisperers, and phantom paints used to draw vanishing images. The most fascinating piece is a ghost clock, which is a monstrous amalgamation of several clocks, including sundials and hourglasses, all rolled into one, with at least three ticking hands and a shrieking wraith that appears roughly every thirteen minutes.

"Ghost time runs differently," the ghost who came up with it explains to me. "We all live on our own timelines."

I have to trust her on that, because this clock is pure madness.

After an extensive tour, we sit on the steps in front of the Grand Palais and take a breather. Théo and Gaby have to take me between them to prevent people accidentally stepping on me. As for the ghosts, there are too many of them to return the favour.

Gaby and I read through Théo's notes and add our own comments, while Théo takes out a sketchpad. When I finally glance over his shoulder, I gasp. "Théo, that's amazing!"

Who knew he was so talented? Somehow, he's recreated the old Palais des Industries and put some people in period dress in front of it. It's not photorealistic or anything, but it definitely captures the vibe and glory of the World Fair.

"How did you know what it looked like?" Gaby asks, gasping as well.

"The palace?" Théo asks. "Oh, you can find a few sketches and old pictures online. I based it on those, then added Alix's descriptions." He holds it up to block out the sun and asks, "Is it close enough?"

I snort. "Absolutely! It's amazing. You pretty much hit the nail on the head." I point to the sides of the door. "They actually have plants there."

As I describe them, he quickly adds them to his sketch.

"You're in charge of the pictures," Gaby tells him. "I'll even put the references together." A task everyone hates.

Laughing, Théo continues his sketch. Gaby and I smile and go back to the notes, which we'll eventually have to find references for to support my ghost testimonies.

"Do you think we can use ghost references when all this comes out?" Gaby muses.

I chuckle, amused. "I don't know. Definitely not without some cross-referencing. Even if people believe ghosts are real, that still doesn't mean they'll necessarily believe me. I mean, I could make up all kinds of shit and no one would be the wiser."

"You're gonna need at least two independent peer whisperers or something like that," Gaby muses. "They'll come up with something."

"Yo, History Girl!"

I look up to see Dix crossing the road, trailed by Sébastien. Smiling, I wave as they approach. "Hey, boys."

Next to me, Gaby and Théo squint, reminding me they're having trouble seeing us whisperers properly in the resonator's field.

Then suddenly, Gaby gasps. "Oh my god, I think I can see Dix!"

Perplexed, Dix halts in front of us. "You can?"

Théo cocks his head. "Teenage boy, blue eyes, shock of blond hair? Yeah, I think can see him, too."

Sébastien joins Dix, frowning slightly. "What's going on?"

"Can you hear me, too?"

Gaby and Théo share a look. To my great surprise, Gaby nods. "It's a bit muffled, but yes." She looks at me. "Alix, what does that mean?"

They all look at me as if I have the answers. I don't, but I have a few theories. Nodding at Gaby's wrist, I tell her, "The ticket probably works to some extent. You can't see full ghosts or the spectral structures, but Dix's more alive than most of them. So, he probably appears to you like a ghost whisperer." To Sébastien, I say, "They can't really see us while we're in Eiffel's field. Only if they focus on us."

Sébastien's frown lifts as he huffs in amusement. "That's fascinating, also slightly disturbing."

Meanwhile, Dix glows as if the sun's dawned on him. "People can see me! They can hear me! I'm not... quite so dead."

"Slow down, Pinocchio," says Sébastien, earning himself a jab in the side.

Gaby giggles. "You're a real boy." She takes my hands, her eyes shining. "You *must* bring Petite Alix to the fair. I want to see baby Alix."

"You're impossible." I shake off her hands and stand. As I'm a step above Sébastien and Dix, I have the rare experience of looking down on them. "How's the investigation going?"

"False alarm," Sébastien says. "We gathered some information, but there's no need to act on it. All the whisperers we've noticed are here because they heard about the fair and were curious. And, more importantly, they heard about the catacombs section. That's where they'll all be for the next few days. The Chevalier's having a big reveal on Friday."

I wince. "Let me guess, we're going to be there, too?"

"If we want to win him over to our cause." Sébastien shrugs. "It would also be a good idea to see what he's up to."

Unfortunately, I have an idea of what the Chevalier might want to present to the world. I really have no interest in seeing reanimated animals again.

"Have you spoken to the whisperers? Won any of them over?"

"None of them are GoPol France and they didn't exactly talk to me." Reluctantly, he admits, "They seem to know who I am and won't trust me with anything."

They probably assume—wrongly—he's his father's loyal man. "Should *I* talk to them?"

"I'd rather you didn't," Sébastien admits, with a sigh. "I'm not gonna stop you, but they're agents, trained in combat and manipulation. It might be dangerous, especially if I can't be seen near you. But if you think it would help our cause, I'm not gonna stop you."

It's surprisingly sweet. He worries about me, and yet knows better than to try to keep me from it. I'm tempted to run to some foreign agents and find out if their agencies treat ghosts any better. I guess it's something we'll have to fix ourselves. Besides, it's bad enough I have one GoPol agency on my heels. I don't need any more if they turn out to be just as horrible.

While we've been catching up, Gaby and Théo have been grilling Dix. He's soaking up their attention like a sponge, beaming from ear to ear. Gaby leans over and asks him something quietly. They both look at us, and Dix shrugs.

"Him, yes. Her, I don't know."

"What are you two talking about?" Apparently, Gaby and Dix meeting spells trouble for me.

Gaby gives me a cheeky smile. "It's a secret." Behind them, Théo grins.

I narrow my eyes before pretending I don't care and looking away. I'm about to burst into a grin when I notice someone else instead. "That's the woman who shot at me!"

Sébastien immediately spins around. "What?"

I point ahead of us. "The former GoPol agent who works for the Chevalier. Samira, or whatever her name is."

"Samara," Sébastien corrects me absently. His face has turned ashen as he stares at who I assume is a former colleague of his.

"You know her?"

"That's my missing partner," he admits hoarsely. "The one I thought was dead."

"Your..."

I swallow as my mind conjures up a faint memory. It's been so long since he told me he'd recently lost his partner in the catacombs while investigating the Chevalier. He even gave me her spare gear to keep me safe. I want to punch myself for not making the connection myself when I met her and heard her story.

"Shall we go over?" I ask, almost timidly, insecure for some inexplicable reason.

Sébastien is already in motion, although he very much looks like he's sleepwalking.

"I assume that's a yes," I mumble.

Just as I start to follow, Gaby pulls me back. "This Samara… is she a ghost?"

"No, she's a ghost whisperer. I met her during my short-lived time in the Résistance. She never truly liked me though, thought I was a child and—"

"I really think she's a ghost."

"What? Why?" I glance over. Could it be her whisper ghost? No, that one's several years younger, but I can't find her in the crowd.

Gaby's eyes widen. "I don't see her. At all."

My eyes widen as understanding hits me. Alarmed, I run after Sébastien and catch his shirt "Be careful, she's—"

Samara has been talking to a ghost who's shown her sheets of paper—a blueprint or something. Now she's turning around, staring straight at us.

"—dead."

Samara's eyebrow rises as she looks me up and down with her usual derision. But then she dismisses me and smiles at Sébastien.

"Looking good, Séb. Let me guess, your father sent you to check up on me?"

Sébastien's still in a weird trance. He heard me earlier and is frowning deeply now. "I... I don't understand. I thought you were dead..."

"Well, as your little pet has already told you, I am dead." She snorts. "How did you get back into GoPol's good graces?"

"I didn't," I protest sullenly.

Her gaze wanders back to Sébastien, completely unimpressed. "You and her?"

All three of us seem to hold our breath, unsure where each other's loyalties lie.

Dix strolls over and nudges Samara's shoulder. "You're dead. What happened?"

"She did." Once more, her searing gaze hits me. "I'm dead because of you."

Chapter 15

It's as if I've run head-first into a brick wall. In fact, Sébastien reaches out and steadies me when my knees buckle. Did I hear that right? *I'm* the reason Samara's dead? How?

I only realise I've asked the last question out loud when she rolls her eyes. "If it weren't for the mess you made of the Résistance, I'd still be alive. Also, I refused to kill you."

"What?" I feel like I'm in a bad dream, where monster trucks appear from nowhere and hit me repeatedly in the chest.

Sébastien's frown deepens, but before he can say anything, Gaby and Théo join us, looking confused. "What's wrong?" asks Gaby. "You look like... I guess like you've seen a ghost. But then you see them all the time."

I'm finding it hard to breathe, but Gaby's voice is like a lifeline. I stare at her, taking in her worried face in until I finally manage to make a sound. It comes out as, "Ughm."

"Give us a moment with Samara, okay?" Sébastien says. "I'll look after Alix." He looks at me. "Unless you'd rather go with Gaby and Théo and have a nice coffee."

As tempting as that sounds, I shake my head. I've just been accused of being directly responsible for someone's death—again—and it's because they refused an assassination attempt on my life. An *assassination* attempt! Coffee won't fix this. Answers will.

Gaby reaches out and gives me a quick hug. "Call me as soon as this is over, okay?"

I manage to nod and watch her and Théo leave. When I finally lose them in the crowd, my head snaps back around. "Who wanted to kill me?"

Samara watches Sébastien as she answers, "Charles Roubert."

"When?" Sébastien growls, giving nothing away.

I'm confused. Samara's on our side, isn't she? She was running with the Chevalier, using her apparent death to escape GoPol's clutches. Was she caught in the raid and offered to prove her loyalty by killing me? To whom is she loyal now?

"Where do you stand, Séb?" she asks. "Still set to take over GoPol one day? Or did she drag you down, too?"

Sébastien visibly bristles. "If by 'dragging me down' you mean 'opened my eyes to the truth', then yes, she did. I trust Alix with my life. Any enemy of hers is an enemy of mine."

His words take my breath away. If I weren't so scared, I might even swoon a little.

"With your life?" Samara asks, sounding amused. "Is that how it is?" She jerks her chin in my direction. "And what about you? Who's your enemy?"

My body still thinks it's her, but I force myself to say semi-cryptically, "Same as before."

Her face opens up a little. "Then I guess we're all on the same side. Who'd have thought?" The last is directed at Sébastien again.

He relaxes ever so slightly. "Are you going to tell us what happened now? All of it?"

Samara sighs. "I suppose I can do that. Very well. Let's get the unpleasant part out of the way first." Her gaze returns to me. "I was the one who betrayed you to GoPol. The one who told them where to look for you when you ran off with your whisper ghost."

It's another frontal hit by the truck, and this time, Sébastien puts an arm in front of me and pushes me behind him, as if Samara just announced she was going to assassinate me.

"Relax. My priorities have changed since then."

I stare, wild-eyed. I'd always wondered how the Résistance was crushed so quickly that night. It's just like Jean Moulin always laments—the Résistance would've been more successful if not for the sheer number of traitors in our ranks. "Why?"

"Because I was still working for GoPol," Samara said. "I was a double agent. A real one." She can't get a word out without taking a swipe at me. The rest of her explanation is for Sébastien, whom she actually respects. "The mission was to go underground, pretend I'd defected and gain the Chevalier's trust, find out what he was doing and if he had any plans to overthrow GoPol. Sorry you weren't made aware of that and had to think I was dead." She takes a deep breath, a remnant of her human days. "Then Alix came along and made a royal mess out of everything."

Sébastien glares at her. "She was only trying to survive in a world that had suddenly turned against her. And she did better than most."

Where are all these declarations coming from? I didn't know he felt so defensive—or is it protective?—of me.

Samara snorts. "Whatever. I do my job and turn her over to GoPol, but they screw it up. A second time. So, then I get the order to take her out. And I refused." She sneers at me. "Something I'm starting to regret."

A low hiss shocks me almost as much as her malice. If Sébastien were a dog, he'd be growling at Samara right now.

"Relax." Samara throws her hands up. "I'm not gonna kill her now. Told you we're on the same side now. Sort of." She sounds almost bored as she continues, "So, one night, C-Trente follows me into the catacombs and bashes my head in. Says I know too much and I can't be trusted. I suppose he was afraid I'd secretly gone over to the Chevalier. Or even to her."

I taste bile in my throat, the mere words bringing back images of how Gaspar murdered Margot. My knees feel weak again. How did I get into this whole mess?

Sébastien slides his hand into mine and squeezes it, quietly offering comfort. "He killed you because you wouldn't murder someone?"

"He wanted her dead because she annoyed him. Seems pretty on brand to me." Samara shrugs. "Anyway, now I'm dead and she lives. Oh, and C-Trente is gone. Just like my Sam."

It takes me a moment to understand who Sam is. "Your whisper ghost is gone?"

"Of course. They don't survive our deaths."

I immediately look at Dix, who gives me a lop-sided smile and a shrug. "It's true. You get to be full ghosts, and we get to be... gone."

"Or we're one again," Sébastien says, the faintest note of longing in his voice.

Samara gives him a flat stare. "It's definitely gone." She snorts and shakes her head. "Eight years, and they're all wiped out in one brutal murder. I didn't even get to say goodbye."

My heart goes out to her all of a sudden. While the majority of GoPol only think of their whisper ghosts as tools or extensions of themselves, I can hear how much the loss affected her in her words. She misses Sam, hiding it behind all that venom and spite.

"That must be so hard."

I'm cut off by another vicious glare. "Don't pretend you know what you're talking about. Your whisper ghost is a baby. You barely even know her."

It seems like whatever comes out of my mouth is the wrong thing. Samara hates me, and rightly so, even though I had little to do with what happened to her. This is worse than Hélène blaming me for Cédric's death, because this one's actually tied to me.

Still protective, Sébastien barks at her. "Alix knows more than anyone else about relationships with ghosts."

"Oh, right, is she still fucking that ghost?" Samara grins at me. "Oh no, that's right, it was all very innocent."

I want to go home. My stomach feels sick, and I might burst into tears if she takes another shot at me.

For now, she's focusing on Sébastien. "How does that feel? Being rejected for a ghost?"

"You have no idea what you're talking about," he says coldly. "Listen, I'm sorry for what happened to you. You didn't deserve that, but it's not Alix's fault. We have a plan to bring my father to justice and we could use your help. Where did C-Trente hide your body? Is there any other record or proof that my father gave the order? We're gathering evidence and—"

"Bring him to justice?" Samara laughs. "No, thank you. I don't want any part of whatever this is." She waves her hand back and forth between Sébastien and me. "Death and chaos follow her wherever she goes. From what I'm hearing, not even the ghosts are safe around her. So, excuse me if I'd rather not get involved in any more of her pathetic little schemes."

CHAPTER 16

I manage to hold it together until we get back home. Sébastien puts my numb little self on the couch and promises to make something to eat, while Dix sprints into my room to fetch Malou. No sooner have they left me alone than I start to hiccup. I try to resist, but the pressure quickly builds, and I gasp, tears streaming down my face.

In an instant, Sébastien is back at my side. He kneels in front of me and pulls my head against his chest. I wrap my arms around him, digging my nails into his shirt and crying my sad little heart out.

"Don't you dare listen to her," Sébastien mutters into my hair. "Her anger isn't directed at you. She's just lashing out because she sees you as an easy target. But she's wrong. Yes, things are pretty shitty right now," he admits, "but you're not the one to blame."

"I'm the catalyst," I cry, repeating Nostradamus' words. According to him, I'll eventually destroy the whole of France. "It's all happening because of me."

"Nonsense."

But I only cry harder, and he can't do anything but hold me in his arms until all the pain and despair has poured out. Lacan said in our last session that I tend to shoulder everyone's needs and expectations as well as everyone's trauma, losing myself in the process. And while that's probably true, I don't know how to stop it. How to stop caring so much.

It takes me a good twenty minutes to collect myself, dry my tears, and regain some semblance of control. Breathing still hurts, but I've stopped hiccupping—and I've stopped clinging to Sébastien as if I were drowning.

When I finally manage to look up, Dix stands there with Malou. He immediately holds her out. "Do you want her?"

I smile at the gesture in spite of my dreadful condition. He obviously has no idea how to deal with my breakdown, so he's grabbed the one thing that always helps him. I nod shyly and hold out my arm. "Thank you. Both of you."

Sébastien strokes my head as I sink back into the couch and cuddle Malou. Poor baby has become a full-time emotional support animal.

"How about I prepare a hot bath and you relax a little while I cook dinner?"

He may not have been able to talk me out of my despair, but he sure knows how to spoil a girl. By the time, the bath is ready, I've calmed down enough to hand Malou back to Dix. Something smells good in the kitchen as I enter the bathroom, where I find not just a hot bath with mountains of foam, but also a candle burning. It's just one of his usual vervain candles, but it makes me smile, nonetheless.

I grab my phone to put on some music and find Gaby's worried messages. Instead of fully relaxing, I call her and tell her all about our meeting with Samara, shedding a few more tears as I sink into the foam.

"Alix!" Gaby moans. "Do you even hear yourself? That bitch ratted you out to GoPol. She's the reason you spent a night in jail, that Petite Alix was almost destroyed, and that Gaspar thought he had to try this experimental resurrection to stay with you. If she would've just minded her business, you would've been okay."

I swallow hard at her blunt words. "Well, I would've been a refugee hiding in the catacombs."

"And probably safer for it." Gaby sighs. "Okay, things would still be complicated, but she's the bad guy here, not you. Honestly, you're the sweetest, most caring person in the world. She's just a bitch. That woman *shot* at you! Remember?"

Gaby really has a way with words. She cuts through my whole woe-is-me crap and reminds me of the cold, hard facts. "It's just that so many people—and ghosts—have got hurt because of me."

She coughs, making her next words intelligible, but I'm pretty sure she meant to say Charles.

"Yes, fine, because of Charles and GoPol. I just can't help thinking how little would've happened if I'd just..."

"Rolled over and died?" Gaby asks unimpressed.

"Given up my whisper abilities."

"So, relinquishing Petite Alix?"

I wince. There's no way in hell I could ever give up that poor little soul. The knowledge she'll cease to exist the moment I die is unbearable enough as it is. Perhaps Gustave Eiffel or Marie Curie have an idea on how to prevent that from happening. As I think about it, a strange determination grows. If I die, she'll suffer, too, so the obvious solution is to *not* roll over and die, as Gaby so aptly put it.

"Look," she continues, "you're right. Very little would've happened. Sébastien would still be under his father's thumb, either numbed to the world or killed for Charles' ambition. That monster, C-Trente, would still be around, killing someone else who's bothering Charles. And poor Dix would lose all hope of ever being more than a whisper of the past. But there's more. The ghost community at Père Lachaise might be whole, but they also wouldn't band together either. Ghosts wouldn't be heard, maybe even have rights one day. So yeah, Alix. A lot of things have happened and will happen because of you. They're good things."

Now I have to cry again, but these are happy tears. "You're the best," I whisper.

"I know. So, what are you up to now?"

I tell her about the bath Sébastien prepared and the dinner he's cooking.

Gaby chuckles softly. "Oh, Séb."

"What's that supposed to mean? He went to a lot of trouble for me."

"I wasn't complaining," Gaby says, amused. "You finish your bath, then you go out there and let that man take care of you. Call me tomorrow."

"Bye."

I put the phone down and sink as deep into the water as I can without getting my hair wet. The heat is disappearing by the second, and I only give myself another five minutes before I get out and extinguish the candle. After drying myself, I put on my pyjamas—which are basically an oversized T-shirt with an Idéfix print and shorts so short they're invisible under the shirt. To be a bit more decent, I wrap the bathrobe around my shoulders and step outside.

Instead of setting the table, Sébastien has put the dinner, a tartiflette, on the coffee table, along with two glasses of white wine and another candle.

"Is this a date?" I ask, amused.

He laughs but can't stop his cheeks from flushing. "Just something nice for you. I can blow out the candle."

"No, no. Leave it." I sit beside him and reach for my plate. The smell of cheese and bacon fills my nostrils. "This looks delicious."

"Pure comfort food," Sébastien admits.

His love of cheese is something special, but I have to admit, it's an incredibly easy thing to get used to. The tartiflette is delicious and filling. In addition to the cheese and bacon I smelled earlier, there's a layer of potatoes and onions. Seasoned with white wine and salt and pepper, each bite is more delicious than the last.

I eat much more than I should because it's just so good, but eventually, I have to stop. I take my wine glass and lean on Sébastien's shoulder. "Where did Dix go?"

While we were eating, he's completely disappeared.

"I think he's in your room, playing with Malou. You don't mind, do you?"

"As long as he leaves when I go to bed." I take a sip, feeling quite sleepy after the meal and crying session. "Gaby talked some sense into me."

"Sense?"

I laugh. "Well, maybe I shouldn't listen to the woman who shot at me." Funny how Samara refused to kill me when she was asked to but had no problem risking my life by shooting at me. Never mind betraying me and the entire Résistance. "She's not a good person."

"*Was*," Sébastien corrects quietly. "I..."

"Sorry. You knew her. She was your partner and all." There's a little pang in my heart I don't quite know what to make of.

Sébastien shakes his head. "She was only my senior partner. We weren't close or anything. If anything, she gave me a lot of crap for being a Roubert. Never once questioned how it happened that we had two generations of ghost whisperers. Or maybe she knew and didn't really care. It sounds as if she was a pretty loyal follower of my father until he turned on her."

I don't interrupt him. After all he's done for me, the least I can do is listen to his heartbreak. It's so rare he lets me in.

"It's just... I felt responsible for losing her." His voice cracks a little. "Like I failed her. And Papa... It's not just that he didn't tell me to protect her secret, but... he blamed me."

"What?"

"I got a speech. Or a warning." He swirls the wine in his glass instead of drinking it.

Without even thinking, my hand runs through his hair, gently ruffling it.

"Some nonsense about looking out for each other. I felt horrible. I was devastated. And I was determined to find her, but of course, there was never anything to find." He snorts. "I don't get it. How did I not see this before? Not Samara, but my father being such an ass. The job is tough, yes, but what's the point of making it tougher? It's as if he enjoys seeing me suffer."

I rest my head against his and sigh. "It's about control, I think. Some bullshit to make sure you never relax enough to truly think it all through." With another deep sigh, I muse, "Killing you was an unprecedentedly risky move. Yes, he created his own super-soldier, but that soldier was still a living, breathing being—someone who could turn on him. So, he had to find that balance between making you a competent agent and breaking you down enough so you'd never think of turning against him. Frankly, I'm starting to think your father is quite paranoid."

Sébastien snorts. "As he should be." He drinks the glass, finishing it in one gulp. "He's done so many bad things, starting with the Chevalier or maybe even before. He's got to be looking over his shoulder all the time."

"That sounds about right." Tired, I lay my head on his shoulder, still strangely fascinated by the feel of his short hair. "So, is this how you *have* to run an intelligence service? Do you have to be so ruthless?"

"To a point, I suppose. If it serves national security." Sébastien looks at me and swallows slightly. "But he's doing so much more than that. Making me a GoPol agent? Unnecessary. There are enough natural ghost whisperers out there. You just have to train them. Kill Samara? She was loyal to him. And you?" This time, he really looks at me, his cheek scratching my forehead. "That's a mess of his own making."

I get a little lost in the blue of his eyes. "So, I'm an *actual* threat to national security?" I say jokingly to break this sleepy spell.

Sébastien looks away again and swallows even harder. "If so, he made you one."

I take a sip of my wine and continue to stroke his hair, unable to stop myself. "You've got a lot of good ideas about how GoPol *should* be run."

"Tainted ideas probably."

"Nonsense," I reply drowsily. "Come on, humour me. How would *you* run it if they put you in charge?"

He snorts. "First point of action, I'd hire you as a ghost consultant."

"Not an agent?"

"Nah, you're too valuable for that."

As he continues to paint his picture of a better GoPol agency, my hand drops, and my eyes flutter shut. All I remember is it sounded a lot less scary—and a little noble.

CHAPTER 17

I wake at some point during the night because my neck hurts. As I roll my muscles, I notice my pillow is uncharacteristically hard. Blinking, I open my eyes and sit up, causing the bathrobe to slip off my shoulder.

Wait a minute, why am I sleeping in my bathrobe?

My heart rate quickens when I realise I'm still on the couch with Sébastien. Sometime during our dinner, I must've fallen asleep on him. My cheeks burn when I accidentally brush against the stomach muscles I mistook for my pillow. While I'm half lying on the couch, Sébastien is still sitting, only a little slumped, his head lolling on the backrest.

Moonlight filters through the sheer curtains, painting the sharp lines of his nose and chin silver. Careful not to disturb him, I straighten. His arm drops down to rest against my ass and I nearly jump. I hadn't even noticed it lying across my back before. I blow a lock of tangled hair out of my face, unsure what to do next.

His chiselled profile catches my eye again. Blond stubble covers his chin, the hairs only visible in the moonlight. His lips part to utter the most enchanting little murmur.

I smile, enraptured by his peacefulness. The pain in his eyes is locked away behind golden down lashes, and no frown mars his forehead. Slowly, I sink back against the backrest and watch him sleep. A muscle twitches and another sound falls from his lips. His beautiful, full lips. The faintest trace of his breath brushes across my face.

Time seems to stand still. It's not just the apartment that's fallen quiet, but the whole city of Paris. Not even a single motorist cuts through the silence.

Though it's the middle of the night, I'm no longer tired. I just watch him until our breaths synchronise and the little sounds he make have melted my heart. When a distant car breaks the spell, I raise my hand, cupping his cheek, my thumb a mere millimetre from the corner of his lips.

Startled, I realise what I'm doing, but just as I pull my hand away, he snatches it from the air. His eyes fly open and our gazes lock instantly. In the dark, the depth of his dilated pupils pulls me in. I forget to breathe as he presses my hand back to his cheek, then turns slightly into it and, without ever breaking eye contact, kisses my palm lightly.

I shudder unintentionally. When he lifts his chin again, I run my thumb over his lips. They feel soft as a feather in the dead of night.

Sébastien's mouth parts, sucking in a breath, and I see his throat bop. I push my thumb between his lips, and suddenly, I'm leaning forward, pressing my lips against his. My hand slides down his neck as I pull him closer, eager to taste the dreams he's abandoned for me.

He moans softly, his hand buried in my hair as the arm I've trapped tightens around my ass, gripping my hip. My whole body tenses in delicious anticipation. As my tongue enters his mouth, I swing my leg over his, pushing my knees into the couch on either side of him and cupping his face with both hands.

He tastes of white wine and earnest promises, of safety and longing. I drink him in as if I've been parched ever since we parted in Provence. The ferocity of how much I want him races like lightning down my spine, gathering between my legs. I need him. Need him in my life as much as I need him in my arms.

Sébastien's arm tightens around my back, pressing me against his chest. The grip in my hair hardens, holding me tight so we may never be parted.

I come up for air, only to run my lips along his chin line, savouring the prickle of his stubble. When I kiss him below the ear, he buries his nose in my shoulder, and his hot breath brushes my collarbone. His lips follow the trail soon after.

My bathrobe has fallen off my shoulders, hindering the movement of my left arm. Annoyed, I shake it off and almost immediately sink my hand back into his hair. He drops the hand in my hair, allowing me to pull my other arm out of the robe, too. As the cloth falls to my hips, I press myself against his rock-hard body.

We kiss again, tasting and teasing each other. Sébastien pulls the robe away with his lower hand, just as I slip my hands under his shirt and run my fingers over those delicious abs.

Oh, how I want to make this man mine. For so long, we've been sneaking around each other, never quite daring to dive in head-first. So many lingering glances and unspoken feelings. I confess them all with my tongue. The touch of my fingers claims what he's so quietly offered. He's been mine for a long time, and tonight I'm brave enough to be his.

Heat blossoms on my skin as his hand slides under my shirt and up my side. I shudder and gasp for breath, completely lost in the sensation, as if I've been waiting for his touch ever since he stood in my doorway, offering me his heart and his soul.

"Shit! Sorry, I'll…"

Sébastien and I fly apart at the sound of Dix's voice. The whisper ghost quickly exits, leaving the two of us breathing hard.

The reality of the situation hits me like an avalanche. I just kissed Sébastien. Much more than that. I practically threw myself at him. My throat tightens as the one who's held my heart for so long comes to my mind.

"Gaspar." The name puts a wall between us that he won't try to—and I can't—cross.

"I'm sorry," he breathes, still panting slightly.

I shake my head violently. "No, no, it was me. I'm…"

I pull the bathrobe around my shoulders and bite my lip. Tears sting in my eyes. In my mind, Gaspar stares at me the way he did after that first unplanned kiss under the opera. Back then, I was exalted to be alive. Now, I have no such excuse.

"I'm sorry," I blurt out, then all but run from the room.

"Alix," he calls after me, his voice betraying the pain I'm causing.

As I slam the door behind me and throw myself into my bed, I'm overcome with hatred and shame. I've taken advantage of Sébastien and betrayed Gaspar all in one fell swoop. It's not like I didn't know how Sébastien felt. I'd have to be blind not to notice. But I was with Gaspar, and Sébastien always respected that. Now I've gone and torn down the boundaries, as if they never mattered.

What kind of horrible person rejects someone after their confession and then strings them along, anyway? Who would kiss someone while claiming their heart belongs to another?

Hot tears run down my cheeks as I scream my frustration into the pillow. What was I thinking? Why did I touch him? Kiss him? Why couldn't I just have left him alone, slipped away, and gone to bed like a normal person?

Because I was drunk on moonlight and golden down.

The taste of Sébastien's lips still lingers on mine, and for a moment, I get lost in the sensation of that one passionate kiss. Oh, how I wanted him. *Still* want him. My body aches for the touch of his hands, for the firm pressure as he locks me between his arm and his body, for the heat of his kiss.

What if Dix hadn't interrupted us? How far would we have gone?

My legs ache with the loss of him. For a wild moment, I consider getting out of bed, crossing the hall, and continuing where we left off. My mind lashes out viciously by bringing Gaspar back up. My sweet, sweet hedgehog boy.

Move on with him.

Is it really a betrayal if he let me go? Pushed me away? *Into* Sébastien's arms?

But *I* didn't let him go. My heart's still broken, longing to be fixed. For things to go back the way they were. I love Gaspar, even now, after all he's done. I'm still holding on to the hope it's not truly him, that the real Gaspar will return to me one day.

And then what?

Can I drop Sébastien and go back to Gaspar, leaving the latter in the dust? After tonight?

My stomach tightens as my mind goes back and forth between the two and the sheer impossibility of both choices. Guilt, shame, and desire all mix into a toxic cocktail, swirling in my heart as it strains against the confines of my chest. I gasp for air, burst into tears, and moan all at the same time.

How can there be two perfect men for me who feel so right, but are so wrong? What do I do with these conflicting feelings? How do I solve this mess I've got myself into?

The answers elude me, but the questions follow into my dreams, leading to a restless, interrupted sleep, and an emotional hangover that puts all others to shame.

Somehow, I've fallen in love with both men. But I can't have either.

CHAPTER 18

Sébastien saves us the embarrassment of the morning after by leaving early. Ever the gentleman, he's prepared breakfast—bloody waffles and coffee—and written an apology note. As if he's the one to blame for my lapse in judgement.

Sorry about last night. I promise it won't happen again. I know how much he means to you. X Séb.

My cheek twitches as I clutch the note to my heart. Sébastien has nothing to apologise for. That he even thinks he does shows how sweet he can be—or how damaged he is. An aching part of me wishes he'd fight for me. That instead of keeping his respectful distance, he'd act on his feelings and make me forget all about Gaspar.

I shake my head. Apparently, last night's horniness hasn't subsided yet. To regain some sort of control over myself, I scribble a quick reply: *Don't apologise. Not for that.*

I make short work of breakfast before packing my bag and cycling to university. Thankfully, classes distract me from my midnight woes, and by the end of the day I feel almost normal again. Later tonight, I'm going to meet up with Sébastien to enter the catacombs for the Chevalier's presentation, but first, I'm seeing my friends at *Chambelland*.

Marie does the afternoon shift, while Gaby and I spread our stuff at our favourite table. After discovering the Ghost World Fair our material for 1889 far outweighs the other two we're supposed to be looking at. Unfortunately, none of it's been referenced yet.

We work in silence for an hour, supported by complimentary coffee and pain au chocolat. It's an interesting experience to read a history book and then see it come to life in front of your eyes. Every mention of a place I've already visited puts an image in my mind, while every other place goes on my next itinerary, like the reconstructed Bastille, which makes my young revolutionary heart sing.

When we get a coffee refill and Marie has time to sit with us, Gaby leans in. "So, tell me all about last night."

My body goes rigid, and I drop my pen. Flustered, I stoop to retrieve it, hiding my burning cheeks under the table.

Gaby laughs. "Oh, my. What happened?"

"What's going on?" asks Marie, looking back and forth between us.

"Séb ran a bubble bath for Alix and prepared dinner. There was candlelight."

I slam my pen down and lick my lips, my cheeks still burning. "It meant nothing. He just wanted to cheer me up."

"And did he?" Gaby wriggles her eyebrows. "Were you cheered up?"

Despite not knowing the first thing, she's reading me like a book. "I was... cheered. I mean..." Gosh, what's wrong with me? "It was nice. Cosy. Yes. I fell asleep on the couch."

Gaby pouts. "That's all?"

"I didn't say that." I glance at Marie, nervous about what I'm about to confess, but if I can't talk to my friends about these things, who *can* I talk to? Gaby's all ears when I reluctantly admit, "I woke up."

"Come on," says Gaby, "don't make me drag it out of you!"

"Fine!" I say, emphatically, feeling the heat. "We kissed. He fell asleep, too. And then I lost my mind and kissed him... Climbed on him, actually."

Gaby's mouth drops open and her eyes light up. "Girl! Yes, finally."

Across the table, Marie giggles.

"Don't get too excited. Dix walked in on us before we did much more and I came to my senses and... Well, I fled."

Disappointed, Gaby pouts again. "But why?"

"Because I'm with Gaspar."

She snorts. "No, you're not. Sorry, ma puce, but that relationship has run its course. Didn't he practically tell you to leave him alone and forget all about him?"

The words sting enough to drain the heat from my cheeks. "He said that to protect me, but that doesn't mean it's over. I still love him."

Noticing how upset I've become, Gaby reaches out and rubs my back. "Sorry, I didn't mean to belittle your feelings. I know it's complicated."

I sigh. "Insanely complicated." Deciding not to dwell on the pain, I admit, "I love Gaspar and I'm still hoping he can be saved, that we can find a way to fix him. And if that happens, I want a second chance. But I also love Sébastien. He's really grown on me and is such a sweet soul. He's also incredibly hot."

Gaby blinks rapidly. "Uhm, yes, yes, he is."

"So, I don't know. Maybe moving in with him was a bad idea. I know he wants me, perhaps even loves me, and I know he didn't just offer in the hope I'd come around. No, he's not like that at all. It's me who's crossed the boundary. I just don't want to string him along and make him think there's still hope when there isn't."

"Because you're remaining loyal to Gaspar? Even when you have a perfectly good man at your side and feelings are mutual?" Gaby asks. It's safe to say Gaspar hasn't exactly left a good impression.

"Why does it have to be either or?" Marie asks innocently. As we both stare, she continues, "I know society likes to push its hetero-normative views on us, but I believe the human heart is big enough for more than one love. If they both love you and you love them both... There's nothing wrong with that, is there?"

"You know what?" Gaby says, leaving a little pause. "She's right. You should be with both."

The blood rushes back to my cheeks. "I can't have two boyfriends."

"Please. Half your ghosts in the Panthéon had a ménage à trois. What's good for them is good for you."

I want to argue that I can't compare myself to our national heroes, but that's not exactly an exclusive characteristic or what they're known for. Love has always been more liberal, especially in Paris. I mean, half of us are in love with love itself. But while I'd never question someone else's life choices, it's a whole different beast when it comes to me. Can I really be with both?

My mind seems to think so, regaling me with a plethora of hot fantasies, but reality is only a millimetre away. "It doesn't really matter. Gaspar's out of the picture." For now.

Gaby shrugs. "Then be with Sébastien and have some fun."

I'm saved a reply by the arrival of a customer. Marie jumps to her feet, only to find out it's Théo.

He holds up his hand and joins us. "Sorry, I'm late. Guerineau made us stay a few minutes longer to finish a film."

Gaby gives me a long look before turning to Théo. "That's okay. We were taking a break, anyway. How's the 1937 fair coming along?"

"Good, good. I actually found some video footage. Not terribly exciting, but at least you get a feel for it. Not much about the industries, though. It's all very political."

"Well, that's still something," I say, eager to change the subject. "I can only imagine how different that one would've been in the political climate back then."

"Yeah, the Germans and the Soviets basically had a pavilion pissing contest, with Italy trying to get a crumb, too."

It's not my favourite time period with a world already too modern and systematised. I much prefer the chaos of the earlier periods, the ever-changing political landscape, and emergence from the Dark Ages. But Théo loves 20th century stuff, so I'm glad he's taken over that one.

"Anyway, how are we gonna do this?" Théo asks. "Shall we just tell each other what we've found or each write a section, then read and critique, and think about how to combine it into a cohesive thesis?"

"I think we should decide on the thesis first, just to make sure we're all on the same page. But other than that, I like the writing approach." Since we're not only giving a talk but also handing in a paper, this sounds like a fair division. "Here's what I have so far."

Before I can really get into it, the door opens again, and another familiar face enters. "Odi?"

Odile's eyes light up as she notices me and rushes over. "Hey guys." She kisses everyone on the cheek exuberantly but hesitates in front of Théo. "And you are?"

Théo stares. "I... um, I'm Théo."

"He's a classmate," I interject. "And that's my sister Odile, who has yet to explain what she's doing here."

Odile gives Théo a peck, too, before sitting next to me. "Gaby told me you'd be here. I brought outfits."

"Outfits?" Théo asks, probably wondering what my sister's talking about.

"Outfits," she says proudly, before dropping a collection of clothes for Malou on our homework. "I need you to do a photo shoot with Malou and send me the pictures for editing. Use the photo box I left in your room."

I hadn't even noticed she'd left something.

Théo picks up one of the little outfits, a miniature superhero uniform and cape, and whistles. "These are for the hedgehog?"

"The hedgehog?" Odile exclaims in mock shock. "Put some respect on Malou! She's a social media star." With a smug grin, she adds, "Thanks to me and my outfits."

"You made these?" he asks, clearly impressed.

Odile tucks a pink curl behind her ear, showing the slightest sign of embarrassment. "It's a hobby of mine."

He checks out another dress, grinning from ear to ear. "These are amazing. You should do a World Fair themed collection."

"A World Fair themed collection?" Odile looks puzzled. "Is that a history thing?"

Théo's eyes light up. "That's our presentation right there." He pulls out his sketchpad and immediately gets to work. "We'll tell the story of Malou as a time traveller who visits the 1855, 1889, and 1937 exhibitions. I'll build a set, you do the costumes. Like a diorama."

It's quite impressive how quickly he draws these sketches.

Odile looks over his shoulder and quickly loses her initial shyness and points to the sketch. "Make one of her in a hat. I'll make an outfit with a walking stick attached."

Théo complies, much to Odile's delight. "We need little inventions to show off her ingenuity."

"Can you really build a set like that?" Odile asks.

"I have friends at the opera workshop. They can help me make miniatures."

My sister's eyes get even bigger. "Oh, can I come? I want to make some, too."

Marie, Gaby, and I share a glance. All three of us have picked up on a certain vibe between the two. All that creative energy is explosive.

Gaby hides her mouth behind a coffee cup. "Guess we're doing a Malou slide show for class."

Neither budding artist hears. I grin. "At least, it won't be boring." Checking my phone, I notice how late it is. "I'd better go meet Séb and Dix."

"Take the outfits!" Odile exclaims, shoving them into my lap before hanging over Théo's shoulder again.

Laughing, I scoop them up and put them in my bag together with the history books. I sling the backpack over my shoulder and kiss my friends goodbye.

"Have fu-un!" Gaby calls after me, wriggling her eyebrows.

I roll my eyes at her and head out. When I look back through the window, Odile's showing Malou's feed to Théo, who leans in with interest, while Gaby and Marie cuddle and share sweet kisses.

With so much love in the air, maybe I *am* going to have some fun.

CHAPTER 19

I've never seen the catacombs so packed. The Crossroads of the Dead is a busy place on a normal day, but now there are ghostly stalls along the sides and on the upper boulevard. The Chevalier's usual meeting place has become a bustling ghost tavern, packed with patrons. I'm glad they're incorporeal. The centrepiece is a gothic circus tent, with black and grey stripes and bone decorations; the Chevalier's pavilion. On the walls around it, spectral monitors flicker. If they're showing any images, I can't parse them.

It's tight and crowded, and I quickly feel overwhelmed. Fortunately, I have Sébastien with me. He takes my hand to pull me through the crowd.

"We're already at capacity," a ghost warden at the door tells us, and I believe it.

A booming voice shouts from behind me, "They're with us."

"Victor!"

I look over my shoulder to see Victor and Voltaire leading a small group of Panthéon ghosts towards the tent. The crowd of ghosts parts for them, whispering and pointing. One eager ghost excitedly asks for an autograph, while another faints and has to be caught by those around her.

The warden's eyes widen. "Monsieur Hugo. Of course, of course. No problem at all. Just give me a second."

As we wait, Victor nods to Sébastien. "Heard you're taking good care of our girl."

The darkness may hide my burning cheeks, but it can't hide Sébastien's nervous throat clearing. "Um, I'm trying my best." He looks at the small selection of the Panthéon ghosts with increasing awe. "Is that..." he asks but quickly shuts his mouth.

I laugh and decide to introduce him to those he hasn't met yet. "You already saw Pierre and Marie Curie at the fair—"

"Your presentation was awe-inspiring," he says, completely flustered. "I've never thought much about the biology—or I guess, physics—behind the ghost experience, so hearing about spectral energies and stabilisation fields was fascinating."

The two scientists are very pleased, and Marie holds out her hand. "It's not unlike the DNA of the living body. In fact, I'm currently looking into the link between—"

She gets jostled aside by Josephine Baker, who shakes her banana-clad booty. "No science talk outside the exhibition. We had a deal."

"This is Josephine Baker," I say, a little too late.

"Enchantée," she says, holding out her hand for a kiss. When Sébastien dutifully bends over to brush her knuckles with his lips, she leans into me. "That's a fine specimen of a man you've got there."

"Stop it," I hiss, once again glad for the darkness of the catacombs. Before she can embarrass me any further, I introduce the last two. "And this is Louis Braille and Jean Moulin. You might—"

Sébastien stares at Moulin, looking absolutely starstruck. "It's an honour... an absolute honour, Mon-monsieur Moulin." They shake hands and the stuttering continues. "I-I grew up on reading about your... you. You're..." He's completely tongue-tied.

"Your hero?" I suggest, amusedly. Who would've thought something could ever shake the stoic special agent?

"Yes!" Sébastien says, with endearing emphasis.

Moulin grins. "Well, from what our dear Alix here has told me, you're quite the hero yourself, so the pleasure is all mine." He pats Sébastien on the shoulder, which makes me worry he's going to faint, too. "Keep up the good work."

Fortunately for Sébastien's constitution, the tent flap opens, and a group of ghosts run out, chased by the warden. As they shuffle away, I hear them complaining loudly about being first. The warden gives us a big, fake smile. "There's room now. Come on in."

"But..." I feel bad for the other ghosts.

"Don't worry about it. They'll be fine," says Victor, and gives me a little push.

The tent seems bigger inside than it is on the outside. A sign by the entrance declares it to be the 'Miracle of Life' exhibition. Several display cases are arranged in a circle, each equipped with an information panel. Well-dressed ghosts lean over the boxes, pointing and exclaiming in wonder.

My chest tightens and I dread going any closer, but I don't stop Sébastien from pulling me along.

It's exactly what I've feared. Inside are the reanimated animals from the Chevalier's lab. I immediately recognise the squirrel with its twisted spine. It jumps up and down in a box that's far too small for such an energetic creature. A large branch is all that's been provided for its entertainment.

Apart from the squirrel, there's also a snake and a hamster skeleton. Many marvel at the latter as it runs on its little wheel, its skeletal feet making a constant clatter. Meanwhile, a handler lifts the snake out of its enclosure and holds it so it can wrap itself around the arm of an elegant woman.

"You knew about this?" Sébastien asks softly as we move from the skeleton section to the zombie section, as I call the roadkill animals that have been animated with fur but without their skeletons intact.

Bile rises in my throat as I watch various corpses move in unnatural ways. "He showed me once," I whisper.

If Sébastien has a problem with me keeping this to myself until now, it doesn't show.

Dix appears in front of us. "There's a hedgehog." He leads us to the case containing the crushed hedgehog with its broken spines.

"Is it not miserable?" Sébastien asks, watching the little creature with grim fascination. "Don't they feel the pain?"

"Oh, no!" Marie Curie exclaims, sounding terribly excited. She points to the information board. "These experiments aren't truly alive. They're reanimated. They don't feel anything."

"How so?" I ask, not trusting the assessment just because the Chevalier says so. I don't think he cares much for these things.

"Because"—Marie reads a little further—"there's no ghost attached. They run on bone memory. Fascinating. Absolutely fascinating." She takes out her lab book and jots down notes before she moves on, completely enthralled.

Most of the ghosts seem intrigued. From their conversations, I gather this is just another cool World Fair innovation for them. Like the ghost puppies. A snotty gentleman behind me complains it's hardly real life if there's no soul attached, which prompts a heated argument about what constitutes life from Voltaire.

On a philosophical level, all this is fascinating and interesting, but no clever argument could make me feel better when I look at the poor hedgehog that's been brought back to life.

"This is morbid," Dix says, with an unbearable sadness in his voice.

Sébastien just nods and pulls me away to the only display of animals that actually look alive and healthy. We catch up with Marie Curie just as she bends over the mouse and says to Pierre, "There's still no ghost attached to it and yet the mouse retains its perfect shape. I wonder what the reading on the spectral barometer would be for such a creature."

Sick to the stomach, I turn away and stare at the vacant podium and microphone to catch my breath. The first time I saw these creatures, it was eerie, but also strangely captivating. Now all I see is what's wrong with them. Starting with Gaspar, this whole resurrection business is wrong.

Sébastien rubs little circles on my back in quiet comfort, while the ghosts get their fill of witnessing the 'Miracle of Life'.

"Has it been worth coming down here?" I ask Victor, hoping my voice isn't too confrontational.

He has his hands clasped behind his back, his facial expression one of mild interest. "Don't mistake our presence here for support. A wise girl once told me we live too far removed from the ghost community, with our heads in the clouds. This World Fair is quite something. I still remember the original ones and this has been no less inspiring. As far as this particular exhibition is concerned, I think it's important to be on the cusp of things in order to form an informed opinion. One can't judge what you don't know."

I cross my arms over my chest, unable to shake the shiver that runs down my spine. "It's not right."

"On *that*, we can agree." Victor smiles gently. "But for now, let's keep an open mind and enjoy the show."

"The show?"

Sure enough, the crowd parts and forms an excited, chattering circle, pressed against the display cases. To my surprise, the walls of the tent have become transparent and the outside spectators cling to the fabric, peering inside. The spectral screens I saw earlier now show the Chevalier entering the tent from an enclosed area at the back. On top of his usual cataphile gear, he wears a rich purple robe embroidered with arcane symbols. He also wears a peculiar set of glasses, which reminds me of one of those tiny opera glasses, but instead of lenses, it has eerie blue swirls.

Roaring applause greets him as he steps into the centre. I inadvertently take a step back into Sébastien, who quietly puts his arm around my lower back. There's a sense of change in the air, as if we're on the verge of something big and terrifying, yet no doubt brilliant.

"Thank you," the Chevalier says when the ghosts have quietened down as much as they're able. "Thank you all for coming here. Tonight, we'll transcend the boundary of life and death. Together."

Another roar erupts, sending shivers down my arms. Sébastien's fingers tighten around my back, his eyes fixed rigidly forward.

"Until now, death has always been a one-way street," the Chevalier continues. "You live and then you die, and then there's nothing you can do but watch as the world slowly forgets you ever existed. But no more! I'm here today to open the world to you, so you may once again take part."

Who would've thought the Chevalier was such a good speaker? The way he puts it, even I'm inclined to cheer. It's as if he's pinpointed the ghost problem and found the only logical solution: give them back their lives. But once I think about it longer, I feel the wrongness of it all. Death shouldn't be reversed. No matter how tragic. Not even for me.

I have to put my hand on Sébastien's to keep his fingers from tightening any further.

He looks down and releases them with a soft sigh. "This is insane," he whispers.

"Obviously," the Chevalier says, raising his hands to stop the applause and the multitude of questions the ghosts have, "we'll have to sort the logistics before any large-scale application, but we're not here to discuss the hows and whens. We're here to witness the impossible become possible. Throughout this exhibition, you can see various reanimations. From skeletons to cadavers to complete reconstructions from a single bone. They all move and behave like their original forms, but they don't need food, drink, or even air to breathe."

I feel sick thinking about how he tested these claims. While it's good to know they don't feel any pain, it doesn't sit right with me he took the risk in the first place.

"It's an impressive achievement in itself," the Chevalier continues, "but is it life? They look alive, sure. However, they're not the solution to your problem. For what good would it be if I could recreate you from a single bone if you were nothing but a puppet on a string? Or worse, still a ghost, still slowly forgotten, while a clone of you walks the earth."

An uneasy silence spreads through the Crossroads. The whole deal no longer sounds so appealing.

The Chevalier gives them a grim smile. "But this is not the end. What you see here was just the beginning. It's what helped me figure out how to reanimate the body."

One of his assistants rolls over the case with the mouse, and the Chevalier holds some sort of device close to it. "As you can see, there is very little spectral energy in this creature. Even less than we find in the living, such as myself. Now..."

The same assistant brings in another case, only this one is covered with a sheet and towers over the Chevalier on its wheels.

As the Chevalier moves his measuring device towards the secret specimen, the readings are through the roof. Once again, excitement rolls off the walls, and the whole crowd leans forward like a single undead creature.

"I rebuilt the body and attached the soul."

My stomach plummets as I realise what's under the sheet—or rather who.

"Half ghost, half human, with a presence in either world," the Chevalier announces with rising fervour. "My masterpiece. A true resurrection."

The sheet falls, revealing the frame of a display case and the boy who's got my heart in a stranglehold on my heart.

Gaspar.

A cruel little smile spreads across his face, and I sink to the ground while the crowd goes wild.

CHAPTER 20

"He feels warm. Soft."

"And he speaks."

"Was he truly dead, though? What if this is just a living person?"

"I knew him as a ghost."

The ghosts crowd around Gaspar, excited and horrified at the same time, while I crouch on the floor, trying to calm my rapid-fire breath. Sébastien kneels beside me, wrapping his arms around me to protect me from the crowd pressing in. I can't see anything, only hear the multitude of questions directed at the Chevalier, Gaspar, or fellow ghosts.

"Do you want me to get you out of here?" Sébastien asks.

I manage to shake my head. "No, no, we need to talk to the Chevalier. We need his help."

If we want to prove anything to the world, the Chevalier's confession is almost mandatory. Like too often, though, it feels like asking the devil for help. If only I wasn't so torn about the right and wrong of it.

I take another deep breath and use Sébastien's blue-eyed gaze to gather my strength.

"Ready?" he asks.

"Ready."

Together, we stand. Although my heart aches for Gaspar, I know better than to seek him out. I saw the cruel smile. This is not the Gaspar I long to see. Fortunately, there are so many ghosts who want to touch him and talk to him they'll shield me from his sight.

"A foul thing," Victor says beside me, shaking his head. "One shouldn't play God like that. Or promote a false success." He gives me a meaningful look. "His resurrection is hardly the miracle it was made out to be, is it?"

In my opinion, it's still a miracle, but Victor is right. While Gaspar's body has been rebuilt, and his ghost has been successfully attached, something's still off. I doubt any of the excited ghosts around me want to become raging psychopaths and possibly endanger their loved ones.

"We will act against this," Victor declares, and Voltaire nods grimly.

"How?" I ask, pointing at the crowd. "Just look at them. They're going completely gaga over him."

Voltaire snorts. "Once again, you underestimate the power we hold, Mademoiselle Alix. Let them satisfy their curiosity today.

The shine will quickly fade when we reveal the truth. As long as we are united..." He gives Marie Curie a long look as she's about to join the queue.

She clicks her tongue in annoyance. "If the research doesn't stand up to peer review, it'll be thrown out."

"Very well, do your... science thing," Voltaire says graciously. "You should have no difficulty confirming Alix's reports on the young man's behaviour. After all, he stayed with us for a while. We can all tell if his mind has been tampered with."

"Do you think that's it?" I ask, feeling an annoying surge of hope in my chest. "His mind has been affected?"

"Oh, for sure," Victor says. "Question is, was it an accidental side effect or by design?" He nods at me. "Better add that to your questions for the Chevalier."

Sébastien's jaw looks like it's being crushed under the weight of his teeth, but he nods sharply. "There's our chance."

In front of us, the Chevalier has managed to escape the crowd and is making his way back to the cordoned-off area from which he emerged. I notice how he easily evades the ghosts despite their large number. Almost as if he can see them.

"Romain!" I shout before he can disappear.

He turns around and smiles, which is a particularly creepy sight with the blue swirling binoculars he has instead of eyes. "Alix! And the young Roubert. You made it to my show."

"Can we talk? In private?"

The Chevalier looks over my shoulder. "No Victor Hugo or Marie Curie? I could've sworn I saw your ghost friends around."

I don't look over my shoulder, already knowing that if they'd wanted to be there, they would've accompanied me. Instead, I focus on his choice of words. "You can see ghosts now?"

"Ah..." Another creepy smile, then he bids us to follow him. "Come along." Once we're out of sight, he takes off his weird glasses and shows them to me. "Spectral glasses. One of my ghost whisperers worked with Gustave Eiffel to create these. They allow me to see ghosts, but unfortunately, I can't hear them, which makes the whole exercise a bit clunky. I don't think I can interest the two of you in translating?"

"Why don't you just ask your ghost whisperer?" Sébastien asks, sounding rather harsh.

The Chevalier clicks his tongue and admits, "She's gone."

"You mean Samara made that?" I ask. It's the only ghost whisperer I can think of in the Chevalier's vicinity, though rumour has it, he has more at his disposal.

His face betrays him. "I forgot you two met. Yes, she created these. You see, she used to study engineering and had a knack for tinkering before her accident. In my opinion, her talents were wasted at GoPol. But I suppose she liked the pay better?"

"She's dead," Sébastien's voice remains rather cold. "My father executed her."

The Chevalier winces. "Ah, yes, that sounds like Charles. So, he found out about our deal, then?" More like there was no deal to begin with.

Sébastien shrugs, seemingly unwilling to divulge any more information.

I take my cue from him and decide to use the subject to my advantage. "Charles seems to be murdering people left and right. We're planning to stop him. My father is writing an exposé, but we need more witnesses and evidence. Your story could help seal the deal."

Frowning, the Chevalier raises his hands. "Wait a minute. What's this about exposing Charles? You're going up against GoPol?" He looks from me to Sébastien and finds only grim determination. "This is madness."

"Together, we can bring him down. I've already got a ton of ghosts working on it, my father's a pro at finding reliable sources, and Sébastien will get us the proof we need. But your story, your file, would have a huge impact," I urge.

The Chevalier crosses his arms. "I'm sorry, Alix, but if you go down that path, you'll be on your own. I strongly advise you to let it go. You don't want to antagonise GoPol further."

"I can't let it go. *They* won't let me go."

In a way, it's all the Chevalier's fault. If he hadn't set me up to steal his file, I wouldn't have got into trouble with Charles in the first place. Then again, I would've been oblivious to GoPol's dark secrets and might've got myself into an even deeper mess. If that's even possible.

"Again, I'm sorry, but I can't risk what I've built here in a one-woman attempt to take down a government agency. I usually love a good David vs. Goliath story, but only from the gallery. You seem to have thought this out very well, so I wish you luck."

Maybe I've been playing up how well we've been doing and downplaying how much we need his contribution. "Don't you want justice for yourself?"

"Justice won't feed or clothe me." He shakes his head. "Nor will it help me fulfil my dreams. In fact, if this justice you're talking about depends on me exposing my past to the whole world, it'll have the opposite effect. No, I'm afraid I can't help you."

"GoPol's already onto you. You're under active surveillance," I point out, desperate to change his mind. "Won't that interfere with your dreams?"

"Sure, but in over a decade, they've hardly ever caused an inconvenience. Charles is dying to know what I'm doing. Not because he wants to stop it, though. No, he wants to gauge if anything I've achieved could serve him and his agency. If he ever were to arrest me, I'll make him an offer he can't refuse."

Stunned, I stare. "You'd work with him?"

"It's not necessarily what I'd prefer, but if that's what it takes to protect my assets... I'm not picky about my allies."

Sébastien snorts and puts a hand on my back protectively. "Little surprise there. You've always been a self-serving bastard."

The Chevalier looks amused. "As opposed to the ends-justi-fy-the-means kind of agent you and your father are? I guess, after what I've been through with GoPol, I deserve to be a self-serving bastard. Besides, as Alix will surely tell you, I'm not just doing this for myself, but for our community."

"What community?" Sébastien asks. "The ghosts you can't see or hear?"

"Séb, please," I urge.

The Chevalier frowns. "There's more than just ghosts in the catacombs. But we don't distinguish between the living and the dead here. Alix understands."

I hate how he's trying to get me on his side when he's just reject-ed my plea for help. The last thing I want to do is come between the Chevalier, who's responsible for the grotesque resurrections in the tent behind us, and Séb, whom I love dearly. If it weren't for the ghosts involved, it would be a no-brainer.

Instead of resolving their conflict, I choose to ignore it. "So, you won't help us?"

"It's too much of a risk, more than GoPol is to me right now," the Chevalier says, his gaze still locked with Sébastien. With a sigh, he averts his eyes and looks at me. "I'm truly sorry, Alix. If you need a safe place, you're always welcome down here."

"Because that worked out so well last time." We were betrayed within hours of arriving in one of the Chevalier's safe spaces. "Besides, it's not just me who's in danger anymore."

My entire family's feeling the impact of GoPol's prosecution. If I suddenly disappeared, they'd be the ones to suffer, and I doubt I could convince them to drop off the earth and move to the catacombs.

"I understand. I really hope you win," the Chevalier says, with surprising sincerity. "If anyone can pull it off, it's you and your ghosts."

I don't know about that, but it's all I have left. My ghosts, my family, my friends, Sébastien, and myself. Hardly enough to take on a government agency, but maybe enough to get rid of one particular guy.

"Did you find out what went wrong with Gaspar yet?" I ask, trying my best not to accuse him of presenting false results at his show.

"Ah, not quite, but my guess is there's still a problem with attaching the ghost to the re-created body. They're definitely connected, but it seems like the body has its own... version of a soul?" The Chevalier squints, seemingly unsure about his words. "I'll look into it further once the fair has concluded. I promise."

"And yet you're already advertising your services to the ghosts," Sébastien says, still annoyed about the Chevalier's lacklustre response to our request for help.

The Chevalier looks tired. "It was too great of an opportunity to pass up, but you're right, I'm not yet ready to grant any requests." He nods at me. "Tell the Panthéon ghosts they can be first in line once I've ironed out the kinks."

I keep my mouth tightly shut to avoid telling him about Victor's and Voltaire's knee-jerk reaction. A reaction I'm very grateful for, even if it's a bit selfish on my part. Instead, I give him an unimpressed look and turn to leave.

Sébastien keeps his arm around my back, as if the Chevalier is about to stab me from behind. Without even waiting until we're out of earshot, he says, "Well, that was a disappointment."

"Yeah."

So far, we've achieved exactly zero. If we don't get results soon, there won't even be a clash between David and Goliath. It'll just be Goliath crushing me before I've even showed up.

"So, what's this about ghosts on the case?" Sébastien asks once we're back in the crowd.

"Oh." I forgot to tell him about Père Lachaise and what went down there. "I might have acquired an extensive spy network. Moulin is running it for me."

The jealousy on Sébastien's face is almost comical. He so wants to be part of Moulin's spy network. Certainly something to add to his dream version of GoPol.

"Anything good yet?"

"A few minor leads. And..." My voice tapers off as my gaze falls on Gaspar.

He's standing in front of us, blocking our path. "Heard you were around," he says in a voice that makes it hard to tell whether he's the bad or good Gaspar.

"Wouldn't miss it for the world," I say, carefully. "Are you... okay with this?"

Gaspar frowns and Sébastien's fingers tighten around my hip, a subtle sign he's ready to protect me from whatever happens next. "With what, exactly? You two?"

It's not what I meant, but my guilty conscience rears its ugly head, causing my stomach to cramp. "You said..."

"I know what I said," he snaps. Definitely bad Gaspar. He snorts. "And you wasted no time following my ill-placed plea. Even moved in with him, I heard. The very same day."

"It's not like..." I stop myself. Arguing with this version of Gaspar is pointless. Whatever I say, he'll twist it around and use it to hurt me. "You know what? If you're ever yourself again, there's a place for you there, too."

And with that, I walk past him, chin held up proudly. Sébastien pats him on the shoulder and follows me out. There are many more wonders to see in the underground World Fair, but I'm too exhausted to take any pleasure in them. What I need is a real-world solution, not a ghost one.

CHAPTER 21

After our frustrating and pointless trip to the catacombs, I visit my family on Saturday. Or rather, I meet up with Papa and Odile at home, while my mother is out shopping with Hélène. They both listen with great interest to my description of the Ghost World Fair and its continuation in the catacombs.

"Unfortunately, the Chevalier won't provide us with a testimony. I wish I still had the photos, but I suppose it would be unethical to publish those without his consent."

"Highly," Papa confirms. He leans back in his chair and frowns. "I have to be honest, it's not looking too good at the moment. Without a high-profile case or hard evidence, I'm afraid no one will take this seriously. It'll just be an account of random people who believe they can see ghosts and a Boogie Man agency no one really knows about."

"So, there's no evidence GoPol exists?"

He sways his head a little. "The building is registered as Interpol: GPF, but there's next to no information about what the letters GPF stand for. Hardly anyone has even noticed it exists."

"Well, it is an intelligence agency, right?" Odile says. "It's only natural they're all secretive and all that."

Papa sighs. "Yes, but we'll dig further. How's Sébastien doing?"

"So-so. His father had his privileges revoked, so he doesn't have access to any important files. He's been making an effort to talk to other ghost whisperers to find out how they got the job and see if anyone might be sympathetic. It'll take a while before he can press them for real information."

It's a tough task for Sébastien, who's so much younger than the other GoPol agents and socially awkward, but he said last night he's actually met some interesting people.

"Yeah, I'm afraid this'll drag much longer than I'd hoped," Papa admits, sitting straight again. "It's not unusual in my line of work. Good work takes time. I'm just afraid Roubert will get ahead of us at this rate." He gives me a pointed look. "Has he approached you or said anything to Sébastien?"

I shake my head. "No, for once, no threats."

If I were the optimistic type, I'd hope that meant I'd be safe from him. We were both there when Gaspar killed Margot, and there were four witnesses to how far Charles was willing to go. But if the last few weeks of gathering information have taught me anything, it's those accounts won't matter. If Gaby, Marie, and I decided to go to the police tomorrow, we might get lucky and meet a sympathetic police officer, but as soon as the higher-ups get wind, it'll be buried. And then we'd be soon after. Or at least I would.

"What if he comes for me?" I ask, picking at my lip. "Like one day, just turns up at Sébastien's door with the police and has me arrested."

"Alix!" Odile looks absolutely terrified.

Papa's face darkens. "I have friends in high places, too. He won't get away with this. I won't let him."

I love my Papa, and while I don't doubt he has government contacts, there's still the whole problem of weighing the risk I pose against the one Charles does. Or maybe...

An idea strikes me. "The higher-ups probably know what Charles has done. They sanctioned it. They protect Charles because he's helpful to them. They tolerate his brutal approach since it gets them the results they need."

"What are you getting at?" Odile asks.

"Maybe instead of trying to prove protecting Charles is riskier than neutralising him, I could be more helpful."

Odile squints at me. "You want to take over GoPol?"

"No, of course not. Just..." Maybe this wasn't such a good idea after all. "The way GoPol works now is highly inefficient. By limiting themselves to their whisper ghosts and the rare police ghost, they lose out on all the gossip. People, I mean, ghosts don't like engaging with whisper ghosts much, at least not GoPol's ones.

They're too removed, and they have too many agendas. They're not part of the ghost community. But if they were to accept the ghost community, GoPol could find ways of working with them and utilising their considerable manpower."

"What a load of horseshit." Hélène's in the doorway. She's still in her pyjamas and looks down at us with disdain. "Nobody will care. They're ghosts. People don't believe in ghosts, not even those who know about them. Except you, of course," she adds belatedly.

Papa draws in a sharp breath. "Hélène, be nice."

She snorts, but her eyes shimmer suspiciously.

"Why are you even here?" Odile asks, sounding disgusted. "I thought you went shopping with Maman."

Hélène hugs herself, remaining in the doorway. "I wasn't in the mood for retail therapy. Money won't fix this. Nor will you if you're trying to appeal to the chief of police to use your ghosts instead of trained whisperers."

As usual, her comments are so abrasive they make my skin itch. "Thanks for your input."

"I want to help."

"Of course you do—Wait, what?" Did I just hear that right?

She sighs and comes over, taking the chair next to Papa, the one furthest from me. "It was Charles, right? That's what made Cédric think he'd get promoted. I know, it was. He was so eager. He told me his dream was finally coming true. I thought he was going to work for GoPol as a normal field agent, not... But Charles let him down, didn't he?" She looks at me for confirmation but finds only stubborn reluctance. "Very well. I know I'm right."

"You usually are," I say, with a heavy dose of sarcasm. "Older sister privilege and all."

"Alix, please," my father warns. He puts his hand on Hélène's and squeezes her fingers. "You want to help Alix?"

Hélène stares at me again, swallowing. "I want Charles behind bars for what he did to Cédric... and my sister."

I raise my eyebrows, unimpressed. Once, I might've been moved, but now I don't trust her enough. If Cédric were still alive, she'd still be trying to rip me a new one.

Papa smiles. "That's wonderful. You could help me with the research—"

Stubbornly, she shakes her head. "No. I heard what you said."

"Looks like eavesdropping runs in the family."

I cross my arms and sit back, waiting for Hélène's brilliant idea for how she's going to get us all out of my mess. Odile gives me a mock-gasp for lumping her in with Hélène.

Hélène just stares as if she hasn't slept in weeks. "Whatever." Finding no excitement on my side of the table, she turns her attention to Papa. "You don't have any real leads. Sébastien may or may not produce something, but his testimony is the only valuable thing you have, and he's biased, because he's related to Charles, and I highly doubt Charles documented how he killed and brought back his own son. Just as he didn't document asking

Cédric to hang himself." She blinks rapidly, trying to hold back the ever-threatening tears. "But there's another way to get hard evidence."

Papa frowns. "What do you mean?"

"By offering myself to him." This time, she doesn't search my face. "You've done it, Papa. Wearing a recording device and sneaking into secret meetings and stuff."

"Wait, you think if you go up to Charles, he'll happily talk to you about his crimes?" I ask. If that's her big idea, she's clearly out of her mind. No surprise there.

Hélène clicks her tongue. "Of course not. But if I go to him and tell him how much I hate you, and that I want to join GoPol in Cédric's stead, he might attempt to make me a ghost whisperer to spite you."

"That's a shockingly bad idea," Odile says, mirroring my thoughts. "He's never gonna trust you."

"You think he won't believe I hate my sister, whom I blame for my husband's death?" Hélène asks, her voice gaining some strength.

Put like that... "You won't even have to pretend."

Hélène's gaze flickers towards me, but she averts her eyes so quickly I nearly miss the pain in them. "I can be convincing, Papa. I'll get you the proof."

"You're not qualified for this," I tell her. If she doesn't rat us out to Charles straight away, he'll see right through her.

"And you are?" The bite is back. Hélène presses her lips together and takes a deep breath. "I know you don't trust me."

"Gee, I wonder why."

"Alix," Papa warns again.

Hélène closes her eyes, her lids fluttering. "I can do this. I know I can. For Cédric."

I snort. "Oh, okay, if it's for Cédric." Despite my father's pleading look, I get up. "Well, knock yourself out. Just try not to screw things up for me again. I've got to get to work."

I still have plenty of time before my shift starts, but I can't stand being in the same place as her. I don't need my big sister to swoop in and rescue me. Not when she's the one who threw me under the bus in the first place.

Chapter 22

For the rest of the day, I'm in a particularly foul mood. I manage to keep up my guide smile for tours, but my voice lacks any of the usual excitement. I can't wait for the day to be over so I can go home and cuddle with Malou while I rant to Sébastien about my infuriating sister. Unfortunately, a work day also means a therapy day, so it'll be even later.

The ghosts, of course, notice my behaviour fairly quickly. I barely look at them and ignore their usual injections. Rousseau pouts unhappily when I refuse to explain his philosophical ideas to an interested tourist, telling her instead that I know little about philosophy. A blatant lie. You can't listen to Rousseau and Voltaire arguing all day without picking up a thing or two.

"Do you want to tell us what's bothering you?" Victor asks as I angry-clean the plaques at the end of the day, as if Hélène had sponsored them.

"Not really."

I'm all but bursting with anger and this is a safe space. So maybe...

"There's someone for you, Mademoiselle Dubois!" Jean Lannes, the Napoleonic general, says as he hurries down the stairs.

"You have to be a bit more specific," I bark back. Catching the disapproval in Victor's eyes, I shrink a little. "Pardon, Monsieur Lannes. I didn't mean to be rude."

He waves me off impatiently. "You think I've never had a superior yell at me? Please." Instead, he salutes me. "Jean Lannes, reporting. The woman appears to be a few years older than you, with long brown hair, not too different from yours. She looks... exhausted, as if she's been crying a lot."

It can't possibly be, can it? "Are you saying my sister is waiting for me?"

"I don't know your sister, I'm afraid."

"Hélène Du... Villeneuf. She... Doesn't the Panthéon still turn away people who bear me ill will?"

Jean Lannes is visibly shrinking in front of me. "I couldn't detect any ill will in this case. Just a desire to talk to you. She's on the stairs."

"You let her get that far?"

A hand falls on my shoulder, and I look up to see Victor. "What's going on?"

Tears sting in my eyes. "That's my sister. She hates me." In front of me, Jean Lannes bites his tongue, as if he's yearning to protest. "Fine, she doesn't hate me. She just does and says a lot of terrible things in the name of caring for me. Better?"

He raises his hand. "It's not for me to say…"

"Talk to her," Victor says, gently but firmly. "She didn't come all this way to hurt you."

"Can you all stop taking her side? What she did…" I swallow hard, feeling my throat tighten. "Her husband is the reason GoPol is after me, and she supported him. She always chose him over me."

Victor sighs heavily. "The blinder our love, the more tenacious it is. It is never stronger than when it is completely unreasonable."

I roll my eyes hard and drag my feet upstairs. Just as I'm about to open the side door, my phone vibrates with a message from Hélène: *Hey, are you still at work? Everything's closed up. I thought we could grab a bite.*

Ugh, if the closed doors won't deter her, she really wants to talk. With a sigh, I unlock the side door and stick my head out. No Hélène. Confused, I step outside and find her waiting on the stairs, as if she's expecting the main entrance to just open after closing time.

I could pretend I've already gone home, but there's a risk she'll turn up at Sébastien's next, and I really don't want that. So, I pull up my big girl pants and stroll over.

"What do you want?" The words are barely out of my mouth before I realise how rude they sound.

Hélène turns to me with a wobbly smile. "That was quick."

"The ghosts told me you were there before your text got through."

The smile wavers, just as I knew it would if I mentioned my ghosts. Unsure, Hélène glances around. "Are the... ghosts here, right now?"

"Don't be ridiculous. They have far better manners than that. We're alone, so what do you want?"

I can't. In my head, I'm all polite and determined to keep an open mind, but when the words leave my mouth, they're harsh and bitter.

Hélène looks as if it's taking everything she has not to take a step back or return the favour with a scathing retort. "I just wanted to talk to you."

"About what?" Maybe I should give her credit for getting out of bed and getting dressed just to see me. "Is it because you hijacked my plan and need more insight?"

"Hijacked," she repeats, her voice wavering. "Isn't it more like Papa's plan?" Before I can protest, she raises a finger to stop me. "No, don't answer that. That was out of line. Again." She takes a deep breath. "I came to apologise."

I raise an eyebrow. "You came here, to my workplace, to apologise? For what?"

"Everything," Hélène replies, with a sad little smile. "Are you done? How about I take you for dinner?"

Sweetening the deal by throwing money at me. Classic Hélène move. "Sébastien's making dinner at home. And I still have to work."

"Oh, I... Do you have a few minutes at least?"

I cross my arms and shrug. "Maybe."

"Can we at least sit somewhere?" Hélène asks, her voice approaching a whiny tone.

"If you don't mind the stairs." There's a table and chairs in our break room, but I'd rather not invite Hélène into my sanctuary. Not wanting to give her any other choice, I walk past her and sit down.

With the sun shining on it all day long, the steps are surprisingly nice. If only the wind weren't picking up. Oh well, that'll give me another reason to flee early.

Hélène hesitates, but then sits next to me and lets out a tremendous sigh. She glances over her shoulder and another faint smile graces her lips. "I can't believe this is the first time I've visited you at work. Do you like it—ghosts aside?"

"Usually." It's not like I've ever visited her workplace before.

She sighs again and hugs her knees in a decidedly un-Hélène-like position. "I know you're mad at me, and with good reason. I was horrible to you."

Apparently, miracles do happen once in a while and big sisters apologise.

"I've been thinking a lot about what's happened in the past few weeks. It was either that or cry," she continues, her chin now resting on her knees.

Despite everything, my heart isn't cold enough to ignore the sadness in the words. Since that fateful wedding, the pain has hollowed my sister out, leaving nothing behind but raw skin and this empty shell.

"For what it's worth, I *am* sorry about Cédric."

"That's nice of you to say," she replies, trusting my pleasantries as little as I trust hers, "but you were right. He was using you for his own gain and I was... too blind, I guess. I believed him when he said he'd do everything in his power to protect you. He had this whole line of reasoning that made perfect sense to me at the time. Now when I look at it, there are so many holes, so many warning signs... He didn't just betray you, you know?" Hélène turns her head slightly to look at me. "And yes, I know it's incredibly selfish of me to say this when he actively put your life at risk, but we were supposed to be in this together. That was our wedding night and he... he betrayed us. *Me.*" A tear runs down her cheek. "I was supposed to be his future. But he didn't care. He wanted that stupid job more than me."

I'm sure, on any given day, I would've been completely heart-broken for my sister. The rational part of me recognises she's been through something incredibly traumatic. Her whole life was turned upside down, going from fairytale to nightmare in the space of four hours—just like Marie's cards said it would. The person she trusted most *did* betray her, and the ghost-whispering sister in me wants to steal Sébastien's gun and put a round of salt into Cédric's pathetic ghost.

But the sister I once was endured being pushed away and belittled time and time again. She had blame heaped upon her and experienced her own share of trauma, courtesy of none other than Cédric himself. He hurt so many people—Petite Alix, the ghosts at Père Lachaise, and me—while Hélène looked at him with doe-like eyes and wouldn't hear a single bad word about him. She enabled him, and I've learnt the hard way that burying the hatchet only leads to her ripping it from the ground and throwing it at my back.

All she gets is another lacklustre, "I'm sorry."

Hélène takes a deep breath and wipes her tears. Suddenly, she stretches her legs out, turns to me, and takes my hand before I can hide it. "I'm going to make it up to you, Alix. I promise. That man will never hurt you again."

"You don't know what you're talking about."

Even after what happened to Cédric, I don't believe my sister truly understands the lengths Charles will go to protect his precious agency—or to take revenge on me.

"Maybe," she admits, "but I'll find a way. I'll prove to you I'm still your big sister. I'll do whatever I can to make sure you're safe."

My stone heart cracks a little and I let out a sigh. "How?"

"By getting you the evidence you need. I'll let you know when he'll see me. Then you can tell Sébastien, so he can... I don't know, break into Charles' office or something. Papa said he hadn't managed to gain access to any files yet."

I massage my forehead, trying to give her plan a chance. A distraction would be wonderful, but would Charles really be so gullible? "Don't underestimate him. The man killed his own son and was ready to do it again."

Hélène breathes in sharply. "Don't worry, I know what I'm doing. Papa's provided me with a state-of-the-art recording device. It'll transmit the data straight to his cloud storage. So, even if Charles tries anything, you'll get the recording."

What the hell? I stare at her in horror. "Hélène! You are not going to sacrifice yourself!"

"Of course not." She clicks her tongue. "But I know the risks and I've accepted them. You'll get what you need to take him down." Filled with sudden determination, she holds my gaze. "And you *will* take him down. For yourself and for Cédric."

I couldn't care less about avenging Cédric, but I catch myself before I roll my eyes. "Please, promise me you won't take any unnecessary risks. I don't... I don't want to lose you, too." I may not be Hélène's biggest fan at the moment, but she's still my sister.

A smile spreads across her lips, so warm it fills out some of the hollowness. "I promise. Now, do you really still have to work, or can I at least buy you a drink?"

I may have let my walls down a bit, but I'm not ready to go back to normal. All I have are pretty words. It's her actions that'll show if she's really changed. "Maybe some other time. I... Well, it's not work, but I have... therapy. With a ghost." Why did I have to say that? Now she has new ammunition.

Hélène's eyes widen a little. "With a ghost?" Slowly, her face relaxes again. "I suppose that makes sense. A ghost wouldn't question you about the whole ghost whispering business and GoPol." She smiles sadly. "Honestly, I wish *I* had someone to talk to. I miss Cédric so much." Her voice cracks as more tears stream down her cheeks.

Reluctantly, I lean forward and give her a hug. "It'll be easier. He's not... completely gone."

With a gasp, Hélène pulls away. "Did you see him?"

Great. I already hate delivering messages from normal ghosts to their loved ones, much less ghosts I actively hate. "At the Eiffel Tower, yes."

"How is he? Is he... Does he regret it?"

"Oh yes, he regrets it." Anything else I could say won't go down well with Hélène, so I stand instead. "He asked me to look after you. Anyway, I have to go. My therapist is waiting, and I don't want to miss a session. Ghosts are fickle, you know?"

Hélène looks up at me with such gratitude I don't know where to look. It feels like a scratchy jumper I got for Christmas and have to wear to avoid offending the gift giver.

"Thanks, Alix. I'm sorry I kept you away from your... ghosts." She stands as well. "I'll let you know as soon as I've reached out to Charles."

We kiss each other on the cheeks, then I practically run back inside the safe walls of the Panthéon. Although I know what to expect, I'm startled by Jacques Lacan's therapy set-up in the staff room. It's the same as always, with Lacan sitting in his comfortable armchair, a notepad on his lap.

With a heavy sigh, I drop on the couch. "Have I ever told you about my sister, Hélène?"

CHAPTER 23

"They're in his office now," Dix informs me when he and Sébastien open the door to the GoPol headquarters. I half expect some security guard to tackle me or an alarm to blare, but everything remains quiet—or rather as lively and unbothered as the agency was on my first visit.

I haven't been to the GoPol building since New Year's Eve when I fled with Petite Alix. The only reason I'm daring to return now is because Sébastien's said he's figured out how to get into the archive—and because my stupid sister put the idea in my head.

Right now, Hélène is meeting Charles for a private chat in his office. She thinks she can distract him for at least half an hour, if not longer. Do I trust her? Absolutely not. Is it too good a chance to throw away? Sadly, yes.

"I'll keep watch upstairs, while you do the boring stuff." Dix bounces up the stairs, not a care in his world.

Sébastien rolls his eyes, and we follow him much more slowly to avoid drawing attention.

My heart pumps twice as fast as normal when we reach the stairs. Refusing to look downwards, where GoPol's ghost extermination lab is, I focus on Sébastien. "So, he's really meeting with her?"

"I think he's curious as to what she could possibly want from him."

"Do you think he'll fall for it?"

Sébastien wrinkles his nose. "Her approach was fairly convincing, but if I were Hélène, I wouldn't have any illusions about mutual trust."

"Unless she's going to betray me." Maybe all this is a trap to lure me into the GoPol building.

Sébastien gives me a compassionate glance. "Let's get this over with quickly."

We make it to the floor where his office and archives are located. Sébastien waits two beats, tapping his watch, then steps forward and swipes his access card in front of the archive. For a tense moment, I'm afraid it will be rejected, but there's a click and Sébastien pushes the handle down. It's only once I'm inside, and the door has closed behind me that I allow myself to breathe again.

"I thought your access was revoked."

"*Was* is the operative term here," Sébastien says, a pained grimace on his face.

"Has your father restored your privileges?" That'd be a huge surprise, even with all the effort Sébastien has put in.

"No, but I'm not a special agent for nothing. I've just never had to break into my own agency." He nods around the room. "We don't know how long your sister can keep him occupied, so let's get to work."

Less questioning, more researching. Luckily, that's something I'm good at. Within a minute, I've got a good idea of how this little library is organised. Not by agent name, but by subject, date, and mission code. There's a section on foreign missions, which I immediately discard. While some of the domestic ones catch my eye, I already know where to start.

The catacombs shelf.

I take the oldest, most fragile notebook and open it carefully, making sure I don't put too much strain on the spine, taking great care when turning the pages. As I don't have much time, I skip all the exciting accounts of early exploration of the catacombs and ghosts encountered. I'm just about to close the book again, when I notice a mention of the Quarry Department.

I'd almost forgotten about it, one of the oldest in Paris. According to Marie's uncle, they know about ghosts and actively work against the burden the dead pose for the city—by moving all the bones to a special area, open to sightseeing, producing ghostly abominations in the process. According to Marie's uncle, they don't know anything about GoPol, but this report says otherwise.

"You have access to the catacombs in the basement?"

"We do?" Sébastien asks. He's looking at more recent reports from Charles' era. Noticing the age of my journal, he says, "We only moved into this building a few years ago."

I shrug and put the journal back. "There are multiple build-ings." GoPol could very well have moved from one suitable loca-tion to another. More importantly, they had maps.

It's illegal to map the catacombs, but apparently that doesn't apply to government agencies. I search some more until I find a set of drawers with long flat drawers. Sure enough, that's where GoPol keeps a whole lot of maps. Many of them are of France as a whole or of the various regions. A lot of them are detailed maps of Parisian arrondissements. In the fourth drawer, I get lucky.

A map of the catacombs.

I try not to be too distracted by the intricate network of un-derground tunnels over two levels and the thin lines of the streets above. I guess I've found where the Chevalier got his copy.

I quickly scan the map into my phone. There are a few smaller areas that have been mapped in more detail during missions. When I recognise the Monastery of the Bears, I also notice tiny marks on the edge of the map.

"Check mission CP427, please."

"CP... four hundred..." Sébastien's finger runs along the shelves. "Twenty-seven." He picks up a folder. "Got it." A heartbeat later, he says, "That's Samara's mission file."

"Jackpot."

I look over his shoulder as he opens it. As far as I can see, it contains a bunch of cataphile mouthpieces on the Chevalier. None of them contain any details, although two have been marked as follow-ups, indicating they weren't entirely truthful. The follow-ups were completed by Samara's whisper ghost, Sam, which eventually led her to the Résistance. There's a report of a clandestine meeting, followed by the layout and location of the Monastery of the Bears.

"That's where we lost her," Sébastien said. "We were trying to listen in on the meeting but couldn't get access, even with our ghosts, and then there was an explosion." He points to some data points. "Samara planned it. She used it to get picked up by the Chevalier, leaving me behind." There's considerable hurt in his voice as he realises his partner didn't trust him with the details. Or perhaps less his partner and more his father.

After the explosion, there's a period of radio silence when Samara went undercover. When the reports start up again, there's a wealth of information about members of the Résistance and mention of arcane experiments. To my surprise, they are all about engineering. No mention of resurrecting animals or humans. Seems like the Chevalier knew what he was working with and only shared his innocent research, like the ghost glasses she helped him build.

Then I notice my name.

The intruder at the ritual site has been identified as Alix Dubois, a history student with undocumented ghost whisperer powers, who has since made contact with Sébastien Roubert. Knowing she's not affiliated with GoPol, the Chevalier is eager to get his hands on her. Suggest contacting her first. No sighting of her whisper ghost.

"Go back," I tell Sébastien. Sure enough, there it is. "Let me photograph this."

What I've just found is the murder of Emily. There's no mention of her name in the report. Just an intruder who disturbed the ritual site, where the Chevalier had promised to show Samara the extent of the magic. Thanks to Emily and then myself, it never came to that. But most importantly, it was Samara who shot her: *A regrettable sacrifice to ensure the ritual went ahead as planned.*

In the end, it wasn't the Chevalier. He didn't even know about it until afterwards. By then, it was already too late. Emily was a ghost and had found me.

There are more mentions of me and the Chevalier's growing interest, but as our time is running out, we just take pictures of the remaining pages. It makes me sick knowing there are several reports about me. It's very likely Charles has an 'Alix file' with all the information he could gather on my friends and family. Cédric probably provided half of the information. Of course, that folder is nowhere to be seen in the archive and is probably sitting on a pile in his office.

Samara's catacombs mission comes to a rather sudden end with the account of how she led GoPol to me and half the Résistance. The last note is written in a different hand. One I recognise from the Chevalier's file.

After blowing her cover, Agent Bensaïd was taken out of the catacombs. She refused to take on other duties and has raised suspicion she was corrupted by the subject. As a result, she was dismissed and neutralised.

Dismissed. That's one way to describe a fatal battery you ordered. Sébastien and I know what it means, but it's hardly written proof. Nevertheless, we scan the page and put the file back where we found it. Just as I look at some of the cross-references, hoping to find the file on Samara herself, Dix appears.

"They're wrapping up. You should probably go."

Instantly, the panic is back. My heartbeat is so loud I'm sure it can be heard outside of the walls.

Sébastien reaches out and holds my hand. "Relax. Let's just close up here and go to my office, just as we planned."

His calm voice and the reminder help me centre myself and cross the short distance to his office with Dix by my side, while Sébastien cleans up and closes the archive door. Then we both settle into his office as practised: me in his chair, looking at a map of the World

Fair, and him leaning over me from behind, pointing out features I know by heart.

I dig my fingers into my skirt as I strain to listen to Charles and Hélène coming down the stairs. When the first peal of laughter reaches my ears, I wince. Despite everything she said, I still don't trust this new Hélène. She's too easily seduced by power and money. Things Charles has in abundance.

We can't hear any of their conversation, but whatever Charles is saying seems very amusing to Hélène. It's kind of scary how easily they can shed their skin. Whenever he sees me, Charles is practically frothing at the mouth. With her, he's the charming host. As for Hélène, she's been in mourning for weeks, her fragility even softening my heart, eventually. And yet, here she is laughing so loudly the whole floor can hear it. It doesn't even sound fake—or at least no more fake than her usual finance laugh.

I'm just about to relax when the door to Sébastien's office tears open. "What's the meaning of this?"

I try not to flinch when I hear Charles' voice. Someone must've told him they saw me for him to leave my sister to fend for herself and storm into here. Maybe that someone was my sister.

Sébastien takes a moment before looking up, as if he was preoccupied. "The meaning of what?"

Charles stands in the doorway, his head looking like an angry tomato. "What is *she* doing here?"

"Oh, Alix?" Because there are so many other women in the office. Sébastien smiles innocently. "Alix is working on my case as a ghost consultant."

"She's not a ghost."

Sébastien chuckles. "True. But she knows a lot of ghosts, such as Gustave Eiffel and Charles Garnier. Without her connections to the ghost world, it would've been a lot harder to get to the World Fair."

Charles narrows his eyes. "You didn't run this past me."

"I ran it by Marcus. You know, my superior."

I have no idea if this part is true, but Sébastien brings it up with such charm and confidence that he'd be in real trouble if this Marcus didn't back him up later.

Sure enough, a vein pulsates in Charles' temple. "You report to me! And you do not bring civilians into GoPol. Our work is too sensitive for that."

Frowning, Sébastien straightens his back. His hand comes to rest on my shoulder, as if to tell me to relax. "Was there policy change today? Because Justine had her daughter here yesterday, and I know Mathieu downstairs was showing his parents around the offices. And—"

"You know very well *she's* not welcome here."

She is sitting here, wisely keeping her mouth shut and letting Sébastien fight this battle for her, because it's all I can do to avoid freaking out.

"She wasn't on the list." Apparently, there's a list for undesirables.

"An oversight," snaps Charles.

"Or a faulty system," Dix whistles. He's standing on the other side of the room, enjoying the fact his father can no longer see or hear him. Looks like I was on the list—until I wasn't.

Charles snorts. "I don't have time for this. Get her out, or I'll have her dragged out. And put her on that damn list!"

The door slams shut, shaking in its frame. Dix gives Charles the middle finger, and I don't know whether to sigh in relief or laugh. The result is an oddly strangled sound.

Sébastien visibly relaxes and leans back against his table. "That was fun," he says in a decidedly unfunny voice.

"You did beautifully."

I'm a bit proud of him, not just for holding his own, but for how much he knew about his fellow agents. It's a far cry from the reclusive junior agent who spent Christmas at the office.

That smile on his lips is also something else. Much freer, full of true happiness. Sébastien may not know it yet, but he's blossoming. After what he's been through with his father, I love it. "Nothing I said was a lie. You should be working here as a ghost consultant."

"Not as long as your father is in charge." I stand up again, taking a deep breath. "I..."

"You have to go. I'll show you to the door."

I appreciate the gesture, not putting it beyond Charles to make good on his threat. The moment I'm safely out of the building, I let out a big sigh of relief. That went a lot better than I thought.

Hélène waits for me three blocks down at a little café, looking a little pale. Not a sign of the laughter she shared with Charles minutes before in sight.

"And?" I ask anxiously.

"He hired me."

Chapter 24

Later that day, Sébastien and I settle on the couch with our collected evidence between us. I've already sent a copy of everything to Papa, but it's time I saw it for myself. I wouldn't exactly call our break-in a huge success, but between the maps of the catacombs and Samara's mission report and documented observation of me, we finally have something to go on.

"Did you report on me, too?" I ask Sébastien, as I reach for the bowl of crisps and shove one into my mouth, frustrated by this scary intrusion into my privacy. She even mentioned my love affair with Gaspar.

Sébastien gives me a one-shoulder shrug. "Of course."

Not the answer I was hoping for. "Thanks. I suppose."

"Look, your name coming up in the reports isn't necessarily a bad thing," he explains. "When I met you, you were an undocumented ghost whisperer."

"Because that's such a crime."

"No, not a crime. But it is GoPol's policy to keep a running list of anyone who's capable of talking to ghosts. I'm not saying it's a good policy, especially when combined with enforcing who can and can't see ghosts. As you know the standard procedure is to check nearby hospitals and eliminate whisper ghosts before the ghost whisperer even knows what happened. The system in place is pretty robust, which makes cases like yours much rarer. Since you have several years of experience with ghosts, the ideal course of action would've been to recruit you. When that failed, you became a person of interest."

Leaving aside my own personal feelings on the matter, I'd probably agree that this is a sensible policy. *If* you see ghost whisperers outside of the organisation as a problem. "Is that how everyone else is recruited?"

"Pretty much, yes. I've talked to a few colleagues about this and about half of them were ghost whisperers *before* GoPol got to them and were offered some kind of deal. Not all those recruited this way become full agents, though. Most of them are used as field agents in their community, the ones we station in hospitals. If someone has the makings of an agent, they're trained. And some are offered other jobs, like administration."

And yet, they never offered me that one.

"What about the other half?"

"They were police or intelligence officers before they became ghost whisperers. So, naturally, they were funnelled into GoPol and given a crash course in ghosts, the GoPol version. That's how my father got recruited."

Frustrated, I munch on some crisps. "They're probably the preferred whisperers. Easy to mould."

Sébastien grimaces. "Yeah, just as we prefer to work with law enforcement ghosts. It's a terrible bias," he adds with a wry smile, "and severely limits our potential."

I bat at his arm. "Stop flattering me and tell me what was in your report." If there was a file on his interactions with me, I didn't come across it in the archives.

"Not much, to be honest: where I met you, what you said about Ossa Arida, and your experiences with ghosts. I looked into who you were and where you lived in case I needed to contact you later, and I looked up Gaspar after you mentioned him. Also, that you didn't have a whisper ghost."

Sounds like the report was a lot more extensive than he's trying to make it sound. "Is that normal?"

"In my line of work? Pretty standard, yes. You were the first person I tried to recruit, so I was bound to make mistakes. According to my father, I gave you too much time and should've brought you in sooner, but you'd just found out the guy you fell in love with had been dead all along. I didn't want to push too hard."

"It felt pushy when you kept asking about my whisper ghost."
He eventually found out where and how I almost died.

Sébastien bites his lips. "I'm sorry. I was just trying to do my job, not realising how screwed up it really is."

I reach out and squeeze his wrist. "I know. And even though it feels super intrusive, I know it's a basic security measure."

Nodding, he adds, "The problems started when my father wouldn't take no for an answer and decided to eliminate you rather than hire you." He leans over to pick up his wine glass and takes a sip. "Did you know I got into trouble because I'd failed to recognise you'd already found your whisper ghost and had hidden it? He wouldn't let me live it down that it was Cédric who gave him the information, whereas I'd failed with my slow and gentle approach. Then he sent me on that mission in Père Lachaise to prove my usefulness."

"You'd better not show your face there for the next decade."

The ghosts of Père Lachaise remember him as one of those who salted them without remorse. Perhaps if I explained the situation to my grandmother—or rather Beatrice, as my grandmother is still catching up—I could persuade them to forgive him for his role. Then I could introduce him to my friends there...

Wait, why am I thinking of introducing Sébastien to anyone? Introduce him as what?

He cocks his head, frowning slightly. "What is it?"

My cheeks flush and I reach for my phone. As if on cue, Dix appears. He swings his legs over the back of the couch and sits on top of it, squeezing between Sébastien and me.

"Did you want to hear how the meeting between Papa and Hélène went?"

"I want you to take your feet off my couch," Sébastien grumbles.

"Your couch, my couch. Stop hogging all the furniture. Besides, my feet are squeaky clean, right, History Girl?"

I can't help laughing. Dix has always had that kind of effect on me. "Can't say I've ever smelled stinky ghost feet."

"There you go."

Sébastien won't have it. "It's not about the dirt, it's about manners." He looks at me helplessly, as if the distance between us upsets him more than Dix's general presence.

"What Séb's trying to say is there's plenty of room for you to sit somewhere else, and yet you've chosen the small gap between us," I say, amused.

Sébastien's mouth falls open while Dix chuckles. "Oh no, did you two want to kiss again?" He pushes himself off the couch and walks across the table, dropping into the armchair at the other end. "Happy now?"

I laugh out loud when I see Sébastien's shell-shocked face. His gaze falls on me. "Alix, I'm so sorry, I'm—"

"It's okay," I assure him, moving closer again. "We were just joking."

It's been a week since I threw myself at him. A week in which I found myself lying awake more often than usual, replaying that kiss over and over again. Meeting Gaspar in the catacombs was strangely cathartic. I hate what's become of him and I'll always cherish what we had, but I'm done tying myself to his memory. I'm still going to do everything I can to help him. I just refuse to let him drag me down any further.

Gaspar can't love me anymore, but there's a guy who looks at me as if I were his whole world. A really handsome guy with striking blue eyes that look straight into my soul, as if he knows exactly what I'm thinking.

"So, do you want to hear about Papa and Hélène?" Dix asks, bored by our endless gazing into each other's eyes.

Sébastien pulls away and clears his throat. "Hit us."

"While they were talking, I had a chat with Lys," Dix starts.

I frown. "Who's Lys?"

"Papa's secretary Louise's whisper ghost," Sébastien explains. "She's only fifteen—the whisper ghost, I mean, not Louise—which makes her unsuitable as a field whisper ghost. She's got a bit of a crush on Dix." He gives Dix a stern look. "Which you shouldn't entertain!"

"Why can't Dix have a relationship?" I ask, ready to go to war for my boy. "He has feelings, too."

"Yeah, but not for Lys," Sébastien says. "He's toying with her."

Dix snorts. "She's an excellent source of office gossip, and I'm not flirting. I'm just not ignoring her either." He rolls his eyes at me. "She's a bit immature and can't be trusted. Until recently, I found her pretty annoying."

"Until recently?" I raise my eyebrows, feeling a chuckle rising in my throat. I try to swallow it to spare Dix the embarrassment, but he only gets more flustered.

"Until recently, socialising with other whisper ghosts was discouraged." He glares at Sébastien. "I had a job to do, didn't I?"

"Dix..."

But Dix waves him off and smiles at me. "It was you, History Girl. You made me realise I might be dead on the outside, but not on the inside, you know? So, I started reaching out to other ghosts. Or whisper ghosts. Kind of regretting it with Lys, because man, that girl never stops talking."

"If she's been discouraged to socialise and not sent on missions, she's probably pretty bored."

I've never met this Lys or Louise, but I can't imagine a fifteen-year-old locked in an office year after year being particularly stimulating. I'd have bored myself to fading.

"Yeah, she made it her business to know everyone's business, eavesdropping on other agents, stuff like that," Dix explains. "She would actually make an excellent spy if she could be taught to keep her mouth shut occasionally. I don't trust her with sensitive information, but she's a wealth of gossip."

"You said something about Papa's and Hélène's meeting?" Sébastien asks impatiently.

I slap him on the leg, but it's too late. Dix's already switched back to agent mode. "While we were chatting, I was listening to the meeting. Papa was pretty sceptical at first, but they found common ground when Hélène told him her version of the story."

"Which is?" I ask, warily.

"That you had got into Cédric's head with your ghost stories and told him how one becomes a ghost whisperer. As usual, you had no regard for his safety, just grandstanding, but it messed with his head. And though she doesn't know what you did, she's convinced you triggered him to try it at his wedding. It's a bit suspicious that it was you who found him. Maybe you wanted to bring him back, but how? In Hélène's opinion, you did something extremely reckless, and Cédric paid the ultimate price."

It's a lot to swallow. I know my sister has to lie to in order to gain Charles' trust, but it hits a little too close to the truth. If it even is a lie. And that's the whole problem. After everything that's happened, I can't trust her. Who knows she's not really playing me while she plots her revenge with Charles?

Dix smiles sadly at me. "It must've been an act. The worst thing is how Papa didn't correct her, but acted all shocked and outraged on her behalf, as if it wasn't his idea that landed Cédric in hot water."

"What did you expect?" Sébastien says quietly. "She basically begged him to manipulate her with that cover story."

"You think it's all an act?" I ask, not so convinced.

Sébastien reaches for my hand. "That was the plan, wasn't it?"

"She could still double-cross us. Our entire plan could fall apart if she tells Charles everything."

Now I think about it, it's a bit suspicious how quickly Hélène changed her mind. One moment, she's inconsolable over Cédric's death, the next she's ready to walk into GoPol to meet and laugh with Charles to help me. What if he sent her a message, offering her a chance to destroy me, and she decided to take it?

"It's going to be alright," Sébastien says.

"You don't know that!" My hands become clammy, and my breath is getting choppy as I imagine Charles' reaction to the article. Will he hurt my father? Or just threaten and blackball him? "Papa is risking so much. So are you, and—"

"You?" Sébastien asks sympathetically. He tugs at my hand, pulling me closer, so he can put his arm around my shoulders and hold me against his chest. "Breathe, Alix. Hélène is on our side. This is all part of the plan. You knew she had to lie about hating you so they could find common ground."

I'm not convinced, but the steady beat of Sébastien's heart in my ear eases my anxiety a little bit. "She betrayed me before."

"Cédric did. Hélène didn't know any better."

"Because she never listens to me."

He brushes a lock of my hair behind my ear. "This time, she listened."

"Right!" Dix announces loudly. "I'd better go find Malou. See if she wants to go for a long walk outside... all night long. No need to wait for us."

I can't help but chuckle at his dramatics while Sébastien sighs. "And you said Lys was immature."

Dix heads for the door and grins. "I'm considerate, not immature. Have fun!"

As soon as he's gone, I lift my head from Sébastien's chest and shake it. "Does he really think we're going to have wild sex the minute he's out of the house?"

Sébastien coughs, his face suddenly beet-red. "What?"

I laugh, but the sound fades far too quickly. Unhappy, I sink back into his arms. "It wasn't going to happen, anyway. I'm a mess."

He snorts. "Bet you I'm the bigger mess."

"Fine, you win." Who can compete with a murderous father?

"It's not the Trauma Olympics," he says with a sad smile, but then he leans his head back and closes his eyes. The twitching of his muscles tells me he's reliving some of his more recent memories.

I snuggle a bit closer again. "You know, lately, I've been seeing a therapist. Jacques Lacan. He's a ghost, of course, so it's easy to talk about all the stuff that's happened in the last few months. Well, as it easy as it is to talk about it."

"Does he take other clients?"

Surprised, I look up at him. "You'd go to therapy?"

After Gaspar scoffed at my offer, I didn't expect Sébastien with his toxic father to entertain the idea.

He opens his eyes again. "It might be a good idea." He's not comfortable with it, but there's a kind of desperation in his eyes. "I want to be better," he admits. "For you, for Dix, for myself. Right now, we have to take care of my father, but I've been thinking. If we succeed, if we really change the world… I want to be a part of that. I want to hang out with friends, meet interesting ghosts, fall in love, maybe even have a family one day. Like a real, proper loving one, like yours." Before I can say anything, he flinches. "I'm afraid I can't. That I'm too broken. Too messed up. I mean, you don't want me, and—"

"I do."

"What?"

I have to swallow before I can repeat myself. "I *do* want you Sébastien."

"But Gaspar…"

"I want Gaspar. The real one, I mean. But I also want you. And I know that's selfish and inconsiderate of your feelings and his, but"—now it's me who has to close my eyes and swallow again—"I love both of you."

My eyes fly open as I suddenly feel his lips on mine.

Startled, Sébastien pulls away before I can even process the kiss. "Sorry, I didn't mean to—"

I pull him back to me, look him deep into his eyes, and kiss him softly on the lips. Unlike that fateful night, there's no urgency, no rush of overwhelming passion that wipes away every thought and doubt. This kiss is sweeter, full of contemplation and commitment. It tastes of hope.

"You..." Sébastien breathes. "I love you so much my heart aches just looking at you, knowing I can't... I couldn't have you."

My body melts into him and my stomach flutters. "I... I know."

"Of course you do." He pulls away a little. "I don't want to take you away from Gaspar. You know, in case he comes back to us."

"Us?" I ask amused. When his cheeks turn red, I laugh. "Wait, do you like him, too?"

I expect a shake of his head or a flash of panic behind his eyes, but all get is a shrug. "I don't know. I had so little time to get to know the real Gaspar. He seemed great before the whole resurrection thing, but you only had eyes for each other then. While he lived here, though... it was nice." He swallows. "That's all I know. Look, I'm not exactly experienced in this sort of thing. Much like Dix, I"—he bites his lip, looking at me as if I have all the answers to his inner turmoil—"was dead inside."

Unable to bear so much sadness, I throw my arms around him and bury my nose in his neck, breathing in the faint scent of vervain I've learned to appreciate from his ghost candles. "But you're not,"

I mutter. "You're not dead, inside or out. You're alive. And you're allowed to live and love and be."

He closes his arms around me and holds me tight. "I'm trying. For you. And for me."

And maybe for Gaspar, if he's still out there.

Chapter 25

Even after several visits, I still can't get enough of the Ghost World Fair. It's too big and there's too much to see. Every time I come here, I discover something new. Today, I'm on the green in front of Les Invalides with Gaby, Marie, Théo, and Odile. To my surprise, I'm the fifth wheel on this outing. Gaby and Marie are attached at the arm, but at least they're listening to me rave about what I'm seeing. The same can't be said for Théo and Odile, who are severely lagging behind, their eyes glued to his phone. He seems to be showing her miniatures he's started to build. Judging by Odile's excited squeals and cooing, the miniatures are as fabulous as his drawings.

"Odi and Théo, huh?" Gaby asks, looking over her shoulder and giggling. "Are they...?"

"I don't know." I laugh, momentarily distracted from the housing exhibition taking place. To my great relief, the Colonial Village has been completely revamped. The same nations are present, but this time they're the exhibitors instead of the exhibits. Apparently, Garnier launched an architectural competition to combine the two attractions. Instead of clichéd dirt huts, there are imaginative, Afro-futuristic designs, each grander than the previous.

If only I could take pictures. But not only is it impossible to photograph ghost buildings, my phone's also hanging on the charger at home, where it's no use to me.

Gaby takes another glance at the maybe-couple. "Do you think it's weird Théo might be interested in Odi, after... you know?"

"After he had a crush on me?" A crush that was never anything more. "I don't think he's into her because she's my sister or looks a bit like me or anything like that. They connect on a creative level. I'm telling you, within a month, he'll have his own channel and will be showing off his art. Or maybe a history channel with art?"

Marie's eyes light up as she exclaims, "I want to watch that." She nudges Gaby. "Maybe I can learn a thing or two about history."

"Says the girl whose family has thousand years of history to look back on."

Marie throws her head back laughing, and the two of them kiss. In the four years I've known Gaby, she's had her fair share of relationships, but I've never seen her this happy. Turns out, defying authority together brings you closer.

A little nervously, I look at Odile, but she's still busy, staring on Théo's phone. "I'm happy for her."

"For Odi?" Gaby asks in surprise.

"She's been a bit heartbroken lately. An unrequited crush." Best friend or not, I'll never betray my sister's feelings to Gaby. "I think she's finally moved on. So, yes, I'm happy for her. Don't get me wrong, I'll still kill Théo if he ever hurts her, but I think they'd make a cute couple."

"Speaking of cute couples," Gaby says, her voice barely containing her excitement. "How's life with Sébastien?" She's barely finished the question when her eyes widen. "You're blushing!"

Suddenly, the sun feels a little too hot. "No, I'm not." I rub my cheeks—as if that's ever helped. "It's... er, you were right."

Gaby bursts out laughing. "Right about what?"

"Living together, it's... We kissed again."

"I told you, a double love line. Two lovers," Marie says wisely.

It's been a while since she's read my palm. Despite the double love line, she also said I have to make my own destiny, which suits me much better than Nostradamus' silly prophecy.

Gaby waves her hand impatiently. "Come on, girl. We want details!"

"Look, I'm just saying it's hard."

"Who? Sébastien?"

"Gaby!" I slap her arm, but she manages to jump out of the way, almost tripping Marie in the process. All three of us burst out laughing. My cheeks are definitely burning now. "What I mean is, he's always there, always around, and it's nice. Comfortable. As if we've been together for ages."

"Oh no, comfortable is not what you want."

I roll my eyes. "Yes, yes, it is. A safe space and comfort is exactly what I need. It also doesn't hurt I occasionally see him coming out of the shower."

Gaby's mouth widens. "Shut up! Oh, yeah, I can see how that might be hard to ignore."

"Very hard to ignore."

Even with all the ghost sights around me, my mind would rather focus on the time Sébastien stepped out of the bathroom with nothing but a towel around his hips. Droplets of water had collected between his sculpted shoulder blades, and it had taken everything in me not to run over and dry him off.

"Sooo, does that mean you two..."

"Please don't ask me to define what we have," I say, blinking to banish the vivid memory. "We... um, I told him that I liked... both him and Gaspar. And Gaspar said I should move on with Sébastien. I still love him, it's just... Sébastien is right there, and Gaspar is... not himself. I have no idea what I'm gonna do if we ever get him back, although Sébastien... it didn't sound like he was totally against a... you know." Why is my mouth so dry? And why is my mind now imagining kissing them both? "It's all hypothetical, of course." Unless the Chevalier figures out a way to fix what went wrong with Gaspar, he won't ever be back.

Gaby suddenly throws her arms around me and squeezes me so hard it hurts. "I'm so proud of you, ma puce! Get that boy! Or both of them!"

"Please stop!"

My brain is already in overdrive without Gaby adding to it. Houses. I should be looking at houses. To my right, there's a beautiful building with bright-coloured patterns between smooth steel runners. I hyper-focus on the fascinating curvature of the upper floors and the thoughtfully placed greenery when I suddenly hear Marie gasp.

"Did you see that?" She's got both hands clapped over her mouth, eyes wide with shock.

"See what?" I try to look in the direction she's staring, but there's nothing there except another ghost pavilion. Not that she can see it.

She and Gaby suddenly jump to the side, avoiding a pair of ghosts strolling down the promenade. "Where did all those people come from?"

"Wait, what?" I stare at the two of them before checking on Odile and Théo.

They're so stunned Théo's phone has dropped out of his hand and none of them move to retrieve it. Then they blink and Théo bends down to pick up his phone, while my sister frantically searches for hers and starts filming around her, exclaiming loudly, "It's back."

"What's happening?" I ask, still confused. My chest feels like it's going to burst from anxiety. "Gaby, plea—"

"Alix!" Suddenly, Dix's running towards me. One moment, he's still thirty metres away, the next, he's suddenly in front of me, timing his arrival with another shriek from Marie. Only this time, she's looking straight at him. "Something's wrong!" he blurts out, grabbing my arm. "Sébastien's looking for you."

I stare at him, then at my friends. "Can you all see him?" Marie and Odile have never received a ticket from Garnier and shouldn't be able to see him, yet Marie nods, her eyes still wide. "That boy's just teleported."

Dix looks unnerved, which is such an alien look for him, my worry spikes instantly. "The World Fair. It's spilling over. People are seeing us... all of it."

My suspicion confirmed, I bite down hard on my lips. "Why?"

"I don't know. Séb just told me to get you. You need to talk to Eiffel or something."

"Eiffel's resonator." He'd mentioned that turning up its power could imprint the ghost world on the real world. But if that's what's happening... "People are in danger."

Dix bounces up and down on his toes. "I know, let's go!" He pulls on my arm.

Gaby hurries me along. "Go! Go!"

"Secure the parameter," I yell at her as Dix pulls me away. "You know the extent of the World Fair!"

"I'll try!" she shouts back, looking just as panicked as I feel. There's no way she can secure anything, let alone the entire perimeter of the World Fair.

But there's no time to lose. If I don't shut down the resonator, people could die.

CHAPTER 26

After a hard sprint that I definitely hadn't planned for today, I fall into Sébastien's arms at the foot of the Alexandre III bridge, almost knocking him over with my momentum.

He catches me and helps me regain my balance. "There you are."

He knew I was going to visit today. We were supposed to meet afterwards, so he could take me out for dinner, but that's definitely not going to happen now.

All around us, people are screaming. Some are running, others are sitting on the banks of the Seine, rubbing their eyes again and again. Quite a few are filming. I'm scared to find out whether they capture anything substantial.

"What's going on?" I ask.

Sébastien shakes his head. "No time, come on."

"I can't run anymore." On my bike, I can be quite fast, but on foot I have no stamina.

He takes my hand and gives me an encouraging smile. "We'll walk fast."

Sighing, I follow his lead. Sweat runs down my shirt and my legs are starting to hurt from the exertion, but I know time is of the essence. As far as I can see, the overlay happens in short bursts, like a flickering light bulb. While the living can catch a glimpse of the dead, there are moments when I can see both. Each time it happens, I'm startled anew as the crowds suddenly double and the objects overlap.

My brain spins in circles, switching between panic and more productive thoughts, like trying to remember what Eiffel told me about his resonator. We're still a few hundred metres away from the Eiffel Tower when it hits me.

"Stop."

"What?" Sébastien asks, a hint of impatience in his voice. "Is something wrong?"

I hold up my hand and take a moment to catch my breath, then I call out to my trusted generals, starting with Alexandre de Beauharnais.

"Alix..." Sébastien looks at me as if I've gone mad. "I don't think we need any more ghosts in this place."

"Exactly."

Alexandre strides up to meme. "You have a request?"

"Yes. Close the World Fair. Send the ghosts home. Or send them to the catacombs. Just make them all go away. Evacuate them, I mean." To Sébastien, I say, "The resonator relies on the spectral energy of the present ghosts and their memories. No ghosts—"

"—no overlap." He nods sharply. "Good thinking."

It'll take time for the World Fair grounds to be completely emptied. The sooner we start the better. Alexandre and the other ghosts salute me and immediately set to work, calling other ghosts from various walks of life to their aid.

I look at Sébastien and take a deep breath. "We can continue."

This time, I manage a slow jog, and a few minutes later, we finally reach the Eiffel Tower and resonator pavilion. There are so many people here, dead and alive, that Sébastien and I have trouble making our way through the crowd.

Dix has no patience and rudely pushes people out of the way, shouting, "Out of the way! Let us through!"

Finally, we break through. People have formed a tight ring around the pavilion, which is the most stable object apart from the real-world ones. Inside it, Eiffel and two other ghosts are desperately trying to turn the big handle, which appears stuck at the maximum level.

"What happened?" I ask, completely out of breath.

I'm vaguely aware of a bunch of cameras pointed in my direction. Sébastien notices it, too, and closes the pavilion's tent flaps behind him. "How can we help?"

"I'm not sure you can," Eiffel snaps. "It's jammed. Someone sabotaged it!"

Curious, I take a closer look. From what I can see through the ghosts' limbs, it doesn't look any different, but then I have an idea. "It's visible."

"Yes, I know. It's superimposed itself on the world of the living."

"You're ghosts. Séb, help them."

Without wasting another second, Sébastien approaches the resonator and takes the place of one of the assistants.

"Together. Now!"

The men groan. Muscles bulge. The machine hisses. Finally, the lever moves. In a matter of seconds, it releases completely and flips over to zero, dropping Sébastien and Eiffel on their butts.

The pavilion flickers out of existence, exposing us once again to the onlookers—or at least, Sébastien and me.

"Is it working?" I whisper as I help Sébastien up, hyper-aware of the cameras.

Dix walks in front of a tourist and waves his hand. "Yep, they can't see a thing."

If only that were true. Far too many people can see me and Sébastien where minutes ago a pavilion stood.

Meanwhile, Eiffel is still grim-faced. "Someone's tampered with the resonator. Someone who knew how it worked. I'll have to check on the others." He walks straight through the people, not bothering to avoid them.

"The others?" Sébastien asks.

"Just follow him." I put my arm around Sébastien's and press myself against his body, trying to avoid looking at anyone directly. What are they still filming for? Is any of this live?

Sébastien reaches into his jacket and pulls out a badge. "Make way!"

Reluctantly, people shuffle out of the way, but their cameras follow us to the southern leg of the Eiffel Tower.

An employee runs up to stop us. "You can't—"

Sébastien's badge stops her cold. "We have to get up there now. It's important."

She nods and steps out of the way, holding back the more persistent gawkers so we can join Eiffel in the elevator. As soon as the doors are closed, a blissful silence spreads.

I lean against the wall and take a deep breath. Eiffel is pacing, muttering under his breath, while Sébastien is furiously texting, only to be interrupted by a call.

"Yes, I'm on it. You need to send the gendarmes and secure the perimeter." He holds the phone away from his ears and winces, then simply shuts it off.

I take a wild guess. "Your father?"

He stares at me darkly, confirming my suspicion. I want to ask him what's going to happen now, but by then the elevator has arrived and we race up the stairs to Eiffel's little research station. As a ghost, he makes it there first.

"Damn it!"

"What?"

"It's gone. Someone stole the portable one." He walks around, rubs his face, stares at the empty spot, and starts pacing again.

"Can anyone explain what we're doing here?" Dix asks.

I quickly tell him and Sébastien about the smaller resonator and the issues with it. "Whoever has it can do actual damage."

"Didn't they just do that with the big one already? How much worse could the little one be?"

"It's a hundred times worse!" Eiffel snaps. "Once activated, it'll suck up any ghost too close to it to power itself. With the big one, we only had temporal overlays, visibly stunning but not actually corporeal. That changes when you use the small one. While it works on a much smaller radius, it'll superimpose the past for as long as the resonator is running. It only takes three to five minutes for the memory to be strong enough to erase the present structure, including anyone trapped in a wall, a piece of furniture, or worse."

Sébastien frowns heavily. "Sounds serious. Who knew about this?"

"Only my assistants. Four of them. A ghost whisperer showed some interest, but she—"

"She?" I call out.

One look at Sébastien and we both blurt out, "Samara!"

Eiffel frowns. "That is indeed her name. We worked together on a project for the Chevalier before and she's been curious about my plans, but that was before I ran into problems with the smaller ones. And she wouldn't have access to these."

"She received a blueprint," Sébastien says, reminding me of when we first met her near the Palais des Industries. "I overheard others talk of a great reckoning but couldn't pick up any details yet. Lots of ghosts dismissed it, but the rumour persisted."

Eiffel sinks against the steel barrier, looking tired. "So, Samara set off the big resonator and stole my little one? Why?"

Sébastien's eyes widen. "GoPol. Her target is GoPol. Jamming the big one was a diversion. Half of GoPol are currently on their way here to take control of the situation, leaving the rest of GoPol practically undefended. Meanwhile, Samara will place the resonator under GoPol and bring down headquarters by reverting it to an earlier iteration of the building. Possibly killing everyone left inside."

"Which would be?" I ask, not quite panicking yet.

"Leadership. They'll all have gathered to coordinate the crisis response. People from Interpol or even a minister or two will probably join them soon."

"So, all the people who don't give a shit about ghosts or whisper ghosts, including Papa," Dix says in a low drawl. He crosses his arms behind his head. "I say let them die."

Sébastien snaps at him, "There's also the office staff, the surgery downstairs, the solicitors, the people who live next door. We're not going to let anyone die."

"She'll be in the catacombs," I think out loud, trying to project calm. "Likely at that entrance under GoPol."

"Which we haven't found yet," Sébastien points out. "The ones I know of are too far away from GoPol. It'll take us hours to get there, while Samara can simply pass through stone."

"I did," Dix says again.

"You did what?" Sébastien has no patience with him today.

Dix glares at him. "I found the entrance under GoPol. Weeks ago."

"Weeks ago? How did you even know about it?"

"Lys."

Sébastien stares at him, slack jawed. "So, you know—"

I grab his arm and shake him out of his daze. "Stop questioning Dix and let's go. Is your bike close by?" The GoPol office isn't too far from here, but it would still take us at least half an hour to walk there, if not more, and I don't think I have that in me after the sprint here.

He nods sharply. "Just across the river."

"Any last important details?" I ask Eiffel, realising he won't come with us if there's any risk of the resonator sucking him in.

"Once it's consumed a ghost, it'll produce a strong electromagnetic field. You shouldn't be in it."

Well, doesn't that sound fun?

"Then we'd better get there before she activates it."

Chapter 27

Sébastien rides his bike like a madman, weaving in and out of traffic, with narrow misses aplenty. I hold on to him and squeeze my eyes shut. It may block out some of the immediate danger, but it only highlights the much greater one we're heading into. To stop Samara, we'll have to run through the very same building she's trying to blow up. Even if we manage to survive and stop her from pulverising GoPol, there are the looming consequences of what just happened in front of hundreds—if not thousands—of cell phone cameras. There's no doubt the sightings will go viral. And then what? What theories will people come up with? Will GoPol speak out? Will my father hit publish on a piece that isn't done to seize the moment?

I shake my head. Thinking about the future is irrelevant right now. People's lives are at stake. They're not people I particularly like, but they're people, nonetheless.

The bike comes to a sudden stop as Sébastien pulls up right in front of the GoPol building. He's practically begging for a ticket. But that's another problem for the future.

Sébastien takes off his helmet, looking nearly as frantic as I am. "Maybe you should sit this one out. Go home and—"

"I'm coming!"

He opens his mouth as if to protest but nods sharply instead.

Meanwhile, Dix waits for us on the steps. "Finally! Let's go!"

We both run up the stairs as fast as we can. Thanks to the brief break on the bike, I've recovered enough. Dix runs through the door, while Sébastien practically slams his card against the reader, then almost breaks through the door when it won't open fast enough.

I follow behind, noticing a bunch of confused looks. Someone tries to ask Sébastien something as he runs after Dix, but they're cut off with a quick, "Evacuate the building!"

Just as he reaches the stairs—Dix's already down there—he smashes the glass of the emergency button. An annoyingly shrill siren starts wailing.

I've only been down here once when I broke in to rescue my whisper ghost. Looking at the door, knowing what happens there on a regular basis, I feel a sudden urge to let Samara have it all. But no, I have to be on the good side of history and be a decent human. Because that's served me so well so far.

Dix runs past the labs and goes even deeper. "Through here."

"The generator room?" Sébastien asks but swipes his card anyway. The reader flashes red. No access. "Damn! I don't have clearance."

Dix rolls his eyes and steps through the door.

"Helpful," Sébastien complains, his nerves clearly frayed. "Very help—"

The door clicks open, and Dix greets us with a grin. "Wanna come in?"

We follow him in. It's much warmer than the corridor outside. The machines hum around us, making me even more nervous. What will happen to them when the past erases them? Outside, the alarm's still blaring, but down here everything's muffled. Dix leads us through the room, past abandoned storage areas until we arrive at another door, completely unmarked, but with one of those buttons top open it from the inside. Dix's on a roll and hits that for us, too. A dark corridor and old metal grates over stone steps lead into the darkness. The catacombs.

Sébastien pulls a torch from his pocket and lights the way. I reach for my phone, only to realise that it's still at home, where it's no use to me. The stairs are quite steep and much longer than I'd anticipated. Worse, they end at the top of a well. Dix heads down without pausing.

He's already out of sight when we hear his voice. "It's not deep, but you'll end up in a shallow cave, so duck your head as soon as your feet touch the ground."

Oh, how I didn't miss this particular future of the catacombs. No wonder this entrance isn't GoPol's standard one.

I let Sébastien go first, holding the light for him. Sure enough, he doesn't climb much further than three metres before he waves up, asking me to drop the light. As soon as he's snatched it from the air, I begin my descent. The well might be shallow, but it's tight. So tight I can feel the vibrations of what must be a Métro passing nearby.

Gritting my teeth, I press my hands and elbows into the walls, while I search for purchase with my feet. This day has already taken too much out of me, and I feel my muscles spasm. Once I feel like I've managed at least two metres, I drop down the rest. Something crunches under my boot and someone grabs my hand.

"Duck!"

I do as Sébastien says. Dix wasn't kidding when he said the cave would be shallow. It's barely big enough to crawl under, but surprisingly wide, like a hidden floor beneath GoPol. For a moment, I'm paralysed, reluctant to stray from the path up, afraid I won't find the well again if I move too far away. Not that I have any idea where we'd even go.

Luckily, we've got Dix. He's crawled sideways to the left, then suddenly falls over what looks like a hidden ledge. Sébastien grabs my wrist to reassure me before following. Not wanting to be left behind in the dark, I stay as close as I can.

When I finally reach the edge, Sébastien is there to help me down. By the looks of it, we can stand in the next part, where we face a new problem.

"You!"

In a wider corridor, dead centre under GoPol, Samara kneels in front of the portable resonator. From the looks of it, she's not quite finished setting it up, which makes me let out a sigh of relief.

"What are *you* doing here?"

"We're here to stop you," Sébastien says, both hands raised in the air as if he's talking down a criminal with a bomb. Which, I guess, is technically exactly what we're dealing with.

"Why?" she asks, continuing her work. "Didn't you say you wanted to bring down GoPol?"

Sébastien swallows. "Not like this. There are still people in the building. Living people."

"Too bad I'm not one of them," Samara says, sending shivers down my spine.

I understand where she's coming from. The betrayal she experienced, the loss she's dealing with—it's all too familiar.

"Samara, I know you're hurting. GoPol took everything from you."

"And now I'm going to take everything from them."

"There's another way," I say, a little more desperate.

Samara laughs out loud, a sound that echoes off the closed walls. "You mean that little essay you're preparing? You silly naïve girl!

You want to make the world a better place, but you don't have what it takes to evoke change."

After what Nostradamus said, I'm not sure I *want* to.

"All you have are a few friends in high places... all of them dead."

The worst part is it's all true. I'm not a special agent. Or a powerful necromancer. I can't fight or handle a weapon. My only power is the very thing that got us all into this mess.

With a snort, Samara dismisses me and looks at Sébastien with hungry eyes. "You know I'm right, Roubert. Your father's too powerful. He can get away with anything. Her school essay will do nothing but paint a target on her back. And yours. There's only one way to make sure he can't hurt anyone else."

"Séb..." I plead. Behind him, Dix looks away. If it were up to him, he'd pull the trigger.

Sébastien takes a deep breath, his hands shaking slightly. "This is not the way we do things."

Samara laughs again. "Oh, no, that's *exactly* how we do things at GoPol."

"By killing everyone? Every agent, every admin staff, the doctor downstairs, the lawyers?" Sébastien asks, sounding horrified.

"They're all complicit." Samara shrugs. "Leave no trace behind. Isn't that what we've learnt? Do you think your father would hesitate to blow up Alix's apartment block if he thought it would solve all his problems?"

The mere suggestion makes my stomach turn. So many innocent people would be caught in the crossfire, just like they are now. Surely, even Charles wouldn't go that far. Or would he? Is there anything Sébastien's father would actually stop at?

"That would be a bit excessive," Sébastien says, sounding terribly nonchalant.

"But effective. The whole Dubois family. Wiped out in one fell swoop. Maybe he'd even go after that best friend of hers. What was her name? Gabrielle?"

The mention of Gaby's name infuriates me. Does GoPol know everything about me? All because they couldn't handle a harmless ghost whisperer out of their control. Anger courses through my veins and eats away at my patience. Gaby and Marie both witnessed Charles' threat to my life and Margot's experiments on Sébastien. The thought he might turn up on Gaby's doorstep to have a little "chat" makes me sick to the stomach.

"GoPol will do anything to keep their secrets," Samara hisses. "Whatever scandal you cook up, whatever accusation you make, it'll disappear with a wave of the hand. You know your father is untouchable. That man *killed* you. Don't you want to take revenge?"

I bite my lip, nervous what Sébastien might say when his face hardens.

"I don't want revenge. I want justice. The last thing I want is to end up like my father. Blowing up GoPol is wrong."

Samara's eyes are ablaze with fervour. "What they did to us—to all of us—was wrong, too."

"But two wrongs don't make a right."

I breathe a sigh of relief when I hear him reject her proposal. Of course he would. The Sébastien I know has too much integrity to take the easy way out. Now all we have to do is convince Samara to leave the dark path she's chosen and appeal to the companion she lost.

The ghost shrugs. "Suit yourself."

She activates the resonator and flips the lever to charge.

CHAPTER 28

A shock wave goes through the catacombs, and I'm thrown into the wall behind me. Pain erupts in my shoulders and the back of my head. When I touch my hair, my hand comes away wet. I blink rapidly, trying to clear the clouds in front of my eyes and make sense of our new reality.

Arms close around me and hands gingerly touch my face. "How are you feeling?" Sébastien asks. He must've landed nearby and recovered faster.

"Hurt?" I shake off the last of the cobwebs and stare over his shoulder at Samara and the resonator.

Or rather just at the resonator, because whatever is left of Samara is a terribly distorted liquid form of a human that's rapidly being sucked into the machine. A funnel-shaped beam forms on top of it, aimed at the ceiling. Below the funnel, a crackling energy field blocks off access for five metres in every direction.

"We need to stop it!" I push past Sébastien and tumble into the field, only to experience the most excruciating pain, sending me sprawling to the floor.

Sébastien pulls me back almost immediately, hissing in pain as his hands touch the field. "We can't reach it!" His eyes are wide with horror.

"I can."

We both look up at Dix, who's standing there, one arm in the field, looking at it curiously. "It doesn't hurt ghosts."

"It does!" I point at the shapeless blob that's left of Samara's entire existence, quickly dissolving before our eyes. "You can't go near the resonator. It'll suck you in, too."

I hate how dead Dix's eyes are when he says, "We've only got three minutes. Five at most. You heard Eiffel."

"Dix, no." Sébastien stands and takes a step towards his whisper ghost. "You can't do this."

"Yes, I can." A sad smile, far removed from Dix's usual grin, plays around his lips. "It's what has to be done, isn't it? The alternative would be..." He looks up at the ceiling and closes his eyes.

I know part of him wants to say, "To hell with Papa". Part of *me* wants to tell him that. But that's not the boy who was brought up to protect his country at all costs.

Dix opens his eyes again, his decision made. "This is what I was trained for. I'm a special agent. Just like you. And you'd do it."

Sébastien's face falls, the misery etched into every feature. "Dix..."

"You don't have to say anything. It was... fun. Lately." Dix's eyes flicker to me. "Take care of him for me, will you, History Girl?"

"Dix!" I throw myself into his arms, hugging him tightly, as if I could make him stay that way. "Don't..."

Tears stream down my face. Right now, I don't care about Charles or the people who protect him or the innocents I've never met. None of them measure up to Dix, to this beautiful, broken boy who deserves the world, not to sacrifice himself.

"Please."

Sébastien's hands close around my shoulders, slowly but surely pulling me away. "Time's running out."

I stumble back with a strangled sob.

"So long, History Girl." Dix gives me a crooked smile, and I lose it completely.

In anguish, I bury my face in Sébastien's chest, hot tears burning trails into my cheeks. Sébastien's strong arms wrap around me and hold me tight, his heartbeat racing under my chin.

"You..." His voice breaks.

"Sorry, you won't be able to see ghosts for a while," Dix says, his chipper tone like fingernails on a chalkboard. "Give them hell from me."

Sébastien's fingers dig into my side, telling me Dix has entered the field. I shudder, my breaths coming so fast I feel like I'm about to faint.

Pull yourself together. Dix's making the ultimate sacrifice. The least you can do is watch his last moment on this earth.

With a gasp, I tear myself away from Sébastien and stumble to the edge of the field. Reaching out, I feel the pain bite into my skin and jerk away. There's nothing I can do but watch.

Dix's almost at the resonator. Already, I can see the funnel reaching for his essence, hungry for his memory. Oh, what a feast it'd have there. All those tightly bundled emotions behind that mischievous grin. Dix resists the call and wraps his hands around the lever to pull. His muscles tense and I can hear him grunting beyond the crackle of the electromagnetic field.

"Hang on!" I shout at him. "Just hang onto it!"

Samara was sucked away so quickly, but she was willing to give her soul for this. Dix is willing to give his soul to stop it, and so he holds onto this plane of existence, putting his entire weight behind the lever. When it gives way for the first time, I feel a surge of hope. Maybe Dix's strong enough to turn it off before the resonator fully consumes him.

But just like the big one under the Eiffel Tower, the small one seems to be stuck. It only moves with sudden jerks. First, it's a centimetre, then half of that, then just a millimetre. Dix's singularly focused on the lever, but he's fraying. His hip is distorting, pulled towards the machine as he desperately tries to turn it off.

It's almost at the top—halfway—when Dix sinks to his knees. His body is shimmering now, and I gasp. I can see the stone behind him through his torso. The field has shrunk a little, but it's still too wide to breach.

"Come back!" I cry. Surely, half the power is enough to stop Samara's plan. It has to be.

But Dix shakes his head. Even though his fingers dissolve before his eyes, Dix pulls himself up again. With an earth-shattering scream, he pulls the lever a full two and a half centimetres across the centre. As a result, his body sways like a leaf in the wind, becoming even more transparent. There's not enough of him left to complete his task.

I look over my shoulder at Sébastien and see the despair in his eyes, which mirrors mine so perfectly. He's crying, too. I can count on one hand the number of times Sébastien has cried, and it's never been in my presence. Swallowing hard, I reach out to him. He's about to lose a part of himself. The only friend he's had since he was seventeen. His brother in body, mind, and soul. His levity.

"Dix..." he whispers.

And then suddenly, he's sprinting forward, throwing himself into the field. The force of it throws his body to the ground, but Sébastien crawls on, writhing in agony, his determination matching Dix's.

"Go back!" Dix shouts, his voice distorted and faint. "I've got this. Trust me."

But Sébastien pulls himself forward. Centimetre by centimetre. Seizures shake his body, and I scream when I see his skin burst. And yet, he goes on until he can finally wrap his hands around Dix's. "I trust you. Together."

Dix nods, and for a moment, his body seems to strengthen again. "On three. One."

"Two."

Dix grins. "Three."

They both push and pull at the same time. Sébastien screams, blood running down his temple and his biceps. Dix's so pale now I struggle to see him clearly. But the lever is moving. A lot.

Two seconds, maybe three, and it finally clicks back into the off position. The funnel disappears, and the crackling field sizzles out of existence. Sparks fly around the resonator and its hum still fills the cave.

Sébastien collapses on the floor, groaning in pain. As for Dix… he's gone.

"Dix." Sébastien barely takes a moment to recover before he rolls back onto his knees and, ignoring his wounds, cradles something in his arms.

I squint, then widen my eyes suddenly when I realise there's still something of Dix left. It's just very translucent and flickering. "Di—!"

A hand covers my mouth just as an arm wraps around my chest.

"Time to go," a familiar voice whispers in my ear.

Before I even know what's happening, I'm being pulled off my feet and dragged away. I try to scream and wriggle myself out of the iron grip when I see the resonator pulsing blue. A second later, it explodes.

Chapter 29

I have no idea what just happened. There was a blue light. My ears popped, and then I fell. I just kept falling, unable to scream, until I hit the ground. Now the darkness wraps around me so completely it's suffocating me. I'm choking and coughing, as if there's smoke stuck in my throat. My knees ache and my head throbs. Fresh blood seeps into my hair. When did I hit my head?

The explosion. First, the one that threw me against the wall, and then the second one. The one that...

"Sébastien! Dix!"

A growl makes me jump, followed by a menacing voice. "Forget them."

My heart pounds in my throat as I take a step back, only to find a wall behind me. I'm trapped in the dark with someone. Someone I know.

"Gaspar?"

"Took you long enough."

I whimper, realising I'm trapped here with the wrong Gaspar. The one who has no interest in my safety.

Slowly, I press myself against the wall, feeling for an exit in both directions. "What's happening?"

Even squinting, I can't tell where he is or what else might be in the room. I creep along the wall, stumbling over obstacles on the floor. Something rattles and rolls away until it suddenly stops.

"I saved your life."

"Did you?"

Does that mean Sébastien and Dix are both...? I swallow a sob, turning it into another whimper.

My fingers find purchase on an edge, something wooden. I feel around it. A cupboard perhaps. What if it's blocking the way out? I slide my hand behind the wood but find nothing but stone.

"If you're looking for a way out, there isn't one," Gaspar says in a chilling voice. "Unless you're part ghost."

He knows exactly where I am and what I'm doing. What did he just say? No way out? Did I pass through stone?

"You kidnapped me."

Gaspar laughs. It's a harsh, cruel sound. "I thought you wanted to be with me."

In the ensuing panic, I bite my lip until I taste blood. *Don't lose your head now, Alix. You're just trapped in the catacombs with a madman, and no one knows where you are.* Yeah, that does little to calm me down.

"You're mine, Alix. You'll always be mine, won't you?"

What a total creep. Right now, it's impossible to say there was *ever* anything about Gaspar that I loved, but I know this isn't him. Instead of trying to find a way out, I take a cautious step into the darkness, only to startle when I hear the shuffle of tiny feet. Are there rats?

I shake my head, forcing myself not to get distracted. "You told me to move on with someone else. That I should forget you."

"But you didn't." His voice is closer now. "How could you possibly forget me?"

Images of the kisses I shared with Sébastien flood my mind. I hadn't forgotten about Gaspar, but I'd let go of him. "You didn't want me anymore. You—" My outstretched hand meets a body.

Before I can fully orientate myself, Gaspar grabs my hand and yanks me against his chest. "Oh, I want you. I did all of this for us. I built this home for us."

As far as I can tell, there's not much down here. I haven't even found the bed yet. Not that it's high on my list of priorities.

"A home? In the catacombs?" At least, I assume we're still in the catacombs.

Gaspar's hot breath hits my neck, and I shudder. With my eyesight gone, my body naturally reaches out with all its other senses, but the sensations quickly become overwhelming. Anxiously, I lick my lips.

"That's nice, I suppose."

The grip on my wrist tightens as Gaspar growls again. "I know you hate being with me. You have Séb now—or not."

His cruelty makes me whimper again. We've just lost Dix. Sébastien can't be gone, too.

"Why are you being like this?" I ask, regretting it immediately as his grip tightens painfully.

"If I remember correctly, I'm like this because of you."

I shake my head and pull at my hand. To my surprise, Gaspar lets go and I stumble backwards, tripping on something in the process. Found the bed.

"This is who I am now," Gaspar says, his voice fading back into the darkness again. "I'm alive, but I don't have a life anymore. My room has been rented, my job replaced, my enrolment cancelled. If I wanted, I could start afresh. New identity, new city, new interests. I'd just have to give up everything I am. Everything I wanted to be. It's not exactly fair, is it? I could've had a quiet ghost life. It would've been a bit of a shock at first, a big adjustment, but I would've found my pace, made new connections. Instead, I found you."

"So now it's all my fault?" I ask, as if I haven't blamed myself over and over again for what happened.

"Who else should I blame?"

Maybe yourself, I think, but I don't dare say it out loud. Gaspar is the one who was so desperate he didn't wait. Who took the risk? Who then jerked me around, pulled me in, and pushed me away as he pleased. This is one of his tugs. Tomorrow, he'll push me away again. I'm so very tired of this persona who's taken over my beloved hedgehog boy.

"Let me go, Gaspar." Especially now I hear the shuffling noise again. Something's under the bed.

"What?" The word cracks like a whip snap.

I hold onto the edge of the bed, which isn't much more than a collapsible cot, and gather my courage. "I know you, Gaspar. The real you. And the real you would never—"

"When are you finally going to accept this *is* the real me?" he bellows from what must be right in front of the bed.

Centring myself, I stand up and reach out for him. I find his face and cradle his cheeks, smiling even though I feel like dying on the inside. "It isn't. It's not all you are, love. It's your pain and your anger and everything bad that's ever happened to you, living or dead, but you're more than that. You're stronger than that. I know you, Gaspar. I know the real you is still inside you."

Suddenly, his hands wrap around my neck and throw me back onto the bed. "This. This is the real me."

I claw at his fingers as he chokes me. "Ga-ghu—"

There's something I should say or do or... But I can't think. I'm lost in my need to breathe, in the pain, in the panic. Is this how he makes sure I'll never leave his side? Air. My chest hurts more than my throat now. There's a sharp pain in my brain. Why can't I kick him off me?

Just as suddenly as he's attacked me, Gaspar lets go. He scrambles backwards as far as he can. As I suck in the precious air, I hear him breathing louder than me in the darkness.

"I'm sorry. Alix. I'm so sorry!"

Now the tears fall. There's something about his proper voice, the real him, that cuts straight to my heart. "I..." My throat hurts as I try to speak.

A light flickers alive, blinding me. Frightened, I retreat to the wall and curl up, protecting my throat and my head. Slowly, my eyes adjust to the flickering portable lamp, which isn't even bright enough to read a letter. In its light, I see Gaspar cowering on the opposite side between a bedside table and a chair. He's clawing at his own head, tearing at his once-soft hair, his face pure misery.

"I'm sorry," he repeats, sobbing. "Alix, I'm..."

As much as his sight breaks my heart, I'm more interested in getting away. Panic creeps into my throat as I realise there truly is no way out. I do find the originator of the shuffling noise, though. It's the run-over hedgehog the Chevalier brought back. Gaspar is keeping him as a pet, maybe to replace Malou.

My eyes flicker to the ceiling. There! There's a latch. If I use the chair to climb onto the cupboard, I should be able to reach it.

"Kill me."

My head snaps back to Gaspar. "What?" I croak.

He's stopped apologising and is staring at his hands now as if they're alien to him. The hands that choked me just a minute ago. "You need to kill me. It's the only way, Alix. This..." He looks up at me and swallows. "This monster can't be allowed to live. The Chevalier won't do it. I'm his greatest success. His proof that it can be done. He says he's going to find a way to fix me, but... it's not a priority. I can't wait. What if I..." Before he loses it again, his gaze locks in on a nearby backpack. "There's a utility knife in the front pocket. Take that and..." Gaspar licks his lips. "Do it quickly."

"I'm not going to"—a cough cuts me off, brought on by his earlier mistreatment of my throat—"kill you."

Gaspar pulls himself up to his feet, and I shrink back again. He holds up his hands as if I'm a skittish, injured animal. "I'll do it myself. That way, you won't have any blood on your hands."

In front of me? "Don't!" It's a terrible idea. I jump off the bed and block his way. "We'll find a way," I promise eagerly, coughing again. "Séb and I... We'll make it a priority."

I've been too focused on the article, on freeing myself from the Damocles sword GoPol has been dangling over my head. I should've done more to help Gaspar, not kiss Sébastien. Maybe there's an exorcism. Anything!

"Séb might be dead," Gaspar says, swallowing heavily.

I almost slap him. "You don't know that!"

While Gaspar has been playing off his little power game here, Sébastien could be lying in the catacombs, bleeding to death. And Dix could be... Dix sacrificed himself to save people who never cared for him.

"Alix. It's the only way. Quick. I can't hold him down forever."

The threat of the other Gaspar returning at any moment sends me straight into a panic. "Alexandre!"

The revolutionary general appears at my side only a moment later. Gaspar side-eyes him. "He's a ghost. He can't kill me."

"Please," I beg Alexandre. "You need to hold him back. He can't..." I swallow, nearly coughing again. "He can't be allowed to end his life."

Suddenly, Gaspar lunges at me, a wild look on his face. But before his fingers can dig into my throat again, Alexandre has wrapped his arms around him and is dragging him back, kicking and screaming.

"I'm gonna get you," the false Gaspar shouts. "You can't escape me, Alix!"

"What do you want me to do with him?" Alexandre asks.

If only I knew. "Lock him up. Find something to secure him." If we can restrain him, we might be able to find a cure for his predicament.

"I'm not sure... but I'll do my best."

"You and I are bound to each other!" Gaspar shouts. "I'm yours and you're mine, whether you like it or not!"

It's hard to ignore his screams, but the most important thing is to get the hell out of here. I push the chair next to the cupboard and test its weight, only to remember the backpack. I can't leave a knife with him if he might use it on himself—or someone else.

I run back to grab the backpack and take the lamp as well. Practically jumping on the chair, I push his belongings on to the cupboard.

"Oh, you're going to leave me in the dark now? Steal all my provisions?" Gaspar taunts. "You should've just killed me when you had the chance. Now I'm going to kill—"

Alexandre must've gagged him or knocked him out. I don't dare look back or worry about this version of Gaspar. He's moaning, so he's not dead. That's good enough for me.

"Hurry!" Alexandre urges me. "I don't know how long I can hold him."

Is he going to restrain him personally for lack of a prison that could hold a revenant like Gaspar? No, I can't think about that now. I climb onto the cupboard. From there, I can reach the jagged hole in the top. It's a precarious balancing act, but I manage to push both the lamp and his backpack through. Then I grab the sides and pull myself after.

"Alix?"

Suddenly, the Chevalier's at my side. He holds my arms and helps me pull myself up over the edge.

"What are you doing down *there*?" He shines his own torch into the room, blinding Gaspar, who's snarling at us in Alexandre's grip. "Oh."

I'm breathing hard and I'm in no mood to argue with the Chevalier. He has a lot to answer for, but not now. Instead, I shoulder the backpack and grab the lamp. Now what? I don't even know where I am.

"You don't have to happen a map?"

The Chevalier chuckles. "You don't need a map. I already have what you want."

"What?" If this is yet another sick game, I'm gonna lose my shit. "I need to find Sébastien."

"As I said, I have what you want. Follow me. I'll bring you to him."

A million questions course through my brain, but it looks like I'm fresh out of options. I don't know where I am and in which direction the explosion is. Not that it matters if what the Chevalier says is true.

He has Sébastien. And I'm ready to pay anything to get him back.

Chapter 30

Wherever the Chevalier is taking me, it's not far, but the time stretches indefinitely. My legs want to run, just like my heart wants to fly ahead. At last, I can't hold it in anymore.

"Is he alive?"

"Of course," the Chevalier says in a hurry, as if mortified he's forgotten to mention it. "He's a bit banged up, took a knock to the knee, maybe cracked a rib or two, but don't worry, he'll live."

Relief floods me so completely my throat seizes and my legs wobble. For a moment, I need to pause and hold onto the wall, fingers digging into the cracks, so I can catch my breath. Involuntary tears run down my cheeks, turning me into a blubbering mess.

The Chevalier stops and regards me with pity in his eyes. "He means that much to you, huh?"

I shake my head at him. Not because he's wrong, but because I can't possibly talk about it right now. Not when my throat still feels as if Gaspar is squeezing it.

"You're probably wondering what I'm doing here," the Chevalier says when I don't answer. "I was nearby when I heard the explosion. Naturally, I had to check it out. Half the room had caved in, with cracks forming at the wall. I heard Sébastien moaning more than I saw him. There was that much dust in the air."

My heart staggers as I listen to him describing the state of the room he found Sébastien in.

"He was beside himself, searching the rubble despite blood running down his face. I had to drag him out of there before the whole thing collapsed, but man, he was fighting it. But then he found something and calmed a little. I managed to convince him I'd look for you and to let me take care of him first. You want to tell me what you were doing there?"

"Do you know what that room was?"

"The GoPol access. Barely used these days due to its inconvenience."

Since he's so forthcoming with information, I decide to throw him a bone. "We tried to stop it from blowing up."

I push off the wall, ready to go again. The Chevalier nods, accepting my lacking answer, and leads me through a tight passageway into a surprisingly comfy living space. With carpet and a pair of couches, it's almost inviting—if it wasn't surrounded by stone with no access to natural light.

"Alix."

A second wave of relief tries to pull me under when I see Sébastien sitting on one of the couches, cradling something in his lap. He looks up in horror. His eyes are red from crying. Dried blood covers half his face and mats his hair. His clothes are torn, and I can see dark stains under a patina of dust that indicate other injuries, but he's alive. He's alive.

"You're here," he says, and for a moment he has to shut his eyes, lashes fluttering, as he takes a few deep breaths.

I feel the same, nodding eagerly, but then my gaze falls on his lap. "Dix?"

"He's fading," Sébastien whispers, looking at me with such a profound loss I have to swallow hard.

My hands tremble as I force myself forward and kneel in front of the couch to take a better look. I only recognise Dix because I know it's him. His upper body is still mostly intact, but no matter how hard I look, I can't see anything below the hip. His left arm is missing and his face... his face looks as if its features have melted away. I can only make out the grin, because I know he'd be grinning at me.

"Hey, History Girl." His voice is paper-thin, barely even a whisper.

My throat tightens, and I choke back a sob. For a moment, I can't breathe. By the time I manage to swallow, Dix has already faded a little more. "Don't…"

"What happened?" The Chevalier asks. He's the odd man out in this reunion, the only one not crying his heart out.

Neither I nor Sébastien are in a position to explain. I reach out and carefully cup Dix's fraying face. "I'm so sorry, Dix."

"Hey, don't rob me of my moment of glory," he jokes. The mocking tone is another dagger in my heart. "Not that anyone will remember me."

"That's not true," Sébastien says. His own voice has been softened by tears. "I'll never forget you."

Usually, that should be all that's needed to keep a ghost in existence. But Dix's not a normal ghost, and he's experienced something out of this world. There's no bringing back a ghost once they've started fading so severely.

My heart misses a beat, and for a moment, my tears stop. "There is a way."

"What?" Sébastien looks at me in confusion.

When my heart starts beating again, it's at double the speed. I jump up, determination giving me new strength. "There's a way to save Dix. We…"

I close my eyes and think back to the World Fair and the presentation I witnessed in Marie Curie's pavilion. She restored a fading ghost, resetting the clock. All that talk about stabilisation fields and spectral energies...

"Alix? What am I doing here?"

I open my eyes and see Marie Curie standing in front of me. As usual, she's wearing a lab coat. What I don't see is the crystal.

"What is this place?"

I'd like to know that, too, but it's not important right now.

Sébastien's eyes are full of hope. He must remember the same event and has drawn the same conclusions. "Can you help him?"

"That crystal you showcased," I explain, "the Ghost Resonance Crystal. Can it be used to bring Dix back? He's fading fast."

Marie takes a look at the remnants of the whisper ghost and her face softens. "Oh dear. What happened?" she asks as she kneels beside Dix and takes his hand. With a little tool, she measures his essence.

"He got caught in one of Gustave Eiffel's resonators," I explain, hoping some of this information will be useful to her. "The portable ones don't work very well. They feed on spectral energy and there's some kind of overlap?" If only I could remember the technical details correctly. "Dix tried to turn it off, and... it sucked part of him in."

While I'm blurting out every piece of information I can think of, Marie puts her hand in her pocket. Much to my relief, she's got one of the crystals in there. Maybe she always carries one with her or maybe the gesture made it appear there. Whatever the mechanisms, she's got one now and is pushing it into Dix's hands.

"What can you remember of yourself, Dix?"

"I…" His voice is so faint I can't make out the rest. Hopefully, the thought alone will be enough.

But the crystal remains dull, and Dix isn't strengthening the way the young revolutionary did at the fair.

"Why isn't it working?" I demand, my voice shaking so badly I feel the urge to clench my jaw.

Marie folds her hands in her lap and looks like she's preparing to tell me the bad news. "Dix's not a normal ghost. He's not attached to this world like the rest of us, because he only started existing upon his death. So, he has no memories to feed the crystal."

"No," I whisper. "No! This is supposed to work! You brought back someone else. Someone much older. Someone no one remembers anymore."

She looks up at me with infinite sympathy. "He brought himself back. With his own memories."

"What about my memories?" Sébastien asks in a toneless whisper. "You say Dix isn't attached to this world. But he's attached to me. He was me. I mean…"

"That could work." Marie eagerly pushes the crystal into Sébastien's hand. "Try it. Concentrate on that tether between you and call up as many memories from before your separation as you can."

None of the memories from before their separation will be any good.

Not that it matters. Sébastien straightens his back, readjusts his grip on both the crystal and Dix, and manages a smile. "Do you remember when we crashed our scooter? It was wet outside, but we…" The smile falters. Sébastien bites his lip, then forces himself to continue. "Papa had complained… no, he'd shouted at us for failing that maths test. His face was all red and I… we thought that vein of his was finally going to pop. He threw the test at our head, not that it hurt, and then took our phone. Took it into the kitchen and smashed it with that meat hammer he liked so much. Said we wouldn't get a new one until we were top of the class. I think… I think we said something about not wanting a phone, anyway. I mean who would we ever call?" He winces and continues. "So, we stormed out the house and jumped on the scooter…"

I can't help but hug myself as Sébastien unveils more and more layers of abuse. He tried to share one of the good memories, but even the good ones can't stand alone without some messed-up kind of framing. Part of me wants him to stop talking, but there's a soft glimmer in the crystal, and though I might be imagining it, I believe Dix is just the tiniest fraction firmer. As horrible as it is, it's working.

It feels intrusive to listen, so I get up and join the Chevalier, who's making notes in a field book, probably about the parts of the conversation he was privy to.

"Thanks for getting him out of there," I say, still hugging myself.

"No worries." He smiles softly, then nods to Sébastien. "How's our young Roubert—and Dix?—doing?"

"Bringing back his whisper ghost with all the shit they've been through." Who needs therapy when you can pour your trauma into crystals instead?

Sébastien describes the scooter ride, and for once, his eyes light up. "No one on the street. The street lamps reflecting in the puddles. The wind. I don't think we'd ever felt more free. For a little while, there was nothing holding us down. No expectations, no responsibilities. We could just leave it all behind and live a little. And then the wheel slipped, we hit the kerb, and broke our arm." His chin drops. "Kind of like a rude awakening to reality."

I look away. "It's working. Marie Curie developed—"

"A resonance crystal," the Chevalier completes. "Fascinating research." When he catches my questioning gaze, he smiles. "I might not have been able to see the World Fair for myself, but I have others who are my eyes and ears on the ground."

Sounds like Samara wasn't the only ghost whisperer in his ranks. I wonder who else he has, but I know better than to ask. The Chevalier guards his secrets as jealously as GoPol.

"—berated us at the hospital. Called us every stupid name under the sun," Sébastien says, and I hug myself even tighter. Every time I think Charles couldn't get any worse, there's a new detail.

Marie watches them with professional curiosity, while also measuring the spectral energy in this room and taking extensive notes.

"Is it working?" I ask. Dix looks a bit more like himself, but he's still missing half a body and, in a sickening way, I can see Sébastien's legs through him.

She taps her pen to her mouth. "Maybe."

My eyes water again. "Maybe" is not the answer I wanted to hear. "Is there anything we can do to improve his chances?"

"I think he might be stable enough to move him," she says, barely registering my distress.

"Move him?"

"To a more familiar place. Something to remember and anchor him. This isn't where he usually lives, is it?"

"No." Though I wonder if it's where the Chevalier lives.

Marie nods. "I think Gustave was onto something with the familiarity of places and its corresponding grounding effect. We might see better results if we move him to such a place."

"Does it have to be from the past?" I have no idea where Sébastien and Dix grew up.

But fortunately, she shakes her head. "In fact, I believe it might be better to use a recent place, one that Dix knows, too."

"Did you hear that?" I ask Sébastien. "We have to move Dix."

Sébastien shakes his head. "He's still so weak."

"That's exactly why we have to move him."

"Listen to History Girl. She knows what's up," Dix whispers.

Sébastien exhales sharply, then nods. "If that will bring him back." He takes a deep breath and tries to stand, but hisses in pain, causing the Chevalier to step in.

"You take care of the whisper ghost," he tells me. "I'll help Sébastien."

Carefully, I slide my arms under Dix, expecting him to weigh a lot. The opposite is true. Dix is as light as a feather and seems to fold in my arms.

"This may be the most embarrassing moment of my afterlife," Dix quips.

"Oh, shut up."

He laughs hoarsely, giving me hope he'll hold out until we can resume the strengthening. The Chevalier puts an arm under Sébastien's shoulder and pulls him up. Sébastien, unable to let go of Dix or the crystal, moans and hisses, but never complains.

With our hearts clinging to desperate hope, we set off for Sébastien's apartment.

CHAPTER 31

By the time we've settled Sébastien and Dix in their bedroom, I've heard a lifetime's worth of bad memories. I know Sébastien hasn't planned this, he just continues with whatever memory is jogged next. Occasionally, there's a glimmer of light, but it's always quickly tainted by Charles. I wonder if some of these were originally happy memories that are only souring now his eyes have been opened to the truth.

The good news is it seems to be helping. Dix's still quite faint, but his face looks almost normal and his body is much more complete than it was. More importantly, his humour gains in strides as he continues to interrupt Sébastien to make fun of himself. By the time I put him in bed, he weighed the same as a toddler.

Sébastien immediately sits next to him to continue his grim tale, while I fetch some water and the first-aid kit to treat his more serious injuries. All in all, he was lucky to escape with bruises and a few lacerations. At last, I leave them to it.

After checking on Malou and giving her a few belly rubs for my own benefit, I join the Chevalier in the living room. I find him staring into the darkness outside.

When he hears me coming, he glances over his shoulder and smiles. "You look like you've had a rough time, too."

"Don't you know?"

He raises an eyebrow. "Something I did?"

"More like something you didn't do." I grab the bottle of wine from last night. Not bothering with a glass, I take a big gulp, making it clear I'm not going to offer him anything. "I begged you to help Gaspar. Just like I begged you to help me bring down GoPol."

"Hm. Sounds like you did just fine on your own." He shows me his phone, which displays a picture of a badly damaged GoPol building, complete with the headline: 'Sinkhole opens under Interpol branch'.

I'm glad it happened after we'd left the catacombs. "Did anyone die?"

Please let it be Charles. After three hours of listening to how Charles raised and brainwashed Sébastien and Dix, I hope he died horribly.

"No, the building was evacuated an hour before it happened."

Silly Sébastien, saving everyone.

"They're just gonna find a new place to terrorise everyone from."

I'm beyond the point of caring right now. All I want is to cuddle up with Malou on the couch and sleep for two days.

"After today?" The Chevalier chuckles. "How long have you been in the catacombs?" When I shrug, he informs me, "There have been ghost sightings all around the Eiffel Tower. People are speculating wildly, and now this 'Interpol' building had a sinkhole open up underneath? I can imagine Charles tearing his hair out."

Or he'll find a way to dump it all on me. "Now would've been a good time to publish our article."

"Agreed."

I blink, wondering if I heard that right. "What's that supposed to mean?"

The Chevalier gives me a sheepish smile. "This is a fast-moving situation that could go either way. The authorities will try to sweep it under the carpet. If you deny it long enough, people will believe it. Maybe they'll delete the pictures and videos or maybe they'll just leave them up and call it a silly conspiracy theory. There are a lot of witnesses, though. At least a handful of them will be well-respected officials or celebrities with a huge following, so the government might decide to embrace it instead and publicly establish GoPol as the wonderful agency that is." The Chevalier holds up a finger. "But right now, neither of those things have happened, which means we have the golden opportunity to control the narrative. How soon can your father publish the article?"

I have no idea. "We don't have enough evidence."

"Give me your phone."

Curious and a little suspicious, I take my phone from the charger where I left it this morning. There's a flood of messages and notifications and even a few missed calls. Joy!

The Chevalier takes my phone and holds it up to his. A few seconds later, he says, "There we go. My file and all the evidence I've collected over the years."

My mouth drops open. "You did what?"

He scoffs. "Alix, don't you think I would've done everything in my power to protect myself after what the government did to me? Why do you think Charles leaves me to do whatever the hell I want in the catacombs?" Nodding at the phone, he explains, "He's afraid these documents will ever see the light of day. He doesn't know exactly what I have on him, only that it's a lot. So, instead of going after me with full force, he's just trying to find out what I'm working on. Sooner or later, he would've made me an offer to return."

"And you don't want that?" I stare at the phone, biting my lip, wondering if the evidence is as good as he says it is.

"Can you blame me?"

I shake my head. What GoPol did to him is the stuff of nightmares.

"No. Charles thinks he can buy me. That I'm eager to continue my research even if it's under his supervision. And sure, the money would be tempting, but I've got my own benefactors. GoPol needs me more than I need them. And that means I get to decide which side of history I want to be on."

I hold my breath, not daring to hope what he might say next. History. What's happening right now has the potential to be the history of tomorrow. And I'm right in the middle of it.

"I choose the ghosts. The whisper ghosts and the actual ghosts. That means I'm choosing you, Alix. If you'll have me."

A shiver runs down my spine and I feel as if something significant has happened. This was never about GoPol versus poor old me. This is about ghosts, how we treat them and how we work with them. Just thinking about the possibilities makes me giddy with hope.

I try not to smile, but my lips quirk up, anyway. "Of course."

The Chevalier beams before looking down at his phone. "Ah, transfer completed."

I expect him to hand my phone back, but he holds it up to his chest.

"One more thing." His smile fades. "I messed up with Gaspar."

And just like that, the joy is sucked out of me.

"I thought I was ready, that I'd perfected the process, but it wasn't there yet. I'm sorry you and Gaspar have to suffer the consequences. I promise I'll put all my energy into investigating what went wrong and finding a way to fix it. I want you to help me."

"Me?" I point with the wine bottle at myself. "What do you mean?"

"Join Nexus. Help me in the lab. Help me make this safer, so we can use it to help ghosts like Gaspar in the future. What do you think?"

I have the distinct feeling he's holding my phone hostage, and this is some kind of bargaining situation, but what he's said has struck a chord. I want to help ghosts. Not by bringing them all back, of course, but perhaps there's a compromise we haven't thought about yet. Some way of helping them interact with the world of the living again.

"Why do you want *me*?"

"Because no one knows ghosts better than you. No one understands their needs like you do. Even I... misjudged. Come on, Alix. Be my good conscience."

I can't help laughing. "Well, I think there are a lot of ethical parameters to look at, but if we can find a safe way to allow ghosts to partake in the living world—especially now people might believe in ghosts—I want to be involved." At the very least, I can put the brakes on if it veers into the wrong direction.

Nostradamus' prophecy draws circles in my mind again. I didn't cause the chaos tonight, but I was still at the centre of it. Maybe that's what the prophecy is all about. Just as raising the dead doesn't necessarily mean resurrecting everyone. I could be raising awareness, bring their issues to a wider audience—any audience, really. And apparently, the occasional necromancy.

"For the ghosts."

The Chevalier smiles. "For the ghosts." Then he finally hands me my phone and takes his leave. "Keep me posted."

As soon as the door closes behind him, I check what he deposited on my phone. The more I read, the wider my eyes get. The Chevalier wasn't lying when he'd said he'd gathered enough evidence to protect himself. This is it. This is enough to lock Charles away for life and then some.

Giddily, I transfer the data to Papa and tell him to get moving. As soon as that's done, I start reading my messages. Most of them are from Gaby, asking me to get in touch as soon as I leave the catacombs. Just as I'm about to text her back, my phone rings.

"I was just about to—"

"Mademoiselle Dubois?"

My exhilaration flatlines as I hear a male voice. "Who's this?"

"Oh, don't play dumb now."

"Monsieur Roubert."

Why the heck did I accept a call from an unknown number? I'd wonder how he got my number in the first place, but that's probably one of the first things he got. And then I remember I signed a contract with GoPol what seems like ten years ago. Great job, Alix.

"That was quite the stunt you pulled," Charles continues, his voice a constant threat. "I'm impressed you had it in you. And that bomb..."

What's he talking about? Samara's resonator attack? "There was no bomb. And I didn't do anything." Apart from preventing GoPol from collapsing before everyone was evacuated. But even that was mostly Dix and Sébastien.

"Stuff your lies. You've thrown your cards on the table, so let's end this business once and for all. Meet me at the top of the Eiffel Tower."

"The Eiffel Tower?" Why would he want to meet me there? And more importantly... "Why would I do that? It's over for you. You're going down."

Charles gives me a sharp, biting laugh. "With that little article of yours?"

The blood drains from my face. How could he possibly know about that? "Article?" I try to feign innocence.

"A little birdie told me."

"Hélène." How could I forget my beloved older sister?

"Yes. You thought you could plant an informer in my own spy agency. How stupid do you think I am? Now come to the tower, little girl, or that pretty birdie of yours will take its first flight."

I gasp as the call breaks off. Did he really just threaten to throw my sister off the Eiffel Tower? Or is it a trap? A flood of terrible images fills my head. Hélène falling on the ground, blood all around her. Me falling. The gun he pressed against my temple.

My sister's in grave danger. I have to go. But how can I?

My first coherent thought is to tell Sébastien and face Charles together. Maybe he can talk him down or something.

I'm halfway to his room when I remember he can't go anywhere right now. He's got Dix to look after. And besides, there's a good chance Charles will hurt my sister straightaway if he sees I'm not alone. No, this is not something he can help with.

I decide to leave him a little note on the coffee table, telling him where I've gone and how much I love him. Just in case I...

I swallow hard. Everything will be fine. Somehow, I'll make it through tonight. But if not...

Just one more look. That's all I need. I can't leave without seeing him once more, so I plaster a smile on my face and check on him and Dix. It's good to see Dix has become firmer. He's still translucent, but it's hardly noticeable now. Despite the progress, he's still tied to the bed as if he's suffering from some terrible illness.

"Hey." I walk over and put my hand on Sébastien's shoulder. He looks so bone-dead tired. Whatever he's giving to Dix is taken straight from his soul.

"We beat him fair and square, but he kept saying he wanted a rematch and..." Sébastien looks up at me, an exhausted smile on his lips. "It's working."

I force myself to mirror his smile and run my fingers through his hair. How I'll miss the feel of the small hairs on his neck. "It is, but don't forget to look after yourself, too." If I had time, I'd make him some onion soup.

"And you, too!" I tell Dix. "No more stunts like that."

"I'll try not to get sucked into experimental ghost machines again, I promise." Dix's voice carries almost as strong as usual. "Would you like to sit and tell me horrible stories from your childhood? You know, add some variety?"

As so often, Dix manages to make me laugh. "They wouldn't do much for you. Besides, I had a pretty happy childhood."

The mention brings up memories of Hélène and me, thick as thieves as we played and chased ghosts together. Of the many times she made me ask the weirdest kind of questions to the ghosts I met, such as if they still enjoyed the smell of flowers or they preferred rotten graveyard soil. She was such a weirdo back then.

"I can tell you a fond memory I have of you," I offer. "It won't really do much, but maybe..." Maybe it can serve as a break to all this awfulness. Something for both to hold onto.

I jump up and hurry into my room. A few minutes later, I'm back with Malou, carefully putting her into the crook of Dix's arm. "It's not that long ago," I say, keeping my eyes on Malou's curious little nose, "but when you first touched Malou, I saw your heart open. Feeling her tiny heartbeat, the fluff of her belly, the spikes did something beautiful to you. In that moment, you held life in your hands, innocent, untainted life. Something easy to love, something where you didn't have to pretend to be something you're not, where you could just be a seventeen-year-old boy with his first pet." Tears are forming in my eyes, and I blink rapidly, trying to smile them away. Look who's pretending now. Sébastien is watching me, and I swallow hard. "It was exactly the same for you. For one moment in time, you were able to let go of all the walls around your heart, the tension in your shoulders, the pain in your eyes." I reach out to him and squeeze his hand, the smile coming a bit easier now.

"She's a little miracle," he confesses.

Dix nods. "She's the best." He looks down at the little creature and gently rubs her belly, the biggest smile on his face.

It might not have strengthened his body, but maybe I did a little to strengthen his soul. It's all I can do for him.

"All right. I'd better leave you to it again." It's getting harder and harder to hold back the tears, so I lean down and kiss the top of Sébastien's head. "Don't forget that you got out of there. Bye."

"Hey, History Girl," Dix calls out, just as I reach the door.

My heart aches as I look back at these two beautiful men. I love one of them so much it hurts, and adore the other to pieces. "What?"

"Are you good?"

My cheeks have started hurting from the prolonged smile. "Yeah, I'm okay."

Before my mask has a chance to fall, I close the door behind me. For a moment, I lean against it, taking one shaky breath after another. A tear drops on the floorboards, staining the wood dark. I can't believe I'm really going to do this.

No, no more fretting. I have to pull myself together. My sister is in danger, and I'm going to save her. I may not survive the night, but the proof is out there now.

Charles is going down. With or without me.

CHAPTER 32

I've lost all sense of time. All I know is it's dark outside as I cycle through Paris. It's started to drizzle; the light reflecting off the puddles. The Eiffel Tower is a beacon in the darkness, lit up like a Christmas tree. I've always loved this sight, but now it fills me with dread. I get off my bike and cross the Pont d'Iéna, as if those few minutes on foot will make all the difference.

At the end of the bridge, a police barricade has been set up. My heart pounds loudly in my chest as I slowly approach the checkpoint. Are they going to stop me? Or do they all know what's going to happen?

A flashlight points at my face. "Can I help you, Mademoiselle?" a gendarme asks.

I could just turn away and go home. Tell Charles I tried but couldn't get through the barrier. But there's no telling what he might do to Hélène if I fail to show up. So, I grit my teeth and take another step forward, glancing towards the tower. "Um, Monsieur Roubert told me to meet him at the Eiffel Tower." I feel like such an idiot. The gendarme probably doesn't even know Charles.

"Alix Dubois?" he says, surprising me.

I swallow hard and nod. So, they're all in on it.

The gendarme smiles encouragingly and opens the barrier. "I'll let him know you're here. He's got his base set up further in. You can leave the bike here if you like."

Letting go of my bike feels like giving up my only escape. I need it as a crutch, so I can hold onto something, but of course, I can't take a bike up the Eiffel Tower. "Okay."

My legs feel as if they've been sucked into a spectral resonator like Dix's, and I feel so sick I could throw up.

Not a trace of the World Fair remains, which makes me inexplicably sad. Here and there, I see a pair of ghosts strolling, but neither pay me any attention. This isn't something my ghosts would be able to help me with, anyway. Still, I smile when I see Gustave Eiffel dismantling his resonator. What a beautiful thing he did for the ghosts and whisperers before Samara ruined it. I wonder what he's going to use it for next.

As I approach, he looks up. "Ah, Alix. Did you manage to find my portable resonator?"

I'm impressed he even remembers it instead of falling back into his daily trot. "Yes, it... it exploded."

Eiffel stares at me. "Exploded?"

"It consumed a ghost and was about to consume another. There was a force field around it that made it almost impossible to get closer, but we managed to turn it off and then it... Boom." I tell him as if I'm in a trance. None of it seems real anymore.

He rubs his chin thoughtfully and nods. "Thanks for letting me know. That's very helpful. I take it the thief was the ghost that was consumed? Samara?"

I nod and look up at the Eiffel Tower. "Have you, um, seen my... sister?"

"Up there?" he asks, already shaking his head. "I was busy cleaning up the mess, but you're welcome to check."

That's not nearly as helpful as I'd hoped, but that's ghosts for you. You can't expect them to care much about the living.

"Good night." He's already distracted by the time I leave and turn my leaden feet towards the service elevator.

Gone are Eiffel's old-fashioned cabins, while the modern operators have been sent home. Instead, a man, who I assume is a GoPol agent, since he's not wearing a gendarme uniform, awaits and unlocks the elevator. "Bonsoir, Mademoiselle Dubois. They're waiting for you upstairs."

I grimace. "Fun times."

There's no point arguing with these people. Charles would obviously put his most loyal agents at the bottom. If I don't get in the elevator, he'll make me somehow. Since I've already had enough rough treatment today to last a year, I obey the order and wait for the elevator to take me to my doom. As the doors close, I see him pulling out a phone. There's no turning back now. Charles knows I'm here.

My pulse has settled, and I feel a strange calm come over me as I watch Paris at night unfold before me. The city of lights. On top of a city of darkness. Who would've ever thought I'd prefer to be in the catacombs than up on the Eiffel Tower?

As soon as I get out of the elevator, someone grabs my arm. "Thank the ghosts you're here."

Great. Just as I was beginning to accept my fate, I'm forced to spend my last peaceful moments with Cédric. "Just go away, please."

"He's got her at the top. At gunpoint. My poor Léni is going out of her mind. You've got to help her."

Oh boy, this is going to be a long climb—and not because I'm taking the stairs. "That's why I'm here, Cédric. To clean up your mess."

"I know," he whines in my ear. "It's all my fault, I know, but please, Léni deserves better. *I* dragged her into this. She didn't want anything to do with ghosts and I... You know my uncle. He's a monster."

A monster Cédric would've loved to work for. Instead of telling him how it is, I click my tongue. "Again, that's why I'm here. Don't worry. He doesn't care about her. It's me he wants."

"But he's not gonna get you."

I stop cold on the stairs and look up at the dark figure looming over me. It's just getting worse. Gaspar is here.

"How did you get here?" Last I saw him, he was in the catacombs, restrained by Alexandre de Beauharnais.

"Did you really think a ghost could keep me from you? I told you, Alix, we're bound together. I always know where you are."

"That's creepy." Apparently, I'm not even granted the good Gaspar as a last reprieve. "Now let me pass."

"No." Gaspar puts his hands on both railings, completely blocking my path.

I'm about to lose it. "Gaspar! Charles has my *sister*. If I don't go, he'll hurt her. Maybe even kill her. You can have your turn afterwards." It's been a very long day.

He snorts, amused. "Where would be the fun in that?" Then he sneers at Cédric over my shoulder. "So what if Charles kills Hélène? You could be together again. Wouldn't that be great?"

Angrily, I push him. "That's my sister you're talking about!"

Not expecting me to get physical, Gaspar stumbles and lands on the stairs, staring up at me with wide eyes. I've had it to here with this casual cruelty. More importantly, I don't have time for this.

Just as I'm about to run past, he grabs my ankle, almost causing me to trip on the wet steps. "Alix," he says, and I can't quite tell whether it's good or bad Gaspar. "She's not worth it."

If I only count the last few months, then maybe. But just because we don't see eye to eye now doesn't mean I want her dead. She's always looked out for me, even if her methods left a lot to be desired. We're sisters. Quarrels are baked into our DNA. Not that Gaspar would understand.

"I'm sorry if your family never took care of each other, but mine did. Now let go and let me save my sister."

Maybe the reminder of his family brought back the real Gaspar for a second, or maybe he decided I'd be easier to deal with if I were dead. Whatever it is, Gaspar lets go. The very second his fingers loosen their grip, I'm out of there, trampling up the stairs.

"I'll hold him back!" Cédric shouts after me, ridiculously pseudo-heroic as ever. "Just save Hélène."

Gaspar growls, clearly not in the mood for Officer Cédric. Hopefully, it will distract them both long enough for me to do what I came here to for.

I run up the stairs, driven by pure adrenaline at this point. The two of them have cost me precious minutes. By the time I reach the top viewing platform, I'm exhausted.

Just as I'm about to take the last steps, someone whistles at me. "Over here."

I swallow. Charles isn't on the top platform—that'd be far too safe for what he has planned for Hélène and me. Instead, he's on some kind of sub-level, accessible only to engineers and painters. A door hangs on its hinges, squeaking in the wind. It leads to a wide beam that makes my eyes water.

There's enough steel on either side to hold onto, though each bar is wet from the rain. As if the height alone wasn't terrifying enough. I hold my breath as I step towards the dark figures in front of me. Charles is closer to me, his gun cocked and aimed at Hélène, who's trembling at the end of the beam, shaking her head wildly as I approach.

"Go away, Alix! I'll handle this."

"Doesn't look like it." Hélène isn't handling anything, but I appreciate the sentiment.

Charles keeps his gun pointed at my sister while he looks at me. "Took you long enough."

I keep my mouth shut, knowing nothing I can say will ever sway him.

"You've made a real mess of things. Having ghosts appear all over the city? The news cycle is going crazy. Is that what you wanted? To induce a mass panic? Do you have any idea how much cleanup this will require? You've just opened the country up wide to ridicule, not to mention countless attacks. You keep messing with things you know nothing about. But this—"

"Had nothing to do with me."

Charles laughs haughtily. "You were caught on camera! Right in the middle of it. Your name's out there. I'm surprised you haven't made some stupid video to address your new followers."

A lump forms in my throat as I try to imagine the unwanted attention. That must've been all the notifications on my platforms.

I'm in no way as public as Odile, but I do have accounts. Accounts I've kept thoroughly free of ghosts.

"Well, I haven't had time yet, you know," I hear myself say in a strangely distant voice. "After I shut down the World Fair and saved thousands of people from being replaced by images of the past, I rushed over to GoPol to stop Samara from doing the same thing there, whom you murdered because she wouldn't kill me. You're alive because of me. You're welcome."

Turns out, facing imminent death has emboldened me.

Charles stares, then shakes his head. "And you expect me to believe that? You may fancy yourself this little hero, Mademoiselle Dubois, the voice of the people, but what you really are is a disruptor of the most dangerous kind. You don't care what you destroy or who you hurt as long as you get what you want."

Projecting much? "You're paranoid. Everything that's happened is because of your own actions. Today's mess? Because you murdered your loyal agent. Your son turning on you? You murdered him, too. Me being such a giant pain in the ass? Guess what? It's because you're constantly trying to murder me."

"Oh, I won't be trying anymore." Ignoring everything else I say, Charles slowly points the gun at me. "You're going to call your father and kill that article of yours. And then you're going to jump or I'll push you. Either way, you'll die. If not, your sister goes down ahead of you."

Hélène whimpers. "Alix, don't. Just turn around and go. Leave. I don't care if he kills me."

Aghast, I stare at her. "No."

But my sister nods, clinging to her newfound resolve. "The world deserves to know your truth. I'm sorry I gave you such a hard time. I was wrong. Terribly, terribly wrong. He's afraid of you. That means you've got him. Just go." As she pleads with me, Hélène walks slowly towards Charles. "Just let me die. I'll be with Cédric again."

"Hélène, no!"

She lunges at Charles, but he's faster. With his left hand, he grabs her long hair and yanks her towards him. His gun still pointed at me, he shouts, "Kill the article. Now!"

I raise my hands. Hélène teeters precariously over the edge, clinging to his arm as she struggles to keep her balance. The wind sweeps through the structure, making the wet beam vibrate beneath our feet. My heart pounds in my throat, and I feel dizzy, well aware of the height. One wrong move and I'll end up on the ground. Even if I make the right move, like putting my hand in my pocket.

But before I can get my phone out, someone grabs my shoulders and holds me steady as they push past me, heading straight for Charles. "You don't get to have her. She's mine!" I hear Gaspar growl as I fall to my knees, holding on to the beam as if the next gust will knock me over. Below me, a maze of steel rungs stretches to the ground.

Hélène screams, and I hear a sickening thud.

I look up to see my sister gone from sight, just as Gaspar rams Charles into a pillar to the side.

"Hélène!"

No longer caring that it's high up, wet, and windy, I run across the beam to where I last saw her. As I peer over the edge, I see her clinging to the much thinner beam below. One leg is hooked over a steel rope, providing temporary relief. Without thinking, I lie flat on the beam and cling to the steel with my legs. The water seeps into my clothes as I reach out my hand.

"Hélène, take my hand."

"Just go!" she tells me, her face straining with the effort. "Please, save yourself."

"I'm not letting you die!" I stretch my arm even further, biting my lip in the process.

"It's okay," she says, though the fear makes her voice shake. "It's not the end, is it? I'd be a ghost... with Cédric?"

Tears run down her cheeks. I get it now. This last-ditch attempt to help me. She was willing to take this risk to make up for what she did and said before, but her heart is still broken, belonging to a man who loved his ambition more than her. Speaking of Cédric. He sits in the rafters below, as if to catch her. Instead of pleading with me, he's fallen completely silent.

"Oh no. No!" Anger courses through my veins, threatening to distract me. "Cédric wouldn't want this for you! He loved you... *loves* you! But he wants you to *live*!"

The ghost hangs his head in shame before nodding. "That's right." Glad he's come to his senses, for once.

My fingers brush over Hélène's arm. If I lean any further, I might fall over the edge before her. But then Hélène grabs my hand, tears streaming down her cheeks. "I don't know if I have enough strength left."

"You're the strongest woman I know," Cédric says, stroking Hélène's hair, unable to make himself known to her. Realising there's nothing he can do for her directly, he climbs up and puts his weight on my legs. "Pull her up."

Taking my cue from him, I tell Hélène. "You can do it. Hélène, you're incredibly strong, and you'll get through this. So, pull yourself up and hold on to your life!"

She grits her teeth. Using her leg as a lever, she manages to push herself up far enough for me to get a good grip on her shoulder and help her wriggle her body over the thin bar below. Her fingers find the edge of the beam, and I readjust my grip to hook my hands under her armpits, trusting Cédric to provide the counterweight.

We labour for a few tense minutes, the slippery conditions causing at least two heart-pounding scares, until finally, she's back on the wide beam and we both cling to each other in that soul-shattering relief that washes over you after achieving the impossible.

"Don't ever do this to me again!" I cry.

"You're the one who came here," Hélène cries back.

That's right. I walked into Charles' trap. Speaking of Charles...

Two quick shots rip through the night.

CHAPTER 33

Hélène and I stare at each other, then we scramble up and run for the stairs.

"Up here!" Cédric shouts from above us.

I want to follow him, but Hélène holds me back. "Alix, maybe we should…" She licks her lip and lets go of me. "You lead the way."

I fully expect to find Charles dead at Gaspar's feet. He's already shown how far he'd go to protect me. Even at his worst, I'm all he cares about.

Hélène and I make it to the top viewing platform and stop short. The one standing is Charles. Blood runs down his face and the arm of his suit is torn, but otherwise, he looks fine. Unlike Gaspar, who's collapsed to the ground, clutching his chest. Blood is pooling around him.

"There you are!" Charles sneers, pointing his gun at me with a rabid look in his eyes.

Hélène clutches my arm as I cover my mouth. Gaspar's bleeding out, but this madman won't let me near him.

"You may have won the war, but you won't live to see the world you created!"

I stare down the barrel of his gun and hear my life ticking away. Just then, the elevator doors open behind him and bright light floods the floor. Hélène pulls me down, slamming my shins into the steps.

"Don't move!" someone shouts as several hard boots hit the floor. "Drop your weapon. Hands behind your head."

My heart is pounding too loudly to recognise the voice at first, but then it dawns on me. "Sébastien?"

Cautiously, I lift my head over the edge of the platform. Six gendarmes accompany Sébastien, their guns all pointed at Charles, who drops his weapon and raises his hands before they're yanked down and handcuffed by his own son.

"You're under arrest for several counts of murder, attempted murder, and treason. You have the right to remain silent." Sébastien leans forward. "Although I know you won't."

His gaze meets mine, and he nods sharply at Gaspar, giving me permission to leave my hiding place. The gendarmes startle when I appear so suddenly, but they quickly put their guns away to secure

Charles' weapon. One of them kneels next to Gaspar and radios for an ambulance before starting to administer first aid.

I rush over and throw myself on the ground to cradle his head. In the bright light, he looks deadly pale, apart from the blood smeared across his face. "Gaspar," I whimper.

This can't be true. He can't die on me again. Good or bad, it doesn't matter. I just want him to live. But as always, he puts me first regardless of his own safety or reputation.

"I love you."

His lips stretch a little, but his eyes flicker. "I..." He reaches for me, and I clasp his hand, eager to offer any comfort. "Sorry," Gaspar whispers. "I'm sorry I... made you cry."

I burst into tears, choking back a sob. With my free hand, I cradle his face and kiss his wet forehead. "Hush. You're going to be alright."

The gendarme throws me a look, and I almost lose it.

Hélène puts her hand on my shoulder and squeezes it gently. "Alix..."

"No, no, no! You came back for me!" I cry at Gaspar. "Don't you dare leave again."

"...always..." Speaking is too much for him, and now there's blood on his lips. "...you."

Crying, I bend over him. My hedgehog boy. My sweet Gaspar. I'll never get the chance to help him. Instead, he's thrown away his second chance at life to save me.

As the sirens wail over the bridge, Gaspar's gaze breaks.

Chapter 34

Two days later, I'm huddled up in front of the TV in Sébastien's apartment, numbly watching the news. A lot has happened. Dix was the one who realised I was up to something. He'd told Sébastien to check on me, which is how the latter found my note. As his bike was still parked in front of GoPol and he had no other means of transport, he'd had to call a taxi. On the way, he'd called my father and gave him the number of a senior Interpol contact.

He'd never told me about this until now, but apparently, he didn't just make friends in the agency, but also made contact with Charles' superiors and Interpol agents. It turned out Interpol was already actively investigating. They swept up Charles' son all too gladly, but it was a delicate operation, which found its success only after he handed them the Chevalier's notes.

With an emergency arrest warrant in his pocket, Sébastien met with the gendarmes, dealt with Charles' man downstairs, and took the lift to the top floor to arrest his own father, arriving just in the nick of time.

Meanwhile, my father has been in contact with various government officials and Interpol, signed half a dozen contracts, and published a conservative but nonetheless revealing article about ghosts, ghost whisperers, and Charles' dark leadership of GoPol. What we'd hoped for came to pass. Charles was deemed the greater risk to national security and was thrown under the bus by his superiors. He's now in jail, awaiting a court date that will very likely see him locked up for life. Being caught in the act of another crime was the icing on the cake.

As for Gaspar, the police didn't quite know what to do with him. Officially, he's a John Doe. Interpol knows the truth—at least as far as his name is concerned. They think he never truly died in the first place.

My name has been kept out of the article, replaced by an alias to protect my privacy and GoPol's integrity. It also takes it from a single incident to a wider problem. My notifications have dwindled—largely because I haven't replied to a single one—one of the many stipulations by Interpol, though one I heartily approve of.

Sébastien's phone, however, constantly rings. He's hardly ever home, meeting with this and that person as they uncover the depth of Charles' malicious practises at GoPol France. I'm under no illusion more bodies won't be buried or those willing to work with him are entirely blameless, but short of a full-blown revolution, that's the price of national security. Some sacrifices must be made. As long as they're not as callous and personally motivated as they were under Charles' regime and we manage to change some things for the better.

No one knows what the future will bring. The news is full of ghost pictures taken that day and my father's article. Some clever historian has correctly identified the 1889 Exposition Universelle, although no one can explain why it would appear all of a sudden. At the moment, everyone's guessing. The existence of ghosts is far from proven, and many remain sceptic, though many more enjoy the speculation. An abundance of ghost experts and mediums are trawling talk shows and cited by less reputable news sources. They all try to explain what ghosts are and why we saw what we saw. It's all rubbish.

"Why are we watching this shit?" Dix asks as I watch yet another quack talk about unfinished business. He's still weak on his feet and willingly sits next to me, resting his head on my shoulder.

I turn off the TV and look at him. His body is no longer transparent and his weight feels right, but he looks drained. "I don't know what else to do."

"We could celebrate," Dix offers. In a soft, wondrous voice, he adds, "We won."

"Yeah." But not without great loss. My heart aches, and I lean against him for comfort.

He puts his arms around me and strokes my hair. "He's still out there somewhere."

Gaspar's ghost didn't stick around for long. This time, he couldn't ignore his death. Or maybe he couldn't ignore the short, cruel life he'd lived. One look at me and he bolted. I have no idea what kind of man he is now. Has death changed him? Or ruined him beyond redemption? Are there two ghosts? One for Gaspar and one for the monster he was tied to?

Despite everything he did to me, I still miss him. Then again, I've been missing him for a long time now. It's not a fresh wound, but a deep pain I'll always carry with me. He no longer holds my feelings hostage. What happened to Gaspar is a tragedy, but I refuse to let it hold power over me.

My phone buzzes and Gaby's name flashes. With a smile, I extract myself from Dix, turn off the TV, and pick up the phone.

"Hey, ma puce. What are you doing?" Her cheerful voice is balm to my soul.

"Dix and I are just chillaxing on the couch, watching ghost experts flout their opinions."

Gaby giggles. "Found any real whisperer?"

Part of the reason I'm watching all the quacks is to see if anyone like me comes crawling out of their hole. But if such a person exists, they know better than to paint a target on their back by going public.

"No, but I'm loving all the theories."

It's probably for the better if the reality of the ghostly afterlife is kept under wraps for a little longer. Give the people some time to come to terms with the fact ghosts are real before we hit them with the specifics.

"I bet. Yesterday, I saw a poster at Sorbonne. Someone wants to start a ghost hunter club."

Dix pulls the most hilarious face when he hears that.

"Typical," I say, rolling my eyes. "If you can't deny it, you have to destroy it." Though my comment isn't that serious, it reminds me of my older sister. "Speaking of denial, Hélène desperately wants have dinner."

Gaby's enthusiasm wanes. "Are you ready for that yet?"

"I don't know. Part of me thinks she proved herself. She didn't betray me to Charles and was willing to die in my stead. Then again, I can't help thinking she did it mostly to be with Cédric again. I don't doubt she wanted to make amends, or that she cares for me, just—"

"Try to make things right with you before dying and joining Officer Cédric in death? Man, the power this creep has over her."

"She really loved him. He did, too." Though not enough to let go of his GoPol dreams. I sigh. "Look, I get it. While I'll never understand what she saw in Cédric, I get loving someone so much you're wilfully blind to all their faults."

Without a word, Dix puts his arms around me and hugs me tight.

Gaby sighs. "Have you heard anything from him?"

"No."

And part of me is glad, considering how badly my last few meetings with Gaspar went. But while my mind is well aware of how toxic our relationship had turned, my heart still yearns for him.

"Give him time," Gaby says, the usual advice. "Alright, I have to go. Work." She sounds less than enthused. "But I'll keep my phone on if you need to talk some more."

She's such a gem. "Love you."

I put the phone down, just as the door opens and Sébastien walks in, also on a call. "I'll tell her, but I can't make any promises... Yes... Okay, I'll get in touch as soon as I know more."

He drops off a bag of food we desperately need. Unlike Dix, he looks as if he's recovered quickly from the ordeal. If anything, he looks energised. There's a smile on his face when he sees us on the couch, as if he's just found his favourite people. I know he has.

"So, I've got some news." His voice is a little shaky. Whatever it is, it's big.

"You always have news," Dix complains.

Sébastien scoffs at him. "I was offered—"

"GoPol?" I ask.

"The Paris unit, yes. I'll be reporting to an overseer from Interpol, but I get to run the Paris office once it's moved to a new building, and I'm invited to the talks regarding new policies. Plus, I get to work closely with the commander-in-chief to roll them out all across France, maybe even the EU." His grin widens. "We're going to make it better, Alix."

I mirror his grin. This is excellent for him. Abuse or not, he's trained his whole life for this job. He deserves this more than anyone. "That's wonderful."

"Ugh," Dix groans. "Looks like our days on the couch are over."

I slap his knee. "As if you aren't bored already."

Sébastien joins us, sitting on the side, so he can face us. Or rather me. "They want you, too."

That's not such good news. I swallow and brace myself. "Do they?"

"Not as an agent, but as a ghost consultant. And a historian. Someone needs to go through what's left of the archive and sort it all out. It's a full-time job. Very well paid."

"You know I don't care about that." Not when it comes to GoPol. "I can't be bought."

Sébastien nods. "Well, they'll try, and you should definitely use that for more benefits." He takes my hands and smiles. "You'd work with me to forge an alternative path for GoPol. This is our chance to change the world. Change the way we treat ghosts. You could teach other ghost whisperers like you taught me."

I love him, and that's why I'm at least entertaining the idea, but my foray into GoPol has scarred me for life. I have no doubt he'll rebuild the agency from the ground up, but I've decided intelligence work is not my thing.

"Look, I appreciate the offer…"

"But?"

"But I'd rather stay independent. Happy to receive a contract, like for the archive, or a running case, maybe even training, but I won't join GoPol."

Besides, I've still got a year of my Master's left and my Panthéon job. Neither of which I'm willing to give up for this.

Sébastien smiles and leans forward to kiss me softly. "I wouldn't have expected anything else."

I wrap my arms around his neck and pull him closer. Tasting this new motivated and optimistic Sébastien, knowing he'll do amazing work, being as ethical as he can afford to be, does something funny to my stomach.

Next to us, Dix clears his throat. "I don't want to disturb you or anything, but there's a ghost at the door."

We immediately break off our kiss and get up. Sébastien grabs his salt gun, ready for anything. It'll be a while before we adjust to this new reality where no one wants us dead.

I gasp when I recognise our intruder.

Gaspar's in the hallway, a squished-in hedgehog in his hands. Blood still covers his chest, and the shadow of the injuries sustained in his first death hovers over him. He smiles sheepishly at us. "Hey."

"Hey," I whisper back, simultaneously reaching for Sébastien's arm. It's only been two days since Gaspar tried to kill me.

Pain flashes in his eyes, and he lowers his gaze. He opens his mouth once, closes it again, looking as if he's about to bolt again, then decides to speak after all. "I heard there's still a place for me here."

Afterword

He's back!

You can't imagine how relieved I am to have Gaspar back for book 7. Of course, there's going to be a fallout, and things are going to be complicated for a while now Alix has somewhat committed to Sébastien in this book. Knowing Sébastien, he'll likely retreat immediately. Let's just hope Alix won't let him.

Aren't you relieved Dix's still with us? To be honest, I had sort of planned for him to "die" in book 4, but things didn't work out (thankfully!) and I thought he was past the point of danger. And then the plot for this book came together and Dix's death was back on the table. Luckily, Marie Curie came up with a way to save him. Sorry to scare you there for a minute!

I'm glad we've finally reached the end of the GoPol arc. Obviously, GoPol will still play a big role in the last three books, but now ghosts are officially a thing, there'll be many more ghost shenanigans. The Chevalier has been patiently waiting to get his game going and, boy, does he have big plans for Alix.

If you've ever wondered where all the royal ghosts of France are, then stay tuned, because book 7 is *Ghosts of the Monarchy.* We're going to visit St. Denis, where most are buried and meet all their delightful personalities. Any guesses on which royals will take centre stage?

As always, a huge thanks to my beta readers, Tina, Jojo, Perry, Paula, and the new kid on the block, Madeline. You've done a fantastic job finding all the inconsistencies and errors in the original draft.

Thanks to Jackie, my proofreader and favourite writing buddy. I love our weekly dates, even if I just puzzle, while you finish up my latest work.

Last but not least, thank you to my children, especially Kai, who's endlessly lobbied for "Squishy" to join the cast, and to my husband, who listens to all my woes and joys as I cobble these books together.

See you next time at the Royal Ball! (I think I might've just given myself an idea ^^')

Love,

Janna

Book 7: Ghosts of the Monarchy

A Force of Nature (Spirit Seeker 1)

A supernatural adventure through Europe

A Drop of Magic (Ashuan Greed 1)

Magic, Demons and High School Drama

ABOUT JANNA RUTH

Once upon a time, Janna Ruth studied the plate boundaries of this world. Now, she's creating her own worlds. Born in Berlin, Germany, Janna lives in Wellington, New Zealand, writing both English and German books.

Janna's writing career kicked off when she won a writing competition for German publisher Ueberreuter. Her first self-published novel "Im Bann der zertanzten Schuhe" (Melody of Curse, coming in June 2022) went on to win the 2018 SERAPH for "Best Independent Title". She debuted in English with her witchy novella "Witching with Dolphins" in 2020 and has since published urban fantasy, YA sci-fi, and contemporary coming-of-age novels and series.

When Janna isn't writing, she has a plethora of hobbies, such as aerial acrobatics, cake decorating, drawing, reading, and anything crafty you can throw her way.

Find out more about Janna and her books here:

Website: www.janna-ruth.com
BookBub: www.bookbub.com/authors/janna-ruth
Facebook: www.facebook.com/authorjannaruth
Reader Group: www.facebook.com/groups/storyseeker
Goodreads:
www.goodreads.com/author/show/16513923.Janna_Ruth
BlueSky: https://bsky.app/profile/janna-ruth.bsky.social
Instagram: www.instagram.com/janna_ruth
TikTok: www.tiktok.com/@jannaruthwrite
Pinterest: www.pinterest.com/jannaruthwrites